THE RUSTED SUN

The Rusted Sun

Michael Zimmer

FIVE STAR
A part of Gale, Cengage Learning

Farmington Hills, Mich • San Francisco • New York • Waterville, Maine
Meriden, Conn • Mason, Ohio • Chicago

GALE
CENGAGE Learning®

LIBRARY OF CONGRESS CATALOGING-IN-PUBLICATION DATA

Names: Zimmer, Michael, 1955– author.
Title: The rusted sun / by Michael Zimmer.
Description: First edition. | Waterville, Maine : Five Star Publishing, a part of Cengage Learning, Inc., 2017.
Identifiers: LCCN 2016037256| ISBN 9781432832308 (hardback) | ISBN 1432832301 (hardcover)
Subjects: | BISAC: FICTION / Historical. | FICTION / Westerns. | GSAFD: Western stories.
Classification: LCC PS3576.I467 R87 2017 | DDC 813/.54—dc23
LC record available at https://lccn.loc.gov/2016037256

First Edition. First Printing: January 2017
Find us on Facebook— https://www.facebook.com/FiveStarCengage
Visit our website— http://www.gale.cengage.com/fivestar/
Contact Five Star™ Publishing at FiveStar@cengage.com

Printed in the United States of America
1 2 3 4 5 6 7 21 20 19 18 17

THE RUSTED SUN

★ ★ ★ ★ ★

PART ONE:
THE STRANGER

★ ★ ★ ★ ★

CHAPTER ONE

Gil Ryan was a tall man on a winter-lean sorrel, wrapped in a cocoon of pain. In spite of the bitter weather, perspiration beaded his forehead below the wide brim of his hat, and his flesh felt hot and swampy under his heavy wraps. He knew he'd have to find shelter soon. Dark clouds were rolling in from the north, mud-thick and laden with snow, and the wind that had been prodding at him all afternoon was strengthening.

He didn't know the name of the town he was entering. He wasn't even sure of the territory anymore. He knew only that the day was drawing to a close and that, if he was lucky, there might be food and shelter ahead for both him and his horse. And maybe something to ease the ache that was drilling into just about every muscle and joint of his body, pounding at his skull from the inside until it felt as if his eyes were pulsating.

The town, strung along a single, broad street, wasn't especially impressive. The only thing that stood out was the way the entire business district sat along the east side of the thoroughfare, facing west. Across the street from the block-long row of storefronts stood a trio of uniquely disparate structures. Farthest south was a low-roofed adobe building with a wooden platform across the front and a sign above the door proclaiming *Larkspur Depot, Elevation 6290*. North of that was a two-story frame dwelling resembling either a mansion or an elegant hotel, only with its windows boarded over and one of the porch treads so badly warped it had pulled free of the stringer. Lastly stood a low, flat-roofed stone building with bars on the windows and a sign needlessly affirming its function as a jail.

Gil returned his gaze to the depot. There were no steel rails approaching the structure's wind-scoured platform, nor even the hint of a roadbed. Just the empty building with its weathered schedule board and shuttered ticket window, a few dried weeds torn loose and huddled like old men in the corner of the front door alcove. It was as if the entire west side of the street had been abandoned years before, while the east side flourished.

Although the street was deserted, the town wasn't. With his shoulders hunched to the buffeting wind, Gil studied the sixty or so homes scattered through a grove of cottonwoods behind the east-side row of businesses. Larkspur's residential section looked like an easy melding of log, frame, and adobe dwellings, none of them arguing for undue wealth or influence. Even though no one was in sight, most of the chimneys were spouting columns of wood smoke into the sky, tattered ribbons curving horizontally to the south, as if fleeing the approaching storm.

Gil felt woozy enough that he didn't pay much attention to the businesses he passed. He was aware of a livery at the north end of the street, its livestock apparently driven inside out of the biting wind since the corrals and holding pens behind the barn were empty. A saloon farther down had its lamps already lit against the creeping twilight. As Gil rode past, a stocky man in a bear-hide coat watched from the window. There was no welcome in the man's piercing stare, nor did Gil expect any; he was a stranger here, and didn't intend to stay longer than it took to wait out the blizzard.

He reined up in front of a mercantile midway down the block, his eyes narrowing at the figure he saw in the window's reflection—wind-honed and bone-weary, his right arm slanted across his chest as if that might somehow protect him from the elements. He wore a sturdy mackinaw coat and had a woolen scarf wrapped around the lower portion of his face, masking a winter's scruff of beard. A flat-crowned Stetson shaded the details of his face—the solid wedge of his jaw and full brows, the smoldering eyes—and deer-hide gloves, once tan but now almost black from grease and hard use, covered his hands. In a scabbard jutting past the sorrel's right shoulder was a heavy Winchester rifle, but there was no bedroll tied behind the cantle, and the saddlebags lay flat and empty against the rig's skirting.

Gil stared at the image for a long moment, wondering what he would look like with the heavy coat removed, his frame exposed for the first time since losing his packhorse and most of his supplies crossing the Big Sandy River nearly a week before. Then a fit of coughing seized him, bending him nearly double as his lungs contracted. Squeezing his eyes shut, he reached clumsily for his saddle horn, hanging on until the paroxysm had passed.

When he could breathe again, he spat weakly, then dismounted and looped the sorrel's reins around the hitching rail. His legs felt heavy and unwieldy as he climbed the steps to the front entrance, and his ears hummed with congestion. He paused inside with his back to the door, his eyes adjusting to the store's gloomy interior. A potbellied stove sat in the middle of the room, its inch-thick window of isinglass glowing like butter from the flames within, and he moved eagerly toward it. The woman's voice startled him.

"If you're looking for the Sun, you've come to the wrong place."

Gil jerked to a stop, irritated with himself for not having noticed her sooner, for letting fever and aching muscles cloud good judgment. She stood behind a counter along the north wall, handsome and full-bodied and nearly as tall as he was, with wheat-colored hair and a smooth, lightly tanned complexion. Not like someone who worked outside on a daily basis, but like a person who enjoyed the sun and the out-of-doors just for the pleasure of it. There was no welcome in her frosty blue eyes, though. Not even after Gil pulled the wool scarf down off his face in an effort to make himself appear less intimidating. He couldn't do anything about his voice. It sounded like something dredged from the bottom of a muddy river, cold and ragged.

"I've come a long way looking for the sun, but didn't expect to find it on a grocer's shelf." He tried a smile, but that didn't seem to blunt her wariness, either. He was moving toward the counter when another surge of coughing caught him midstride and nearly bowled him over. Gasping and red-faced, he stumbled sideways into the end-panel of a row of shelves and leaned against that until the dizziness passed. When he looked up, wiping his lips with the mackinaw's sleeve, the woman was gone. He caught a glimpse of her yellow hair disappearing into a back room. A moment later he heard her voice and another's reply, then a middle-aged man with the same crisp blue eyes appeared from the rear of the store. He had salt and pepper hair and deep furrows above his brows. As he made his way down the rear of the counter, Gil noticed his expression. Where the woman's had been hard and unyielding, the man's appeared more cautious, as if expecting trouble he somehow hoped to avert.

"My daughter says you might be looking for the Sun."

"Your daughter is wrong." Gil replied over a throat that felt as if it had been scored with knives.

The storekeeper hesitated as he took in the younger man's appearance. His gaze lingered on the beads of sweat and the fevered bloom of his cheeks. "What are you looking for?" he asked guardedly.

"I'm looking for a place to stable my horse until this storm blows itself out, then maybe a room for myself, if there's one available."

"The town has a livery, but there aren't any hotels. Not unless you count Quinlin's empty shell across the street."

"The one next to the depot with no train?"

The storekeeper nodded solemnly, then glanced out the window as if to reassure himself that the deserted buildings were still there. It had started snowing in the few minutes Gil had been inside, tiny grains pelting the glass in the windows like birdshot fired from a distance. A gust of wind rattled the door, and the storekeeper shivered and looked away.

"The livery's at the north end of the street. Bannerman will probably have a room he can rent you."

"Bannerman?"

"Owns the saloon." He tipped his head toward the wall behind him, and Gil remembered the lighted window and the baleful glare of the man standing inside, watching him pass.

"I'll be needing some supplies, too. A bottle of whiskey and some honey and lemons."

"I've got brandy and honey, but no lemons. I can sell you a little tin of dried peel, although I doubt it'll be much help." He bit thoughtfully at his lower lip. "Look, it's none of my business, and I'll sell you whatever you want, but we have a pretty good doctor here who'd probably do you a whole lot more good than a bucketful of hot toddies."

Gil's attempt at a reply was cut short by another coughing jag. He leaned into the counter until it passed. When he looked up, tiny red dots were dancing in his vision. "You're probably right," he allowed hoarsely. "Where . . ." He stopped when his lungs twitched warningly, waiting for the need to clear his chest to pass.

"Doc works out of his house at the north end of town," the storekeeper said. "You came in from the south, right?"

Gil shook his head. "No, from the north."

"Over the Saddleback?" His brows rose questioningly.

13

"Over a low pass with a lot more snow than I wanted to buck. Stirrup deep in places."

"That's . . ." He stopped and shook his head. "It doesn't matter. If you came in from the north you probably rode right past Doc's place. It's an adobe house set back in the trees. Blue trim on the wood and flower boxes under the windows."

"I didn't see it."

"It won't be hard to find. About a hundred yards past Offerman's Livery. If he has room, you can board your horse with Offerman. He'll take good care of it."

"Thanks," Gil replied. "I'm obliged."

"If you decide you want that brandy and honey, come on back. The lemon peel, too. My ma never used lemons when I was growing up, but I know a lot of folks do."

Gil pulled the scarf up over his mouth and nose. "I'll likely be back before I settle in. I'll need some food to pad the brandy."

He went outside and loosened the sorrel's reins. "Let's go, Rusty," he said to his horse—speaking to the rangy gelding had become a habit on his long ride south. "Let's go see what the doc has to say, then we'll find some place to hole up until . . ."

That was as far as he made it before another deep, raging cough tore at his chest. He hung onto the saddle until it passed, then climbed exhaustedly into the seat. The snow was sweeping in almost horizontally now, and Gil tipped his head forward as he reined into the wind, his eyes only partially protected by the Stetson's brim. As he came even with the saloon, one of the wide, double doors was flung open and the stocky man in the bear-hide coat stepped onto the boardwalk.

"Hey," the man bellowed above the wind's icy hum. "Come here."

Gil looked but kept on riding. The man moved to the edge of the walk to scowl after him, but he didn't say anything more, and after a moment Gil turned his back on him.

14

Looking for it, the doctor's house wasn't hard to find. Had he not been so addled by fever and lightheadedness on the ride in, Gil probably would have noticed it right off, a low adobe structure with bright blue trim and a tidy yard. The flower boxes were empty, but the dirt inside had been freshly turned and was ready for planting. Gil could hear the sawing of a fiddle from inside when he reined up, then, after listening for a moment, he decided it wasn't a fiddle but a violin—small difference to the instrument, he supposed, but usually significant to the person playing it.

He tied up at an ornate iron hitching post out front, then knocked at the door. It was opened by an older woman with plump cheeks and gray hair who took one look at the sweat wiggling through the thick mat of Gil's beard and immediately stepped out of his way.

"Come inside," she said authoritatively, then called over her shoulder, "William."

She led Gil through a small parlor toward a door at the far side. A man Gil took to be the physician appeared before he and the woman were halfway across the room. He was carrying a violin and a bow in the same hand, but quickly set them aside when he saw the deep flush of Gil's cheeks. Like his wife, the doctor was older and gray-haired and stoutly built. He was also just as quick to take action. Putting a hand on Gil's shoulder, he guided him toward the back room. "Let's get you into my office and see what's going on."

The woman stopped in the parlor. "I'll be close by if you need me," she said.

The doctor nodded his appreciation and the woman turned away. After closing the door behind them, the physician motioned toward a narrow table in the middle of the examination room. "Have a seat. Let me take your coat and shirt."

Gil shivered violently as he slipped out of his heavy wool

coat, then the lighter jacket and vest underneath. He peeled his shirt off over his head and dropped it on the table at his side. The doctor took his damp outerwear and hung it over the back of a chair next to a small stove. Eyeing the washboard contours of his patient's ribs, he said: "How long has it been since you've eaten?"

"Five days, more or less."

"And this?" He pointed to a puckered scar high on the left side of Gil's chest, the flesh around it still an angry pink.

"Last fall."

The doctor's lips pursed thoughtfully. "What caliber?"

"A forty-five is what they told me. I was unconscious when it was dug out."

"I'm guessing from the extent of damage to the surrounding tissue that it wasn't extracted by a physician."

"It was pried out by a local barber who did a little dentistry and medical work on the side."

The doctor clucked his tongue disapprovingly. "A jack of all trades, no doubt."

"I was damn glad to have him at the time," Gil replied pointedly.

"Yes, I suppose so. It looks like the bullet might have lodged awfully close to your lung."

"I was spitting blood for a while."

"What about now?"

"No, just . . ." Then another coughing fit grabbed him, forcing him to grip the edge of the table until his knuckles paled to keep from sliding off.

"How long has this been going on?" the doctor asked when the coughing subsided.

"About four days," Gil rasped as another shiver racked his gaunt frame. The physician brought a blanket down off a nearby shelf and draped it over Gil's shoulders. Placing a hand against the patient's forehead, he held it there for a moment, then went to a nearby table laid out with an array of instruments and picked up a pencil-sized thermometer.

"Put this under your tongue," he instructed, and when it was in place, he fit a stethoscope around his neck. "I'm William Shaw, by the way. Is there something you'd like me to call you?"

"Gil Ryan'll do."

"A pleasure to meet you, Mr. Ryan. Now shut up and hold still." The doc placed the stethoscope's polished diaphragm against Gil's chest and leaned close, as if those few inches might somehow make a difference. He moved the dollar-sized disk to various locations across Gil's rib cage, then placed it against his back. "Take a deep breath, then exhale slowly."

Gil did as instructed, then did it several more times as Shaw slid the cool metal across his flesh. After a couple of minutes the doctor took the thermometer from Gil's mouth and carried it over to a lamp on his desk. He frowned at the mercury's length of travel, then grunted and shook the thick, silver-colored element back into place before returning the thermometer to the tray atop his desk.

"How do you feel?"

"Like hell warmed over."

The physician chuckled. "Well, at least you're honest. Half the waddies who wander in here with some ailment or another try to insist there's nothing wrong with them. It's tedious having to pry out the information I need to make a diagnosis."

"If information is what you need, I've got a hell of a cough and a raw throat. I feel like I'm burning up, but I can't stop shivering, and I'd swear my skull was about to crack wide open. On top of that, I ache in just about every muscle north of my toes."

"I don't doubt it," Shaw replied gravely. "You have a temperature of one hundred and three degrees, and if you don't have pneumonia yet, you soon will, assuming you don't take steps to prevent it." He paused as if to gauge the younger man's comprehension of what he was saying. "Do you understand the seriousness of pneumonia, Mr. Ryan?"

"I've seen what it can do. Helped bury a few men from it, too."

"Well, Larkspur has a cemetery if that's your choice, but I believe you're young enough and healthy enough—relatively speaking, of course—to kick this thing with the proper care. Understand that most of that will have to come from you, and not from a bottle of medicine."

"I'm not going anywhere," Gil replied. Although he wouldn't have admitted it, Shaw's words struck a chill to his heart far worse than what was traveling up and down his spine. The first man he'd ever buried from pneumonia had been his father, barely thirty-five years old and tough as an oak burl, just too stubborn to stay inside and keep warm and dry, the way Gil's ma had begged him to.

The doctor studied Gil quietly for a moment, then turned away to idly rearrange his stethoscope and thermometer. "Tell me something, Mr. Ryan, are you looking for the Sun?"

"You're the third person who's asked me that since I rode into town," Gil replied as evenly as his congested lungs would allow.

After a pause, Shaw said: "The Sun is Arthur Quinlin's ranch, southwest of here. He's been hiring . . ." The doctor turned and his gaze dropped to the revolver holstered at Gil's waist. "He's hiring men who are proficient with firearms."

"You mean gunmen?"

"Yes."

"I'm just passing through," Gil said.

"Not many people just ride through the Ensillado Basin, Mr. Ryan. There's not really anywhere to go with the Saddleback closed."

"That was the storekeeper's impression."

"Fred?"

"I didn't catch a name. Whoever he was, he seemed surprised that I rode in from the north."

Shaw appeared equally startled. "We've mostly assumed the Saddleback was impassable until well into spring, May at the earliest."

"I wouldn't have come that way if I'd known what it was like."

"And your destination lies . . . farther south?"

"I was in Idaho until a few months ago. I wasn't keen on spending another winter gophered in with snow up to my horse's belly. My horse wasn't looking forward to it, either."

Shaw chuckled and seemed to relax. "So you came south looking for the sun, and now everyone is ready to slam their door in your face when you admit it?"

"Something like that." Gil rolled his left shoulder experimentally, feeling the uncomfortable stretch of muscle around the still-tender bullet wound, and his expression hardened.

"My search was in the opposite direction," Shaw was saying. He'd turned to his desk and was unaware of the effect his question had on the younger man. Bringing a military insignia out of a drawer, he showed it to Gil. "I was a contract surgeon for the army for nearly thirty years, the last fifteen of them in the southwest. When I retired, Alma and I came north looking for seasons. We were tired of constant sunshine and one hundred-plus-degree temperatures for weeks on end."

"Looks like you found what . . ." Gil stopped, breathing shallowly until the urge to cough subsided.

Frowning, Shaw plucked a small, dark bottle and a deep-bottomed spoon from a cabinet next to the examination table. "Try this," he said, filling the spoon to capacity then tipping it down Gil's throat.

The results were immediate, and Gil took a deep but cautious breath. "What is that?"

"Codeine, with a little syrup and flavoring to make it more palatable."

"It sure takes the edge off a sore throat."

Shaw was writing in a small notebook. "You'll need a tablespoon every six hours or so. I'm also prescribing half a dozen tablets of quinine sulfate for fever. Take one every twelve hours. I'd also recommend warm mustard plasters for your chest. Drink as much water as you can to counteract the dehydration caused by the fever, and get a lot of rest. That means staying in bed, not sitting at a poker table in a smoky saloon." He ripped the page out of the notebook and handed it to Gil. "Give that to Fred Somers at the mercantile. He's a pharmacist, and will fix you up with what you need."

"He's the one who sent me here."

"Fred's a good man. Tell him I want you to have the front room over his store, the one above the stove. He'll know which one I'm talking about."

"He said Bannerman had rooms."

"Bannerman does, but I want you to stay with Fred. He has four empty rooms he'll rent to the right people."

"But not to anyone looking for the Sun?"

"No, but there's a reason for that. Tell him you're not riding for Quinlin and he'll be all right. Tell him I'll stop by later to talk with him. I want him to keep a kettle of water on the warmer in your room, and to bring you your meals instead of having you go out for them."

"I'm not helpless."

"You will be before this is over, or damn close to it. Once you start to relax, that fever's going to kick you hard in the hindsights. You'll be glad to have your food delivered then, although you might not feel like eating it."

Too wrung out to argue, Gil shrugged the blanket off his shoulders and started to pull on his shirt.

"I noticed your coat is wet. The jacket and vest, too."

"I went through the ice crossing the Big Sandy," Gil explained, and Shaw whistled softly. "Lost my packhorse, my bedroll, food, all my extra clothes. I kept looking for my horse, thinking I could rescue the pack even if the animal hadn't made it, but the ice became thicker the farther downstream I went. I never did find it or my gear. It was dark by the time I got a fire going that night, and everything I was wearing was coated with ice. When I woke up the next morning I was already starting to feel hot."

"You'll feel a lot hotter before that fever breaks," Shaw predicted. "Just keep the codeine handy and the mustard pack warm and moist, and stay under as many blankets as you can stand. I'll stop by to see how you're doing after I talk to Fred."

"What do I owe you?"

"A dollar if you have it, or you can chop some firewood for us when you're feeling better if you don't."

"I've got it." He drew a coin from his pocket and placed it on the desk. "Thanks, Doctor."

"You're welcome, Mr. Ryan." He clamped a hand over Gil's shoulder and walked him to the door. "Fred has a stable behind his store that he's not using. You can keep your horse there or at Offerman's Livery, although I'd recommend boarding it with Fred. Offerman has a contract with the Ensillado Stagecoach Company to take care of their teams at this end of the line, and he already has a full barn. Larkspur Feed and Supply rents a few stalls, but that's owned by Art Quinlin. Art doesn't think the town knows it, but we do. If you don't keep your horse with Fred, board it at Offerman's. He'll take good care of it until you're back on your feet, and you won't be putting money into

Quinlin's pockets to hire more troublemakers."

Gil nodded but didn't reply. He didn't have any interest in either the man named Quinlin or the town's problems with him, but he'd keep the sorrel with Somers if the storekeeper was willing. He liked the idea of having Rusty close by, where he could look in on him from time to time.

After buttoning the mackinaw to his throat and wrapping the scarf around the lower portion of his face, Gil stepped into the icy blast of the wind. The snow had tapered off while he'd been inside, but he could sense the storm's nearness in the clouds, unfurling overhead like sheets of gray wool. The cold was deep and penetrating, and crept effortlessly through his damp clothing. There would be more snow when the wind died, he thought, and probably a lot of it. This late in the season, the odds were good that it would be wet and heavy, although not likely to hang around long. He wasn't sure of the month, but thought it had to be late March or early April. The long, dreary days of winter were nearing an end, and the warmth of spring lurked just around the corner. As far as Gil was concerned, it couldn't happen soon enough.

CHAPTER TWO

It wasn't quite full dark when Reece Ward guided his horse into the small barn behind Fred Somers's store and dismounted. The fingers of his left hand tingled with numbness from where he'd held onto the reins on the ride into town. With his horse secured out of the wind, Reece jammed both hands into the pockets of his heavy winter coat and stamped his feet in the dust to restore some circulation. It had been miserably cold coming in and it was going to be worse going home, but he figured it would be worth it for a few minutes alone with Peggy Somers. At least if her father didn't catch them.

Reece's lip thinned with resentment as he recalled his last brush with that overbearing tyrant. Fred had treated him no better than an Irishman, and all but called his daughter a tramp to her face. The memory of that evening burned in Reece's belly like hot embers; there hadn't been a night since that he hadn't relived the encounter in his mind, visualizing all the things he should have said, the actions he might have taken.

Feeling his anger starting to boil out of control, Reece forced his thoughts away from Fred Somers, back to the empty barn with its broken boards and odors of moldy hay and burrowing mice. Leaving his horse hitched loosely by the reins, he slipped outside and across the rear yard. For several minutes he stood beneath the store's looming presence, his shoulders hunched to the cold as he stared longingly at the upstairs window of Peggy's bedroom. The lamplight glowing from within assured him that she was there, and that the store downstairs was closed for the day, their evening meal finished.

He kicked around on the ground until he uncovered half a dozen pea-sized stones from the dirt, then gently tossed the largest one toward the window. It popped sharply against the glass. Reece flinched but nothing happened. The wind was too strong, he supposed. Its constant pummeling was keeping the building's timbers creaking and moaning, masking the sound of the pebble. It took several more tries before Peggy finally took notice. Her shadow appeared across the window and the sash rose. Reece smiled when he saw her. She leaned outside, the wind snatching her long blond hair and whipping it across her face.

"Who's out there?" she called suspiciously.

He stepped backward, into a patch of lamplight.

"Reece!" she exclaimed, still in that heightened whisper that probably could have been heard across the street if not for the howling of the storm. She made a motion for him to stay where he was, then pulled back and closed the window. Reece returned to the barn, out of the worst of the wind. Peggy joined him a few minutes later. The frightened look she tossed over her shoulder before darting inside dimmed his anticipatory smile.

"Reece," she whispered, coming against him. She spread the wool blanket she'd wrapped around her shoulders wide to enclose them both. "What are you doing here?"

"I came to see you." He slid his arms around her and pulled her tight.

"In this weather?"

"In any weather."

She shivered and brought her arms up between them. "You're getting snow on my dress," she complained.

"Let's move into one of the stalls and you can take it off."

"Reece!" she said, and the muscles along her spine abruptly

stiffened. "I can't stay long or Dad will wonder what I'm doing. He asked where I was going and I told him the privy, but I don't think he believed me."

Reece tried to pull her close again but she wouldn't let him, and he said in exasperation, "Doesn't he know a woman needs to use a privy once in a while?"

"Not when he furnishes her with a chamber pot under the bed for nights like this." She put her hands against his chest and he reluctantly dropped his arms. The blanket fell away from him and Peggy pulled it tight around her, closing him out. "What are you doing here?" she repeated, as if she didn't believe his original answer. "You'll freeze."

"Naw, I won't freeze, but I need some medicine."

"For your mother?"

"Yeah. She's been feeling worse lately. Can you get me some laudanum?"

"I think so. I'll pick up a bottle on my way through the store, but I'll have to drop it out the window. Dad would know something was wrong if I tried to leave the house again so soon."

"Wrong?" he echoed bitterly.

"You know what I mean. Reece, please, give him some time."

"I don't think there's enough time left in any of our lives for him to change his mind about me."

"It'll change, you'll see. Right now he's frightened because of what happened to Earl."

"What happened to Earl Quinlin doesn't have anything to do with you and me."

She hesitated, her eyes searching his face in the near darkness. Wondering, he thought. Then she glanced worriedly over her shoulder. "I'd better go."

"Stay."

"I can't." She hesitated. "Les is in town."

"So?"

"He's been drinking. There's a stranger here, too."

That piqued his interest. "What kind of stranger?"

"A rough-looking man. He told Dad he came in over the Saddleback."

"That's bull. There's too much snow up there."

"Then how'd he get into the Basin?"

"The same way everyone does, up Ensillado Canyon." His tone grew caustic. "I'll bet he's another one of Quinlin's gunmen."

"Dad asked if he was looking for the Sun, but he acted like he'd never heard of it."

"Now I know he's lying. Everyone in the territory has heard of Quinlin's Sun."

She took a step back. "I have to go, Reece. I'll drop your mother's medicine out the window. But promise me you'll stay away from Bannerman's tonight."

"I'm not afraid of Les Quinlin."

"You should be, especially when he's with those two friends of his."

"Jackson?"

"Him and Love."

Reece laughed loudly, ignoring the panicked look that came into her eyes. "Odell Love isn't his friend. Neither is Tim Jackson."

"They work for the Sun, so what's the difference?" Then the store's rear door swung open and Peggy gasped. "Go," she whispered urgently, but Reece smiled and raised his hands in a palms-up gesture, as if asking how. The barn didn't have a rear exit. There was just the wide front door and a smaller side entrance that opened toward the mercantile. Either way, her father would see him as soon as he left the barn.

"Peggy?"

Fred Somers's voice cut through the dusk like a whipsaw,

and Reece's hand moved instinctively toward his revolver. Peggy's eyes widened in alarm.

"Reece!" she hissed.

"Go on," he said. "Before he comes out here looking for you."

Her expression was bleak as she turned away. Reece waited with his fingers wrapped around the grips of his revolver, but Fred didn't leave the store. Reece heard him ask Peggy where she'd been and she told him she'd ducked into the barn because of the cold. It was a weak excuse, but Fred seemed to buy it. When the back door slammed shut, Reece let his hand fall away from his revolver. He walked out into the cold and wind, and when Peggy's window flew open several minutes later, he was there to the catch the package she dropped to him.

"I'll be back," he promised, but she'd already closed the window.

Reece returned to the barn to fetch his horse, then rode out into the open. It was snowing again, tiny flakes swirling madly on the wind. He stopped in front of the barn, his gaze as hard as stone as he stared at the mercantile's rear door. He sat that way for probably a full minute, then, cursing, he reined away, flipping the tail of his coat over his gun to protect it from the storm.

On the street, Gil turned south with the wind. Full dark was coming on fast and most of the town's businesses were already closed. A few remained hopefully open, their lamp-lit windows like pale smudges in the gloom, closed shutters bleeding amber.

Shivering, he tried to burrow deeper inside the mackinaw, but that did him little good. The dampness of the heavy wool was like a magnet sucking the cold straight through. He was still some distance from Bannerman's, Somers's mercantile half a block beyond, when one of the saloon's front doors swung open and the stocky man in the bear-hide coat stepped onto the boardwalk. Another followed, taller than the first, with a scraggly beard and a face so narrow and pointed it reminded Gil of a fox. Or a weasel.

Bearskin stepped down off the boardwalk and started across the street in front of Gil's sorrel. Weasel stopped at the edge of the walk, his gloveless fingers playing nervously over the grips of a large-framed revolver holstered around the outside of his coat, as if tapping out a tune only he could hear.

Gil swore wearily. Then, as inconspicuously as possible, he loosened a couple of the mackinaw's lower buttons and slid his hand inside. He was carrying a Hopkins and Allen Army Model revolver on his left hip, its butt canted forward for a cross-belly draw. Wrapping his fingers around the revolver's *gutta-percha* grips, he gently loosened the gun in its holster. As he neared the saloon a third man stepped onto the boardwalk, and Gil knew instinctively that this would be the one he'd have to deal with.

The third man took his time descending the saloon's steps. He was the tallest of the trio, slim and young and confident, with curly dark hair spilling over his collar in back and a thin mustache of the same somber hue. Unlike the first two men, bundled in heavy winter clothing, this one was dressed lightly—a thigh-length buckskin jacket with long fringe, flat-crowned hat, striped trousers tucked inside his black boots. Heavy Mexican rowels jingled at his heels, audible even above the moaning of the wind, and the tails of his jacket had been brushed back to reveal the carved ivory grips of a nickel-plated Colt revolver riding high on his right side.

Gil kept Rusty to the middle of the street, his eyes darting among the three men. Although he was expecting the younger man to speak first, it was the squatty guy in the bear-hide coat who started the ball rolling. Raising a hand as if to stop some speeding youngster in his daddy's buggy, he called, "Hold up,

Mister. Les wants a word with you."

Gil reined in, turning his mount slightly to the west so that the three hard cases would be on his left, quickest under his gun if he had to draw in a hurry.

"I hollered earlier," Bearskin continued in a faintly petulant tone. "I guess you didn't hear me."

With his throat still sore and his patience bordering on non-existent, Gil refused a reply. His stony silence brought a scowl to Bearskin's features.

"You deaf, boy, or just stupid stubborn?"

Gil turned to the man in fringed leather. "Speak your piece, Les, or pull off your curs."

The words sounded strangely hollow in the gathering dusk, as if rattling up from the bottom of a deep pit, but the man in the leather jacket laughed loudly, and Gil knew he'd guessed right.

"Jackson, back off some. You're making our friend nervous."

Bearskin's unintelligible grumble declared his opinion of the command, but he did as he was told.

"If you ain't in too much of a hurry, stranger, why don't you come on inside and have a drink," Les offered.

Gil kept his silence. He could feel his chest tightening, and knew a fresh bout of coughing was imminent. He wished he had some of Doc Shaw's codeine, or even a slug of whiskey to help cut the phlegm building up in his lungs, but he was going to have to bull through this on his own. Gracing Bearskin with a calculating stare, Gil nudged his horse forward. At the saloon, Les's expression changed abruptly. He took a threatening step forward, his hand curling over the Colt's fancy grips.

"I made you a friendly offer, mister." Les's voice rang across the street. "I'll consider it damned impolite if you don't accept."

Bearskin's scowl instantly switched to an eager grin. Only

Weasel looked undecided yet, which gave Gil a small measure of relief. If it came to a fight he'd go for Les first, then Jackson, in his bear-hide coat. He'd tackle Weasel last, if it went that far.

With his fingers taut on the sorrel's reins, Gil tried to steel himself against breaking into another cough. "I'm just passing through, Les," he said hoarsely. "I'll have that drink some other time."

The younger man's gaze narrowed. "Who are you?"

It was a brazen question, lacking the courtesy normally expected in this land where aliases were common and a man's business was his own. "You're pushing a hard line, friend," Gil said. "You might want to ease off a mite."

"Did Ward hire you?"

Gil shook his head. His congestion was thickening; he knew it couldn't be denied much longer.

Les's reply was slow in coming. "Do you know who I am?"

When Gil shook his head a second time, Les's lips peeled back in a skeletal grin. Gil tightened his grip on the Hopkins and Allen.

"My name's Quinlin, and around here, mister, when a Quinlin offers you a drink, you'd damn well better take it."

"I'm not from around here, and since I'll be moving on soon, there's no reason for us to get acquainted."

A worm of skepticism rippled across Les's face. "You're just passing through?"

Gil tipped his head in a nod.

"Jackson says you rode in from the north."

"That's right."

Les's gaze shifted to Jackson, then back to Gil. "From the direction of Max Ward's Flying W?"

Gil didn't reply. His head was swimming and the humming in his ears had grown to a low roar. He wanted this conversation to end. He'd prefer to do it without violence, but knew the

violently as before. When he was finished, he wiped his lips with his sleeve. Shaw slid the bottle of codeine from his pocket and handed it over, and Gil took a healthy swallow straight from the vial. The relief was immediate.

"I'd advise some restraint where codeine is concerned," the physician cautioned. "Drink enough of it too fast and it can kill you."

Gil nodded and recorked the bottle, but he didn't hand it back, and Shaw didn't protest when Gil slid it inside the mackinaw's big side pocket.

"This Jackson, is he a drover or one of Quinlin's gunmen?" Gil asked.

"I wouldn't call him a shooter, but he isn't anyone I'd want to tangle with, either." After a pause, he added, "I'm afraid you're going to have to leave the Basin, Mr. Ryan."

"It was Quinlin who drew first," Gil said. "I fired in self-defense."

"I believe you, but Art won't care. He'll want revenge, and he has the men to see that he gets it."

Gil looked away, his thoughts fragmented by fever and violence, while the pain from his long drop from the saddle continued to rumble through his already aching frame like a slow freight train. "You've got a jail, haven't you?" he finally asked. "You must have a sheriff."

"We have a man who wears a badge, but I wouldn't say he represents the law."

"Hal Keegan is another of Art Quinlin's apple polishers," Fred Somers explained, coming over with his hands thrust deep inside the pockets of a heavy wool coat. "You'll get no help from him."

"Then who do I talk to?" Gil persisted. "I'm not going to run, not when it was Quinlin who drew first."

"It was the kid's doin', all right," the bartender said, joining them in the middle of the street. "Les and them two curs of his rode in this afternoon, sore as spring bears because of something Joel said or wanted them to do. I never did get the straight of it, nor much give a damn, but when Jackson spotted this jasper ridin' in from the north, they figured Max Ward must've hired him. That got Les riled up all over again."

"Gil Ryan, this is Ira Bannerman," Shaw said. "Ira owns the saloon."

"Ryan."

Bannerman's greeting was brusque and without interest, and his gaze never left the physician's face. Gil didn't bother replying. A wave of nausea flowed over him and he leaned weakly against the sorrel's shoulder. He recalled Doc's admonition to go easy on the codeine, and vowed to use more restraint the next time he needed a swig.

"He can't stay," Ira continued adamantly. "Quinlin's gonna raise sweet holy hell when he finds out what happened to that boy of his, and we don't need that kind of trouble here."

"We know that, Ira," Shaw replied patiently, then turned to Somers. "Fred, we have to get this boy out of town, and the sooner the better. He's going to need food and medicine. He says he has money, but if he doesn't have enough, I'll cover what he can't pay for. I want him well supplied when he leaves here."

"I'm not going anywhere until this is straightened out with the law," Gil said.

"There isn't any law up here to straighten it out with," Somers replied. "If you stay, you'll be dead by this time tomorrow."

"That ain't no empty promise, either," Ira added solemnly.

Gil looked at Shaw. "I'm not running."

"There's no other choice, Gil. If you stay, Quinlin and his men will kill you. It's as simple as that. After you're out of the

Basin you can report this to a United States Marshal, if that would make you feel better. There's one in Albuquerque and another in Santa Fe. Tell them that if they have any questions they can write to me here in Larkspur. I'll confirm Les Quinlin's guilt in . . ."

"Doc," Ira interrupted, nodding toward the saloon.

Gil turned in time to see the man he'd dubbed Weasel climbing onto one of the horses in the alley. Shaw ordered him to stop, but Weasel drove his spurs into the animal's ribs, barreling out of the narrow passage like a cannon ball. He'd picked up his revolver along the way, but had it holstered.

"Go to hell, you sons'a bitches," Weasel yelled over his shoulder. Then he raised a fist in the air and shook it at them. Thirty seconds later he was gone, swallowed by the gloom.

Shaw swore and turned to Somers. "Can you outfit him?" he asked, inclining his head toward Gil.

"Sure."

Doc recited a list of supplies he wanted Gil to have, including a pint of codeine, the quinine, and some mustard plaster and cheesecloth for poultices. "He'll need a heavy bedroll and enough food to take him out of the Basin, too." He glanced at Gil. "Have you got matches, a change of clothes?"

"All I have is what you see. Everything else is at the bottom of the Big Sandy with my packhorse."

"I'll take care of it," Somers said, then hurried toward the store where the young woman was still watching them from the boardwalk.

"Ira," Shaw said to Bannerman. "Can you have someone remove these bodies?"

"I reckon I could. Where do you want 'em?"

"The feed store is as good of a place as any. Lay them out in back where it's cool." Ira nodded and took off in his long-legged stride, motioning for a couple of men standing in the light from a nearby restaurant to follow. When they were alone, Shaw said, "It's a regrettable situation you've been forced into, Mr. Ryan. I feel badly about it, but I think in the end, your leaving will be for the best."

"For who?" Gil asked quietly.

"For everyone, including you. We've had a growing problem around here for quite a while. I suspect Lester's death is going to bust everything wide open."

"Quinlin?"

Shaw nodded. "Art seems determined to drive the settlers and small ranchers along the Basin's north rim out of the valley. He says they're stealing cattle, although he's never offered any proof of it. For the last year or so, he's apparently decided he doesn't need to." He shook his head in frustration. "I used to think Art was a good man under a gruff exterior. I'm finding that harder to believe lately."

"You said there's a marshal in Albuquerque. Get him up here."

"We've sent for a marshal. More than once, but nothing's ever come of it. The last Deputy we had up here made it clear he didn't want to be called back unless we had legitimate proof to back up our accusations, rather than baseless speculation." A morose smile tugged at the physician's lips. 'Baseless speculation' was his description, mind you, not ours."

Gil could see Somers returning with full arms. The mercantile was a black hulk behind him, the light from its windows blurred by the developing storm. The woman came with him, bundled in a red capote with the hood pulled up over her wheat-colored tresses. Shaw went to help Somers, lifting a huge bedroll from the storekeeper's shoulder and sliding it across the skirting behind the cantle. The woman stepped over to where Gil was standing next to Rusty's shoulder, a burlap sack cradled in her arms.

38

"There are mustard poultices, a packet of quinine sulfate, and codeine in here," she said, "and Dad added a bottle of brandy and some honey and lemon peel for hot toddies. He says you should use the codeine first, but if you're still feeling poorly when that's gone to try the brandy."

"I will," Gil said, accepting the sack and looping it around his saddle horn.

"I . . . I'd like to apologize for the way I treated you earlier. I thought you were one of Quinlin's men. I'm sorry I misjudged you."

"It was a simple enough mistake," he replied, then, after a pause, "I'm afraid I don't know your name."

"It's Peggy, Peggy Somers."

"And Fred?"

"My father."

"I appreciate everything the two of you have done, Miss Somers."

She nodded, then moved back when her father and the doc came over. Somers spoke first.

"I noticed you were carrying forty-four rimfires in your cartridge belt. I took the liberty of adding a couple of boxes of ammunition to your saddlebags. I couldn't tell from the stock what kind of rifle you were carrying, other than that it looks fairly heavy."

"It's a Seventy-six," Gil said. "Forty-five-seventy-five caliber."

"Heavy enough," Somers agreed, then glanced at Peggy, who headed for the store without further direction.

Gil dug a buskskin poke from an inside pocket of his coat. "What do I owe you, Mr. Somers?"

"Eighteen dollars ought to cover it."

Gil counted out the money and dropped it in the merchant's hand. By the time he returned the pouch to his coat, Peggy had reappeared with four boxes of .45-75s—eighty rounds altogether. Gil glanced at Somers, then inclined his head toward the extra ammunition.

"It's already covered," Somers said.

Gil nodded and stepped alongside his horse. He took a moment to gather his strength, then placed a toe in the stirrup and heaved himself awkwardly into the seat, his leg dragging across the massive bedroll. Shaw came over as he was leveling his reins along Rusty's neck.

"If it was light, you could follow the road, but I doubt if you'll be able to find it in the dark. You might not see it tomorrow, either, if we get a lot of snow."

"My horse'll find it."

"Just remember there's only one practical way out of the Basin at this time of year, and that's through Ensillado Canyon, at the southern end of the valley."

"How far?"

"Right at sixty miles."

Gil's jaw tightened at the thought of sixty frigid miles, his head already swimming just from the effort of mounting. Other than that, he kept his face blank.

"I suppose if there's any silver lining to your situation, it's that when you reach the canyon's mouth you'll be nearly a thousand feet lower in elevation." Doc smiled bleakly. "Warm weather and plenty of sunshine."

"Desert country?"

"Prickly pear and mesquite. It's a hot, hard land, but it doesn't often snow." He took a step back, his expression taut with regret. "I wish it could be different, Mr. Ryan. Good luck."

Gil felt a strange, hollow ache in his gut as he nodded his goodbyes to Doc and Fred and Peggy, the only ones left now that full darkness had settled over the town. Ira Bannerman had seen to the removal of the bodies, and the townspeople along the boardwalk had returned to their homes and businesses.

Gil's sense of loss seemed misplaced considering the short amount of time he'd known these people. A couple of hours, at most. He told himself that it was because of all the lonely miles he'd traveled coming south out of Idaho, the days and weeks with just himself and his horse to talk to, but he knew there was more to it than that. He sensed a simple kindness in these folks that he hadn't experienced in his years knocking around the northern mining camps, an easy acceptance of who he was based only upon what he said and how he acted. That had been lacking in Idaho, where a man's every motive was met with some degree of suspicion. Especially by those who'd found color in the icy streams—a small percentage of the total population, really—or who believed they were about to strike it rich, which included just about everyone else.

Gil's chest rattled threateningly, and he quickly reined away. Tapping the sorrel's ribs with his heels, he rode out of town at a jog. Although the rough gait aggravated his lungs, another quick sip of codeine tamed that bobcat. He returned the bottle to the mackinaw's side pocket, then pulled the woolen scarf up over his mouth and nose. He didn't look back, but he sensed the others were still there, watching him out of sight.

He rode south for nearly thirty minutes. The winds calmed but the temperature continued to sink. After a while the snow began to fall in earnest. Not the small, pebbly stuff that had tormented him off and on all afternoon, but big flakes, solid with moisture. They swirled through the air and curled under the wide brim of his hat to lodge along the rim of his scarf, sticking to his flesh, blanketing his shoulders and back. If it kept up like this, Gil anticipated several inches by morning, maybe a foot or more, and all of a sudden he knew he wasn't going to make it. Not in the shape he was in. Sixty miles was too far with his fever burning hot and his chest drawing steadily tighter. He'd be lucky to see the southern end of the Basin, let alone

41

make it down through Ensillado Canyon to the warm desert below. With a ragged growl, he pulled his horse around and started back the way he'd come, into the face of a storm he wasn't sure he'd be up to handling.

CHAPTER THREE

A gust of wind swept away the veil of falling snow to reveal a campfire in the distance. It was a large one, its flames roaring skyward like leashed panthers. Although chilled to the bone and eager to share in the fire's warmth, Odell Love halted his mount well out on the plain. His relief at finding the derelict horse camp in the middle of a blizzard was tempered by a sizable dose of foreboding. He didn't know how the boys were going to react when they learned of Les Quinlin's death.

No, not his death, Odell immediately corrected himself, *Les's* murder.

He'd need to keep that straight, because if he didn't, someone might start to wonder if Odell hadn't hightailed it out of Larkspur too soon, and he didn't want any part of that. The Quinlins were going to be tough enough to be around without him wandering needlessly into their sights because of some careless slip of the tongue.

Even though it was late, well after midnight by Odell's reckoning, he could see men moving around the fire, and when he listened close he could hear their whiskey-tinged shouts and raucous laughter. Eyeing the camp from afar, he felt a moment's sadness for what the Sun had become since the old man's tumble from grace. The boys were supposed to be rounding up the summer cavvy, bucking the bark off the worst of the stock and readying the whole string for the spring gather. Instead, they were squandering time like they had it to burn. And maybe they did, Odell speculated. Maybe, listening to the old man's grumblings all winter, they'd decided he wasn't all that serious about cattle roundups and calf brandings like he'd once been. Like he should be now, in Odell's opinion.

Not that Art Quinlin would ever give a rat's dragging behind what he thought. Odell had realized a long time ago that Art neither liked nor respected him. He supposed it was enough that the fiery old bastard continued to tolerate his presence on the Sun, even if it was for reasons that had nothing to do with the efficient operation of a cattle ranch.

"Even a bone-headed twit has his place," Art had once explained to his crew, eliciting sputtering brays of laughter from the bunkhouse butt-kissers hoping to stay on the old man's good side. Art hadn't specifically mentioned Odell by name, but everyone knew who he was talking about, especially coming as it did right after Odell had stopped a stampede by accidentally being in the right place at the right time.

It had been a cougar's scream from the rocks above the holding grounds on the north range that had sent the cattle boiling to their feet. Odell, hauling his britches up after one of the cousie's especially spicy chili concoctions, had flown into the saddle without hesitation and quickly brought the stampede under control. Damn near single-handedly, too. Unfortunately, he'd forgotten that in his haste to reach his horse he hadn't taken time to button his trousers or pull up his braces, so that when he rode proudly into camp afterward and swung to the ground like the cock-of-the-walk he'd envisioned himself to be, his pants had dropped unceremoniously around his boot tops, leaving his boney knees and bare ass exposed to the chilly mountain air.

A stunned silence had greeted Odell's unexpected display of pasty flesh. Then the old man had laughed and shaken his head, before mounting his horse and riding out to inspect the herd.

He hadn't forgotten the incident, though, and would bring it up almost religiously whenever he wanted to deflect attention away from some decision he sensed his men were wary of, or to avert a bunkhouse altercation before it could erupt in gunfire.

Arguments descending into gunplay would never have been tolerated when Odell first started riding for the Sun, but that had changed after Molly Quinlin's death. Slowly at first, then with increasing swiftness, the character of the hands the old man hired began to coarsen, and the ranch itself began spiraling downward. It wasn't the size of the outfit or the number of cattle Quinlin laid claim to that declined, but the buildings themselves that were slowly falling apart from neglect. Odell had watched in sad confusion as Molly's flower beds were gradually absorbed back into sage and grama, while a rubbish heap outside the kitchen window grew into a small, fetid mountain that attracted all sorts of vermin.

The old man had become meaner as the years passed, too, and as his mood declined the older hands, the ones who had come into the Basin with him when the grass was belly-high to a tall horse and the Apaches still ran wild and free, began to drift on to other, more distant ranges. It was as if they sensed that, in time, not even the entirety of the Ensillado would be large enough to contain the elder Quinlin's growing tyranny.

Despite the abuse, Odell had stayed. Mostly, he knew, because he didn't have anywhere else to go. Although the other hands had been annoyingly confident in their ability to find employment elsewhere, Odell had lacked their certainty. Way back in the beginning, before Molly's death, he'd been hired on at the Sun as a waddie, someone whose responsibilities were to stay close to the ranch and make sure the repairs were kept up on the buildings and corrals, to fetch water for the missus and wood for the cook, and to keep the horse stalls clean and dry. It was a job he understood, and was a lot more in keeping with his skills. It wasn't until the more experienced cowhands began their exodus that the old man started putting Odell in the saddle on a regular basis.

"Start earning your keep for a change," was how he'd put it, and even though the words had stung like a horsefly's bite, it hadn't been enough for Odell to abandon what he'd for some time been afraid he might never find again—a home of sorts, with decent food, a warm bunk, steady pay, and a boss willing to overlook a man's occasional shortcomings.

Now, sitting his dun mare in the middle of a snowstorm, staring blindly past the swirling, scab-like flakes toward the stuttering flames of the too-large campfire, Odell wondered if he hadn't made a mistake in his decision to stay. Maybe he should have cut his pin with the others and taken his chances somewhere down the pike, before the hard cases starting showing up in ever-increasing numbers, changing the marrow of the outfit as surely as the sun changed the seasons.

A horse's nicker from the summer cavvy inside a large pole corral yanked Odell back to the frozen plain, a half day's ride north of the Sun's headquarters along the Little Ensillado River. Taking a resolute breath, he jabbed his spurs into the dun's ribs. The horse snorted its displeasure, but was too weary after its long ride from Larkspur to do more than give a little crow hop of protest. Odell cursed the horse for its attitude and spurred him again, and the animal broke into a shuffling trot. When he was about 100 yards from the fire, he gave a shout to announce his presence. He might've been dumber than a stump in the old man's estimation, but he wasn't so stupid as to approach a Sun camp in the middle of the night without letting the men there know he was coming in.

An answering hail ordered him forward, and Odell reluctantly rode toward the fire. As he drew closer he began to pick out individuals through the falling snow. Joel Quinlin, the old man's middle son—the last of the three Quinlin boys left alive now that Les and Earl were gone—was standing next to the fire with Brownie Hillman, Samson Hoag, and Wade Palmer. Carl Roth was sitting toward the rear of the lean-to that was the camp's primary shelter, his boots off and a last pipe jutting from the corner of his mouth. Goose Carter was already burrowed inside his bedroll against the back wall.

They were a tough bunch, every one of them, but Odell continued to probe the camp until he spotted Clint Miller standing in the shadows outside the lean-to. The lanky gunman's eyes were fixed coldly on Odell, and a chill that had nothing to do with the temperature skittered down his spine. He was wary of them all, but it was Miller who scared the bejesus out of him, and had ever since he'd shown up not too long after Christmas with a letter from the old man in his pocket, promising half a year's employment at $150 a month. That was five times what Odell was making, although he was honest enough with himself to know he wouldn't have wanted Miller's job no matter how high the pay.

Art Quinlin had made it plain last fall that he intended to sweep all the rustlers and troublemakers out of the Basin as soon as it greened up in the spring—fair warning to anyone claiming land outside of Larkspur's town limits, he'd stated at the time, and a promise that hell would be descending on any cattle thief still in the valley after the first of April.

Even though Odell didn't have any doubts about which side was going to come out on top in that fray, he sure as hell didn't want to be party to it. He was hoping that when the time came, the old man would send him onto the range to keep an eye on the Sun's cattle, instead of night-riding after innocent settlers. Not that he would have termed them as such within earshot of either Art Quinlin or Clint Miller, as testy as they'd both become on the subject.

The Sun's crew had built their fire in front of the lean-to, and had their still-saddled mounts hitched to a rope stretched between a couple of nearby pines. Odell couldn't see the summer remuda corralled back in the trees, but he could hear it. Not any one sound, but a coalescence of subtle noises, as of a single, massive entity lurking just out of sight. No one spoke as he rode up, until Joel took a single, aggressive step forward. "What are you doing here, Love?"

"I got bad news, Joel."

Quinlin's gaze swept past him. "Where's Les?"

"That's what I gotta tell you."

"You'd damn well better tell me he's on his way," Joel said. "If Pa finds out you three slipped off to town and left the rest of us out here to work the summer cavvy on our own, he's gonna peel your hides with a bullwhip."

Odell had been trying to think of a fitting way to tell Joel of his brother's death—his *murder*—ever since leaving Larkspur. Now, with the moment at hand and his pulse thundering in his ears, the best he could manage was to blurt it out like it was something evil to the taste.

"He's dead, Joel. Les . . . Les is dead."

Joel froze, staring at Odell as if unable to absorb the meaning of his words. The others stirred uneasily, and Carl Roth and Goose Carter scrambled for their boots. Carl was strapping his gun belt on over the outside of his coat before Joel spoke.

"What do you mean, he's dead?"

"I reckon it's like your pa figured," Odell replied shakily.

"What? What did my pa figure?"

"That Max Ward hired hisself a gunfighter."

Joel's eyes narrowed suspiciously. "Who?"

"He didn't say. He just come ridin' into Larkspur bold as you please, and when Les tried to talk to him, he opened up like hell's own fire. Shot Les down cold and killed Tim, too, then he threw down on me before I could get a clear shot at him."

It finally sank in. Joel took an unsteady step backward. He was breathing hard and his eyes were wild and darting. He'd been carrying a steaming tin mug of coffee when Odell rode up; he looked at it now as if he couldn't figure out what it was or where it had come from. Then he let the cup slip from his gloved fingers and his hand moved down to cover the grips of the Colt holstered at his waist.

"He caught us all by surprise, Joel. I swear, not a one of us knew what he was up to until it was too late."

"Even after what Pa said about watching sharp for strangers?"

"Well, yeah, we thought about that, but it was real clear this jasper was sick as a dog. Looked like he was barely hangin' onto his saddle."

Joel's brows furrowed. "Sick?"

"Uh-huh. He stopped at Somers first, then went over to see Doc Shaw. After that, when he was riding back through town, Les said we ought to go see who he was and find out what he was doing in Larkspur, in case it was something your pa needed to know about. We all walked outside and Tim went into the street to stop him, and that's when he opened up. Had his pistol out before any of us knew what he was doing."

"You're telling me a sick man, barely able to sit his horse, outdrew Les and Tim Jackson, and you didn't even fire a shot?"

"Ah . . . I . . . ," Odell's gaze shifted involuntarily to the others, but no one came to his aid. They were all watching silently, almost hungrily, as if the entire bunch was turning into a pack of wolves right before his eyes. "I stayed where Les told me to stay, Joel, but I didn't have a clear . . ."

"Bullshit!" Joel turned to the others. "Mount up. We're gonna go put that gunslick son of a bitch under a tall tree, then let him hang there 'til he rots."

The men turned as one, all except for Clint Miller. Clint stayed where he was, staring at Odell as if he could see right through him, picking out the lies like raisins from rice. Then he smiled knowingly and turned toward the picket line. When they were alone, Joel said: "You'd better be telling the truth, Love, 'cause if you ain't, I'm gonna stretch your neck alongside Les's murderer."

"I saw what I saw, Joel, God's honest truth."

Joel sneered. "You saw what you saw, then ran out here to tell me?"

"I'd've been all night reaching the Sun, and maybe given that gunhand a chance to slip away."

"He won't try to get away if he's working for Big Max."

"Yeah, I guess that's true, but I don't . . ."

Joel turned away and Odell stopped talking. Clint Miller rode into the light on his gray, leading a handsome palomino by the reins. Joel took the palomino's reins and stepped into the saddle, then spun the horse around to pin Odell with a dark stare.

"You head on down to the Sun and tell Pa what happened, and you think real careful about what you tell him, too, so that the story he hears from you is the same one I hear when I get into town."

He paused as if waiting for Odell to deny there was anything less than whole hog in his description of what had taken place in Larkspur. When Odell didn't reply, a taut smile played across the younger man's face.

"Maybe you ain't as dumb as everyone thinks, Love. At least you're savvy enough to know when to keep your mouth shut." He glanced over his shoulders at the others, gathered at the edge of the firelight. Half a dozen hard-bitten men, all of them mounted on good horses and ready to ride.

Looking once more at Odell, Joel said, so softly his words

were almost inaudible: "Don't get lost, Love, because if you ain't with Pa when he rides into Larkspur, you'd better have a damned good reason why not. You try slipping away before we sort this out and I'll personally put a five-hundred-dollar bounty on your head. Understand?"

"Hell's bells, Joel, I ain't . . ."

"Understand?"

Odell flinched, then nodded, and Joel dug his spurs into the palomino's sides. He rode past at a gallop, the others streaming after him. They came so close on either side that Odell could feel the wind of their passage against his cheeks. He remained where he was, keeping his horse on a tight rein until the snow-muffled thunder of hooves faded behind him. Then he dismounted on unsteady legs and approached the fire.

Grease was dripping from strips of recently butchered beef propped over the flames, and the coffee pot was still half full. Odell fixed himself a meal and ate it slowly, all the while trying to convince himself that the reason he was trembling was because of the cold. Despite Joel's warning, he did give some serious consideration to making a run for it. He figured the odds were in his favor that he could be out of the Basin, down into desert country, before anyone knew he was gone. The problem was that he knew Joel meant what he said about putting a bounty on his head, and it was just as likely the old man would throw some money into the pot as well.

Cursing his poor luck, Odell drained the cup Joel had left behind, then tossed it into the lean-to. Mounted, he reined toward the Sun's headquarters, still half a night's ride to the south. If he kept a steady pace and didn't get turned around in the storm, he figured he could be there by dawn; if the old man was around and not sunk too deep into a bottle, they could probably be back in Larkspur by midafternoon. Lord knew what they'd find when they got there. Joel could be as crazy mean as his pa under the right circumstances, and Odell doubted it would take much to push him over the edge after seeing his dead brother. With a sinking sensation in his breast, Odell realized hell was on its way to Larkspur. Only time would tell how severely the town was going to be scorched.

Dawn brought crisp blue skies and temperatures hovering right at ten degrees according to the thermometer hanging outside Doc Shaw's kitchen window. The nearly eight inches of new snow that had fallen overnight sparkled like fields of crushed glass in the early-morning sun, and the air was as still as the inside of a casket. It was a quiet, beautiful morning, but as Doc stood at the dry sink staring out at the pristine landscape, he couldn't help wondering how long it would last.

Alma moved quietly behind him, clearing away the breakfast dishes even as she set out jars of last summer's green beans and pickled beets for the noon meal. From time to time Doc would sense her coming close, and he appreciated the occasional gentle touch of her fingers on his arm or shoulder or back. She didn't speak for the longest time, and he was grateful for that, too, but when she finally did break the comfortable silence between them, he was ready for it to be broken.

"It would have happened sooner or later."

"I know," he said.

"Lester Quinlin was always the troublemaker in the family, even before his mother passed away, God rest her soul."

"It was worse after Molly died, though."

"Yes, but with only Arthur's influence on their lives, it's a wonder all of those boys haven't been killed or jailed."

Doc nodded pensively, thinking back to Molly Quinlin's death. Although the culprit had been a burst appendicitis, he was convinced he could have saved her if Art hadn't been so bullheaded about sending for help, if Doc could have gotten there in time to remove the inflamed organ before it ruptured. But Art had told his boys their mother would be fine in a day or two, and allowed the woman to slide too far downward before their eldest son, Earl, snuck away to seek aid.

It was forty miles or more from Larkspur to the Sun, and Doc had kept his old mare at a swift trot the entire way. He could tell from Earl's description of his mother's condition that the situation was critical, but by the time he reached the ranch it was too late. Molly had already slipped into unconsciousness; she passed away even as Doc prepared for surgery.

Although their mother's death had affected all three of the Quinlin boys deeply at the time, Doc hadn't detected any emotion in Arthur at all. He'd buried his wife that same afternoon on a small knoll north of the family's sprawling adobe house, and hadn't even given Doc time to send word back to town so that others might know and share in the service. Although he'd allowed Doc to stay, he'd made it clear he didn't want a bunch of townspeople coming out to the Sun thinking they had to do something to help the grieving family.

"We take care of our own, Shaw, like we been doin' since long before you and your kind started showin' up in the Basin."

Doc had argued that the citizens of Larkspur would only want to offer their condolences to the boys, and to say goodbye to Molly in their own way, but Art wouldn't hear of it.

"Keep 'em away," he'd nearly spat, then stalked rigidly toward the corrals, calling for his sons to saddle up and get back to work.

Only Earl Quinlin had defied his father's command to return to the range. After the others—Art, Les, Joel, and the half dozen or so wranglers who worked for the Sun in those days—had left, Earl came over to where Doc was backing his mare between his buggy's shafts. He was holding out a five-dollar gold piece that Doc at first refused, but Earl had been adamant, and his eyes flashed dangerously.

"Take it," he'd growled in muted imitation of his father's barely contained pain—a wrenching, gut-deep hurt, masked in anger.

Doc had reluctantly accepted the coin, but when he tried to express his sympathy to the boy for his loss, Earl abruptly spun away. He went to the corral where his horse was tied and swung into the saddle. He hadn't looked back as he rode away from the ranch. Not even toward the knoll where his mother was buried.

"Two dead," Alma said softly, bringing Doc back to their little house in Larkspur. At first he thought she was talking about Les and Tim Jackson. Then he realized she was talking about Art's oldest and youngest, both killed by gunfire less than a year apart. Now only Joel remained, as mean as any of them, but more calculating than Les. Had Joel been in town last night, Doc felt certain he could have stopped his brother from pushing so recklessly against a man he didn't know, backing himself into a corner with only his arrogance and a deeply ingrained rage to guide him out again.

Doc thought briefly of Earl. He'd always felt there had been traces of goodness in the Quinlins' eldest son that the others lacked. Perhaps because he'd been exposed to more of his mother's influence than the younger ones. But Earl had been killed late last autumn, shot down less than a mile south of town. Although Art insisted the boy's death had been at the hands of one of the homesteaders crowding onto the northern ranges, Doc had his doubts. A lot of Larkspur's residents did, knowing about Earl and Fred Somers's girl, Peggy, and about Reece Ward, who was Big Max's son. It was all a convoluted mess in Doc's opinion, filled with more speculation than solid fact, but Earl's death continued to nag at him, like an itch he couldn't reach.

Sighing, he set his empty mug in the dry sink, then turned away from the window.

"There's more coffee if you want some," Alma offered.

"No, thanks." He walked into the front room and brought his coat and fur cap down from their pegs beside the door. "I think I'll head on down to the Paris. The others will be there soon."

"Will." Alma waited until he stopped and turned. "You don't have to do it all," she said gently. "Let someone else take charge this time."

"Who?"

"Fred, or Ira, any of them."

Besides Doc and Fred Somers and Ira Bannerman, Larkspur's *ad hoc* citizens' committee consisted of three other businessmen, although none of them had been officially elected to the position. Paul Offerman owned the livery. Henry Fisher carpentered and sold hardware out of a small building behind his house, and Roger Greene had the town's only barbershop and bathhouse, which he ran with his wife's assistance. They were all good men, but they weren't leaders. Doc knew they'd wait half the morning for either him or Fred to take command of the meeting, rather than grab the reins themselves.

Although it occasionally irritated both Doc and Fred, it seemed to bother Alma and Peggy a lot more. The trouble, as Doc saw it, was that if someone didn't take charge, then no one would. Nothing would ever be accomplished, and the small inroads they'd made so far in giving Larkspur a legitimate town council would be lost.

The trouble as Alma saw it, Doc knew, was that her husband had more of a commitment to the town than anyone else, except for maybe Fred Somers.

"They don't care, but you do," she said, helping Doc into his bulky winter coat.

"This is our home," he reminded her.

"It's their home, too."

"Alma . . ."

"Don't you shush me, William Shaw. You know how Art is going to react when he hears of this. Or, heaven forbid, if Joel learns about it first."

"Enough," Doc said, but there was neither animosity nor heat in his tone. He knew what she was saying was true, and that her feelings were rooted in concern for his safety. But sometimes a man had to do what was right, no matter the odds or the consequences, and Doc sensed that, for Larkspur, the time for action was rapidly approaching.

He pulled the badger-skin cap on over his bald head. As he did, his glance strayed into the parlor and a smile twitched at the corners of his mouth. His violin was still sitting on the upholstered chair next to his music stand where he'd placed it last night, after Gil Ryan's arrival. What a foolish pastime, he mused, staring wistfully at the instrument. He'd taken it up when he retired from the military but had yet to conquer even the simplest tune with any real skill. Yet he still loved the instrument. Its smooth, varnished wood and the smell of a freshly rosined bow had the ability to carry him far away from whatever trouble might be pestering his thoughts. In the three years that he'd owned the violin, he'd never tired of his struggle to master it, although he sometimes regretted the torture he put his wife through in his violation of the classics.

Sighing, he turned his back on the parlor. Alma was at his side, smiling to show her support.

"I know you'll do what's right, Will. That's why I love you."

"And I know you'll worry about me. That's only one of the reasons I love you."

He expected a smile but didn't get it. She searched his face. "Do you think Arthur will be in today?"

"I'm surprised he isn't already here." Impulsively, he caressed her cheek with the back of his fingers. "I'd better go. The others will be wondering what happened if I'm not already seated when they show up."

"Be careful."

He nodded and opened the door. "I will," he promised, but he was already stepping outside as he spoke, the words tossed almost carelessly over his shoulder.

The cold was embracing, and more penetrating than he would have expected with the sun already up. He trudged through the shin-deep snow to Larkspur's single, lopsided street before turning south toward the business block. Since the boardwalk wasn't completed all the way, he decided to forge a path to Hannah Brickman's Paris Café along the street, where the snow had been packed down earlier by a horse-drawn dray. A column of wood smoke was already rising from the restaurant's chimney as Doc approached, and he could smell Hannah's fresh-baked bread even before pushing through the front door. Hannah's daughter was standing behind the counter when he walked in, freckled and red-haired, fourteen years old and already as pretty as a spring daisy.

"Hello, Dr. Shaw," she called cheerfully as he paused to stomp snow from his half-boots.

"Hello, Daphne. Am I the first one here?"

"Ain't you always?"

He smiled and moved toward his accustomed spot at the table nearest the window. It would be chilly there today, but worth it for both its familiarity and its view of the street. Hannah came out of the kitchen with her own warm greeting and asked if he'd eaten yet, even though she knew he had. She was tall and solid and had her sleeves pushed up above her elbows. Her hands were dusted to the wrist with flour, with a random streak of it across one cheek that set off her blue eyes like chips of turquoise under rust-colored brows.

"I have," he assured her, "although I wouldn't turn down a slice of something warm to go with my coffee."

"I've got some dried apple pie left over from last night, or I can throw a slice of fresh-baked bread on the stove and toast it."

"Does that toasted bread come with any kind of butter or jam?"

Hannah laughed with loud good nature. "Plenty of Schwartz's butter and any kind of jam you can think of, as long as it's grape or huckleberry."

"There's an offer I can't turn down. I'll take huckleberry, if you please."

Hannah returned to her kitchen and Doc settled back in his chair. He liked the Paris Café. It was a small building, but it was always warm and friendly and clean. Even the silverware. There were red-and-white checked cloths on the tables, and a shelf along the back wall that was always lined with an assortment of recently baked treats—pies and cobblers and fancy breads.

Besides its cleanliness—something of a rarity on the frontier in Doc's estimation—the café's most unique feature was a lithograph that hung prominently above the rear counter, an uncomplicated image of a Parisian street scene at sunset. Sloping veils of rain fell in the distance, and the cobblestones in the foreground had a wet shine, as if the storm had only recently passed through. A horse and carriage were moving away from the eye on the left, toward the setting sun, while an outdoor eatery dominated the entire right-hand side of the painting, men and women in their Sunday best enjoying whatever it was the French ate and enjoyed on rainy afternoons. A small brass plaque centered on the lower portion of the frame read: *L'Avenue des Champs Elysées.*

Doc didn't have a clue what that meant, nor did Hannah, but

it didn't matter. Although small in scope, the illustration had always seemed large in concept. Doc had seen cowboys and laborers alike stare at the painting for minutes on end, as if mentally slipping inside the almost whimsical depiction so that they, too, could wander its rain-slickened streets. Doc was as guilty of this as any of them, and seldom visited the café without spending a few minutes studying the scene, poking around inside the stores in his own mind just for the hell of seeing what his imagination could conjure up.

A shadow flitted across the window and Doc pulled his gaze away from the lithograph. Fred Somers huffed inside, his nose already dripping from the short hike from his store. Like Doc, he paused to kick the worst of the snow from his shoes, then closed the door with a exaggerated shiver.

"I'd hoped winter was over after last week's warm spell," he announced to the room at large, then directed individual greetings to Hannah and Daphne, who had returned from the kitchen when they heard the door open.

"I'm toasting Doc some bread to go with his jam," Hannah said. "You want some?"

"Toast and jam and sugar for my coffee?"

Hannah nodded and disappeared into the kitchen. Fred eased into the chair at Doc's side, his expression somber. "How'd you sleep last night?" he asked quietly.

Doc waited until Daphne had poured coffee for both of them and returned to the counter before replying. "About the same as you, I'd imagine."

Fred regarded the tabletop thoughtfully. "I was wondering . . ." He hesitated.

"Yeah?"

"I was wondering if maybe it wasn't time we fought back. The town, I mean. What do you think?"

The question caught Doc off guard. As hesitantly as it had

been broached, it was still the first time he was aware of anyone on the citizens' committee proposing they stand up to the Sun as a community. It had always been something they'd expected the small ranchers and homesteaders to do, as if unrelated to the town's welfare, but Doc knew that wasn't true. Everything the Sun did, no matter how distant, eventually affected the town. Sooner or later, the citizens of Larkspur were going to have to acknowledge that.

Yet, even though he agreed that it was time, past time even, Doc couldn't deny the gut-deep feeling of apprehension that suddenly gripped him. Art Quinlin was oak-tough and rabid-mean, and he wouldn't look kindly on the town sticking its nose into what he would undoubtedly consider the Sun's business.

After a pause, Doc mused, "I wonder how many men he has working for him."

"Quinlin? I'd bet a dozen by now, if not more."

"More than he needs to work cattle."

"A lot more, and most of them hard cases, to boot."

"If it came to a war, we'd be lucky to muster half that many," Doc said reflectively.

"Out of the entire Basin?"

"Out of Larkspur, at least. Think about it."

"Damnit, Doc, this is our home."

"You don't have to convince me. I told Alma the same thing before I came over here, but I suspect others would pack up and move away before taking a stand against the Sun."

"Not all of them," Fred replied stubbornly.

"Most of them."

"Arnie Hale wouldn't."

"No, he'd probably stay and fight, but think about the citizens' committee. Think about Henry and Roger and Paul standing up to Quinlin. They wouldn't do it, and I'm not sure Ira would, either."

Fred leaned back in his chair, staring moodily out the window. After a moment, Doc joined him, two old friends content to sit quietly while their minds wandered private trails. The lull continued for nearly five minutes before the thud of boots climbing the café's steps interrupted their thoughts. Henry Fisher and Paul Offerman stomped inside, scattering snow from their boots and cuffs across the floor. Roger Greene showed up a few minutes later. Ira Bannerman was the last to arrive, but he generally was, having to stay up later than the others to close his saloon. Ira had barely commandeered his usual seat between Offerman and Greene when Hannah appeared with a platter stacked high with toasted bread. A small wooden tub of butter and jars of both grape and huckleberry jam were carried in a wicker basket dangling from the crook of one arm. Small spoons had been jabbed into all three vessels.

"If you gentlemen need anything else, shout," Hannah instructed, then motioned for her daughter, who was topping off their coffee mugs, to come along. "Let's leave these men alone, Daph. They've got some serious business to discuss this morning." She waited until Daphne exited the room. "Just so you gents know, I have a shotgun in the kitchen that I'm not too shy to use," she said. "That's something you might want to keep in mind as you make your decisions."

"Thank you, Hannah," Doc said gratefully, and the woman nodded once, curtly, then walked away.

"By damned, there's one who'd stand and fight," Fred murmured.

"Fight?" Paul Offerman echoed. "Who's talking about fighting?"

Doc studied the faces of the five men sharing the table with him. He tried to imagine how each of them would react if pushed into a confrontation with Art Quinlin and his gunmen. He didn't think the outcome would be favorable.

They weren't a young bunch anymore. Paul was probably the last to leave the cradle, and his hair and beard were as gray as a steel dust pony. At sixty-four, Doc was the oldest, but Henry wasn't too far behind, and Fred was sliding rapidly toward his mid-fifties. Nor were any of them especially proficient with firearms. They all owned guns and were adequate shots—the land demanded that much—but they weren't anywhere near the equal of Quinlin's crew. And now there was word that Art had brought in a professional, a hired killer from the north whose job was to whip the Sun's ragtag band of hard cases into a cohesive fighting outfit.

Just contemplating it made the likelihood of success seem all the more remote to Doc, and he was glad when Henry spoke up in response to Paul's question.

"Nobody's talking about butting heads with Quinlin," Fisher said. "Fred was only thinking out loud. Ain't that right, Fred?"

Fred didn't reply. He glanced at Doc and the others followed suit. Doc sighed. There wasn't going to be much idle jawing today.

"I don't suppose there's any point in denying it. Fred and I did talk briefly about not bowing down to Quinlin's demands . . ."

"What demands?" Paul interrupted. "Art Quinlin ain't been making no demands I know of. It's the horse thieves and cattle rustlers he wants cleared out, and I can't say I blame him."

"The North Rim homesteaders?" Fred asked mildly.

"Yeah, damnit, men like Max Ward and that bunch." He glanced around the table with a look of belligerence. "By God, that ain't no way our fight."

"I've never seen any evidence of rustling from the settlers along the Rim," Doc said.

"We don't run cattle up there," Paul replied. "Quinlin does."

"There are innocent men up there, too. A lot of them with families."

"There's innocent men right here in Larkspur, and a lot of us have families," Paul retorted.

"All Fred and I discussed was the possibility of taking a stand against Art's aggressiveness, rather than reverting to our usual passivity," Doc said.

"You mean fighting?"

"Not necessarily, but if it came to it."

"Buckin' Quinlin's bunch'd be suicide," Ira stated flatly.

"Do you have a better idea?" Fred asked.

"That second thing Doc mentioned sounded pretty good."

"What, passivity?"

"If that means keeping our heads down and not getting our tail feathers plucked, you damn right."

"All we're doing right now is exploring our options," Doc reminded them.

"There ain't no options that need exploring," Paul said. "We try standing up to those boys of Quinlin's, they'll burn this town to the ground." His gaze swung from Doc to Fred, then back again. "It, by God, *ain't* our fight, Doc!"

Keeping his voice low and his demeanor as calm as his growing aggravation would allow, Doc said, "We're not talking about the people under the Rim, Paul. We're talking about Art Quinlin, and what's going to happen when he shows up in Larkspur with blood in his eyes for Les's death. We need to have some kind of a plan in mind for when he gets here."

"What Quinlin's gonna want is revenge," Ira said. "I don't wanna be the one to tell him we let that drifter slide outta here without tryin' to stop him."

"What happened last night wasn't Ryan's fault," Doc replied. "We can't shift the blame away from where it belongs just to avoid a confrontation."

"Not even if we can shift it onto a stranger who's no longer here?" Henry Fisher asked. "I'm not saying we should, mind you, but you know how Art is, Doc. He's going to be spitting fire, and Lord help us if Joel shows up first. They're going to have a lot of mad to burn off, and I don't want to see them take it out on the town. None of us wants that."

"We're not going to shove the fault for Les's actions onto a sick man," Doc replied stubbornly. "What kind of men would we be to stoop to something like that?"

"Live ones," Ira said.

"Cowards," Fred amended.

"It ain't bein' cowardly to look after your own, Somers," Paul replied. "We'd be idjits to let Quinlin sic his dogs on us for something none of us had any say over."

"Whatever happens today won't have anything to do with who killed Lester Quinlin last night," Doc argued. "Which brings us right back to asking ourselves, how much longer will we put up with Quinlin's oppression?"

"What in blue thunder do you mean, it doesn't have anything to do with who killed Les?" Paul nearly stuttered. "That's the whole damned long and short of it."

"No, Doc's right," Fred began, but Ira cut him off.

"It ain't neither Doc nor Paul who's right, Fred, it's what're we gonna do when the old man comes a'hellin' in here lookin' for someone's hide to peel. I'll tell you straight, I ain't eager on it bein' mine."

"Me, neither," Paul declared hotly.

"The solution isn't to offer a sacrificial lamb to Quinlin's fanaticism," Doc said. "Art Quinlin doesn't have a right to peel anyone's hide, whether it's a stranger's or one of ours."

Ira grunted dismissively. "Tell that to the old man, Doc, see what it gets you."

"Hold on, fellas," Roger Greene said, lifting the fingers of his left hand partway off the table as if wanting to calm the rising tide of antagonism, yet half afraid of getting something bit off if he put it out too far. "Doc, I understand what you're saying, and it does sound noble and all, but Paul and Ira are making pretty good sense, too. We don't have any law up here other than what Hal Keegan brings, and we all know who he'll side with."

"Hal Keegan is out to the Sun right now, swappin' stories with the old man about those North Rim homesteaders," Ira informed them. "The talk I was hearin' last night was that as soon as it greens up for certain-sure, he's gonna start a full-scale war on them boys. Gonna rid the Basin of squatters for good. That's what Les was sayin'."

"Keegan's not on our side," Fred agreed, earning quick nods of assent from the others. "We can't turn to the law on this."

"Tried it already," Paul reminded everyone, although he deliberately avoided eye contact with Doc.

Doc ignored the implied criticism. Everyone, and that included Art, knew that Doc had sent for a United States Marshal the previous summer, pleading for help when Quinlin began making his first tentative raids against the smaller outfits under the North Rim. A deputy had showed up some weeks later to look into the allegations, but by then Quinlin's men had intimidated most of the Basin's witnesses into a stoic silence. The deputy had stopped by Doc's place on the way out of the valley and told him not to write again without solid proof and witnesses who weren't afraid to testify.

"We're on our own up here, no doubt about that," Henry Fisher stated glumly, and no one disagreed with that, either. Not even Doc.

"That's why we've got to approach this problem differently than folks might do elsewhere," Roger went on. "We have to be delicate about it."

"Delicate?" Ira snorted. "We half'ta put that old man off our scent is what we half'ta do. Ain't no other way to handle a hell-raiser like Art Quinlin."

"What are you suggesting, Ira?" Doc asked quietly.

"I ain't been beatin' around the bush, Doc. That stranger that came through here last night killed two men, then rode on outta town like he didn't have a care in his pocket. Quinlin's gripe is with him, not us."

"Unless the old man blames us for letting him ride out," Paul added. "That's what I'm afraid of, and I'll tell you what we should've done, too. We should've arrested Ryan last night and put him in Keegan's jail. That way, we wouldn't all be sitting here worryin' about what Quinlin's gonna do."

"No," Doc said in a voice as cold as ice.

Sensing the change in the physician's demeanor, Paul met his gaze with caution. "What do you mean?"

"It's not Keegan's jail, and it's not Quinlin's decision."

"Doc," Roger said warily, "I reckon you know I've got a lot of respect for you, but this isn't a fight we can win, or the time to try it, either."

"When will that time be, Roger?"

"I don't know. Maybe when we have our own lawman up here, someone who'll support the wishes of the committee."

"One man?" Ira scoffed. "One man couldn't do it, Rog. It'd take an army to stand up to Quinlin now."

"Maybe not," Fred said quietly, and the others looked at him with varying degrees of puzzlement. Shrugging, he added, "The right man could do it."

Paul guffawed and shook his head. "Ain't no one man gonna stand up to Quinlin no more, Fred. Hell, not even Wild Bill would stand a chance against that bunch."

"No, not all at once," Doc agreed quietly. "But maybe . . ."

A shout from the street interrupted his thoughts. Peering past the slush of melting frost on the café's window, he saw a group of horsemen riding hell-for-leather into town, and his heart sank. Across the table from him, Paul Offerman moaned low in his throat.

"Aw, hell," Ira whispered. "They're here."

Chapter Four

Odell sucked in his breath as his dun mare lunge-jumped into the fast-flowing Little Ensillado. The splash from the knee-deep waters was like a sharp slap to his face, and his already icy toes curled even tighter inside his boots. Gasping a string of stuttered profanities toward the deep blue of the sky, he urged his horse up out of the river bottom and onto the lane leading toward the ranch.

Although the twin wagon tracks winding through the sage were little more than shallow indentations in the snow, they were easy enough to follow in the brilliant sunshine. Frankly, Odell wouldn't have minded if they'd been a little more difficult, or if they'd hugged the curve of the river instead of cutting straight across the plain to the Sun's headquarters. Not that the delay would have changed anything, other than to maybe make the old man even madder if he found out Odell had taken any other route to the ranch than the most direct one, and he sure as hell didn't want that. Art Quinlin was going to be pissing fire as it was when he found out Odell had ridden to the horse camp first to tell Joel of Les's death. No, murder, damnit. Les's *murder!*

Odell drew rein at the lower end of a small ridge fingering down off a piney bluff to the south. The ranch lay before him under its blanket of freshly fallen snow. The main house sat atop a small bench about 100 yards away, its white-washed adobe walls peeling clay, the pale red tiles of its roof edging closer toward the eaves with each passing season and no one to look after them. That had been Odell's job, back when Molly Quinlin was alive and the old man had taken pride in the way the place looked. When Odell Love didn't have to ride a horse or carry a gun every damned day just to keep his job.

Where the lane curved up toward the main house was the official entrance to the place. Odell's gaze lingered on the towering crossbeam, metal-strapped atop a pair of huge logs set upright in the rocky soil. Hanging from the center of the crosspiece was what had once been the old man's joy, a massive ship's wheel taken off a Gulf Coast steamer, then modified by a Galveston blacksmith into a crude image of the sun. Although not an exact match of the outfit's brand, it was close enough that no one was going to mistake it for anything else. The old man had brought the giant sculpture with him from Texas, but time and the elements had been hard on the discarded ship's wheel. With neglect, its surface had become pocked with rust, the tips of the sun's rays nearly eaten away by corrosion in the twenty-plus years since the old man had left the salty Gulf Coast air.

Softly cursing his poor luck, Odell hupped his mare into a walk, guiding her up the slope toward the main house. His mood sank even further as he came even with the house corral and spotted Hal Keegan's blue roan gelding standing alongside the old man's buckskin. The snow in the tiny corral was churned and discolored from manure and urine, the hay manger empty, its water iced over.

"Lazy bastards," Odell mumbled, his oath including not just Keegan and the old man, but the whole damned crew. His gaze skipped to the bunkhouse where a thin thread of smoke rose from the chimney, then on to the far corral where the hired men kept their horses. The rear corral was full, and Odell knew that if he checked, that manger would also be empty, the trough frozen.

He brought his gaze back to Keegan's roan and his lips thinned in disdain. He didn't have much use for the Ensillado lawman. He wasn't even sure the position was legal. Sure as hell not very many people in the Basin thought it was. Not that Odell cared overly much. Politics had never held much interest for him. He couldn't have named the president of the country, let alone the governor of the territory, but it did bother him the way Hal Keegan would talk about a number of Larkspur's leading citizens. Especially their wives and daughters. That was going too far in Odell's opinion, and he could remember a time when the old man wouldn't have tolerated it, either. Lately, though, Art seemed to almost encourage the sheriff's coarseness, as if reducing the Basin's citizens to objects rather than human beings made his own ambitions easier to stomach.

Drawing his mare to a halt in front of the *hacienda,* Odell stepped down and looped his reins around a sagging hitching rail—*just one more thing that needed attention,* he thought sourly—then made his way through the nearly knee-deep snow to the front entrance. He didn't knock. That kind of formality only irritated the old man, especially when he had to drag his own ass out of a chair to answer the summons. Had the weather been warmer, it was doubtful the door would have even been closed, but it was shut that morning, and Odell had to push his way inside, then shove the heavy door shut behind him, kicking snow out of the threshold to close it.

"Mr. Quinlin," he called into the *hacienda*'s sprawling interior.

"Who is it?"

The voice echoed harshly through the house. Odell followed the query down a dark hall to a large room at the rear of the house. The closer he got, the warmer it felt, and the first thing he noticed as he entered the room where the old man kept his guns and saddles and whiskey was a blaze in the fireplace as big as a bonfire.

The old man was seated in a leather chair to one side of the hearth, short and skeletal, his hair falling white over his collar, his beard like a spade molded from bone china, although stained yellow along each side of his mouth. His pale gray eyes, set in such a leathery face, were always startling to Odell when viewed in this kind of light; there was something almost nonhuman in their gleam.

Hal Keegan sat opposite him, sharing the warmth of the fire and a tumbler of what was probably some pretty good Eastern whiskey. Keegan was in his mid-forties, thick chested and heavy gutted. He had a pudgy face, and his cheeks were flowered with tiny, broken capillaries. He laughed crudely when he saw who it was. "Damn, I was hopin' she sensed I was talkin' about her, and had come out to visit."

Odell didn't know who the lawman was talking about, and didn't figure it mattered. The old man wasn't as oblivious, though, and his eyes narrowed as soon as he recognized his visitor. "What's wrong, Love?"

Odell hesitated at the brusqueness of the question, then sucked in a deep breath and began his tale, staying more or less on the same track he'd taken earlier with Joel. Twenty minutes later he was saddling a fresh mount for himself while the old man roused the rest of the crew from their bunks and Keegan saddled his roan and Art's buckskin. When they rode out not long afterward, it felt to Odell as if they were no longer cowhands, that they'd finally shed the last vestiges of an illusion no one had believed in for a long time anyway. They were an army now, riding out to conquer a legion of innocents.

They rode in from the west, and with the sun barely an hour into the sky, Doc knew it had to be Joel's men coming from the

Sun's horse camp. Art wouldn't be in until later that afternoon, assuming someone had gone to the ranch to tell him.

After Ira's hushed exclamation that they were here, no one spoke for a long time. They sat staring in dreaded anticipation until Doc finally pushed to his feet. The others followed suit, right down to the look of impending doom on their faces. Although they stepped clear of the table as if expecting trouble, no one there was really up to stopping it. In the heavy silence of the little café, the sound of slowly scraping chair legs and popping knee joints seemed almost comical.

Joel led his men to the saloon first, all of them dismounting out front, then trooping inside as one, leaving their winded mounts hitched loosely to the rails. The citizens' committee stood silently until Joel reappeared a couple of minutes later. His men were still with him, bunched tight with their hands on their revolvers. They paused for only a moment, then turned toward the café. Mumbling under his breath, Paul Offerman took a dragging step backward.

"Don't lose your courage," Fred said softly, advice Paul responded to with a guttural curse. Then the café's front door was shoved open and the Sun's crew tramped nosily inside, spreading out like professionals to cover the entire room.

Doc recognized several of the men. Brownie Hillman and Wade Palmer had hired on late last year, and been in and out of Larkspur on a semi-regular basis ever since. Carl Roth was another familiar face, a German with a thick accent and a huge Bowie carried sheathed on his left hip. The other three were strangers. There was a lanky blond with a drooping mustache, a thick-shouldered African with a full, tightly curled beard, and a tall, slim man with an unusually long neck and prominent Adam's apple. None of them wore chaps or rope-burned gloves, and as Doc's gaze roved over the crew, he thought, *There's not an honest-to-God drover among them.*

Hannah Brickman came out of the kitchen as Quinlin's men marched inside. She paused at the galley's entrance, the door partially open, then made a shooing motion behind her. Doc hoped she was telling Daphne to leave. He didn't know what kind of men Art had riding for him nowadays, but he had to assume the worse.

Moving behind the counter, Hannah said, "Welcome to the Paris, boys. Come on in and have some fresh bread and a cup of cinnamon coffee. It's on the house." She fixed her gaze on Quinlin. "You, too, Joel. I'm real sorry about Lester, but standing there dripping melted snow all over the floor isn't going to help."

"You stay out of this, Mrs. Brickman," Joel said, his face flushed from either anger or the biting cold on their long ride into Larkspur.

"I'm not butting in, Joel," Hannah replied mildly. "I'm only offering some warm food and hot coffee to take the chill off a bunch of frosty riders."

Hillman glanced sheepishly at Quinlin. "Hell, a little grub wouldn't hurt, would it?"

"Shut up, Brownie," the tall blond with the drooping mustache said, and Doc thought, *So that's Clint Miller.*

Brownie's gaze narrowed but he didn't reply. Spying Doc across the room, Joel said, "Where's Les?"

"In the back room of the Feed and Supply."

Joel's chin jerked up as if yanked by wire. "You just tossed him in the back room of a feed store like a god . . ." He threw Hannah Brickman an uncertain look. "Like a sack of grain?"

"We put him there because I thought the cooler temperatures would be easier on the body," Doc replied. "It'll give you and your father time to . . ."

"Pa ain't here," Joel interrupted. "It's me and my boys you gotta deal with today."

"Your pa would agree with Doc," Ira said in an appeasing tone.

"Has he been sent for?" Fred asked before Joel could respond.

Scowling, the younger man said, "Ain't you sent for him?"

"We figured Love would tell him."

Joel shook his head. "Love came to where we was working the summer cavvy. I sent him on down to the Sun to tell Pa, but you boys should've sent someone, too."

"That's true," Paul Offerman said, glancing quickly around the room as if seeking support from the other members of the citizens' committee. "We was real dumb not to think of that, Joel."

In the far front corner of the café, the man Doc had pegged as Clint Miller laughed harshly. As if gaining confidence from the gunman's mockery, Joel said, "You boys had better start thinking better next time. You don't want to get on the wrong side of Pa, and you sure as hell don't want to get on the wrong side of me."

Doc took a step forward, drawing the room's attention to himself, away from Quinlin and Miller. "Would you like to see your brother, Joel?" he asked, and was relieved at the way the chocks seemed to be yanked out from under the younger man's brashness.

"Ah, yeah, I guess I'd better. Is he . . . is Les in a box?"

"Not yet," Fred answered.

"That's something else we should've thought of," Paul said, and Doc found himself wishing he could tell Offerman to shut up as effortlessly as Miller had hushed Brownie.

"It's not our place to make that decision," Fred said, giving the liveryman a cautioning look. "Maybe Joel's pa will have other plans, or like to have a casket made special."

Joel looked baffled, waffling from one emotion to another, in control of none of them. Easing toward the door, Doc said,

"Come on, Joel, let's pay respects to your brother."

A daunted, half-frightened look spread over Quinlin's face. For a moment Doc thought he was going to change his mind. Then he licked nervously at his lower lip and said, "Ever'body just stay put 'til I get back." He glanced at Hannah and shrugged. "I guess maybe we'll take you up on your offer, Mrs. Brickman."

Hannah smiled and turned toward the kitchen. "You gents have a seat," she instructed over her shoulder, then stopped to peg the citizens' committee with a purposeful stare. "And you gents head on back to your shops. We've got a town coming awake, and folks will be needing things." She pointed to the front door. "Go on now, get about your jobs. You've lolly-gagged enough for one morning."

Heads lowered, the townsmen moved quietly toward the door. All except for Doc, who picked up his fur cap from a nearby chair and clamped it on his head. "Ready, Joel?"

Joel nodded stiffly and followed Doc outside, while the rest of the Sun's crew drifted toward seats at the counter. All except for Clint Miller, who trailed Joel into the embracing cold.

"You don't mind me taggin' along, do you, Doctor?"

"That'd be up to Joel," Doc replied, and although he hoped Quinlin would tell the gunman to stay behind with the others, he wasn't surprised when the younger man glumly concurred. Doc knew Joel still thought he was in charge of the Sun's crew, and wondered how long it would be before Miller set him straight.

Larkspur Feed and Supply sat at the south end of town, the last building on the left before the broad street narrowed into the Ensillado Canyon road, the main route through the Basin. The store's location, across from both the train depot and the Larkspur Hotel, was no accident. Although run by an older man named Lloyd Thompson, who claimed majority ownership in the business, everyone knew Art Quinlin was the real power behind the store. He'd fronted Thompson the money to set up the venture nearly four years earlier, about the same time construction had begun on the hotel and depot. All three enterprises had been financed through a company out of Santa Fe called Sunrise Land and Cattle Corporation.

A lot of people assumed Art didn't know that his association with the distant organization, or the local feed store, was common knowledge throughout the Basin, but Doc had his doubts. Art Quinlin might be a ruthless son of a bitch, but he was nobody's fool. He also had enough stooges around the Basin to keep him apprised of what was going on, people who maybe didn't especially like him, but who preferred to stay on his good side.

Although Art may or may not have wanted his interest in Larkspur's business district kept a secret, he'd never made any bones about his desire to bring a railroad into the Basin. In fact, it was rumored—and Doc found this a lot more plausible—that Quinlin had turned a blind eye to both the settlers along the valley's northern rim and the developing town in the hope that a thriving population might help attract the railroad's interest.

In those early years between his wife's death and the failing of his dream to see Larkspur turned into a major shipping center, Quinlin had been almost manic about the Basin's prospects, and the area's residents had rallied firmly behind him. But the railroad had viewed the valley's potential differently, and after sending an engineer to inspect the project firsthand, it had passed on the opportunity to run a spur into the Ensillado. Their argument had been that, as large as the valley was, its scattered population and limited resources wouldn't be enough to support the endeavor. Not with only one viable route into the Basin, and that so steep in places that construction costs alone might bankrupt the operation before it reached its destination.

Although the townspeople had wanted the line as much as anyone, Doc thought only Art had been surprised by the railroad's decision. Perhaps he'd been blinded by his own needs. Everyone in the Basin knew that the person who would have profited most from a spur was Quinlin, who would no longer have to drive his cattle all the way to Albuquerque to find a market. Unfortunately, the railroad wasn't moved by the Sun's difficulties or the town's hopes.

It was right around there, Doc thought, that Art's scruples began to flake. He'd always been hard-nosed—his steely re-action to his wife's death had proved that—but he seemed to sink even deeper into hostility when he realized his dreams of success, so intricately tied to the railroad's presence in the Basin, would come to naught, leaving him and his fake corporation—Sunrise Land and Cattle—the sole proprietors of a vacant hotel and a useless train depot. Only the feed store had survived, and that just barely, supplying hay, grain, and other sundry items to support the town's meager population of milk cows, goats, horses, mules, and chickens.

Doc's tread grew heavier as he and Joel approached the rambling structure. There was a loading dock out front and another in the rear, with smoke dribbling from a tin chimney midway between the two. Doc veered off the street toward the rear platform, forging a path through the unbroken snow. Joel followed, but his pace began to drag as they neared the build-ing, so much so that Miller was forced to a stop every few yards until Quinlin could pull ahead again.

Doc climbed the steps to the rear platform and put his shoulder to the large sliding door, only opening it far enough for them to enter. It was dark inside, the smell, thankfully, of shelled corn and ground oats, molasses and burlap. Had it been warmer, the odor could have been much worse, and Doc wasn't sure how Joel would have reacted to that.

Lloyd wasn't around, but there was a lantern sitting on a keg of molasses that he would mix into the grain to make it more palatable to livestock. Doc lit the lantern, then tossed the match into the snow outside. After Joel and Miller entered, he wrestled the door closed. It was bitterly cold inside the back room, and the light, softened by a layer of soot on the lantern's globe, seemed more depressing than illuminating. Les and Tim had been laid out on heavy planks, held off the floor by a pair of sawhorses. A lightly tarred paulin had been draped over the pair to keep the dust off and the rats at bay. Doc was glad Ira had thought to cover them. He wouldn't have wanted to face Joel's wrath if vermin had discovered the bodies overnight.

Joel halted inside the door to stare at the tarpaulin. "That them?" he asked huskily.

"Yes," Doc replied. "If you'd like to be alone, your friend and I . . ."

"No." Joel licked nervously at his lips, as if trying to remove something stuck there. "That's . . . I've seen all I need to."

"You haven't even looked at him yet," Doc said.

Joel jerked his head around. "That's Les, ain't it?"

"Yes, Les and Tim Jackson."

"Then what the hell do I need to see 'em for? I know what they look like."

"We came here so you could pay your respects."

Doc's words brought a callous laugh from Miller's lips.

"Those two fought like cats and dogs, sawbones. I think ol' Joel here just wanted to be sure he was dead."

Joel flinched at the gunman's words, but he didn't deny them. "Let's get outta here," he said brusquely.

A wave of contempt flowed through Doc. He turned away without comment, shouldering the door open and stepping into the frigid air. Miller followed. Joel came last, and Doc had to remind him to extinguish the lantern before he slid the heavy door closed on its steel rollers. They paused on the platform, Doc and Miller waiting silently for Joel to make the next move. After a lengthy pause, the younger man said, "Let's go back to Hannah's. I want to know what happened here last night."

"I can tell you what happened," Doc volunteered.

Joel started to reply, but Miller cut him off.

"Be warmer inside the café. Besides, I might like to try some of the lady's warm bread and coffee, before we try to figure out who's to blame."

After an annoyed glance at Miller, Joel said, "We're goin' back," as if to reinforce his earlier decree.

The three trudged back through the snow to the street. Joel had the lead now, plowing ahead as if anxious to put some distance between himself and the feed store. Miller brought up the rear. Doc had the middle, his stride returning as reluctant as Joel's had been going, and it made him wonder if this was what it was like to be led to your own execution.

The other members of the citizens' committee were gone by the time they returned, but the Sun's riders were still there, seated along the counter drinking coffee and helping themselves to thick slices of Hannah Brickman's oven-toasted bread. Only Carl Roth and the black man with the tightly curled beard remained standing and alert—Roth at the front window, the African at the door to the kitchen. Most of the crew had loosened their outer clothing in the café's warmth, and Doc was struck again by the singularity of the men who rode for the Sun nowadays, their heavy armament and surly dispositions.

Joel stopped in the middle of the room, heedless of the snow dragged inside on his boots. "Where'd they go?" he demanded, and everyone knew who he meant.

Brownie, melted butter pooled at the corners of his mouth,

mumbled around a wad of dough. "The woman sent 'em home."

"Before we left, remember?" Doc prodded.

"Huh? Oh, yeah, yeah, I remember." Joel squeezed the bridge of his nose between two fingers, then pointed toward a table against the restaurant's rear wall. "You go over there and sit down, Doc. Brownie, wipe that crap off your face, then take Goose and Palmer and round up the citizens' committee. I want 'em back here *pronto.*"

"All of 'em?"

"There's no need for that," Doc interjected. "I can tell you what happened."

"You stay outta this, Doc." Joel looked at Brownie and Goose and Palmer. "You boys get on out there, now. Bring 'em in."

"Just the liveryman," Miller said, stepping forward as Joel whipped around in surprise. "We'll start with him, then move on to the others if we have to."

"I said I wanted 'em all here."

"I know, but we'll start with the liveryman." Miller moved past Joel and the younger man stepped back instinctively, and just that smoothly the balance of power tipped out of Joel's grasp and into Miller's.

"Go on, Brownie," Miller said. "Take Goose and Palmer with you."

When they were gone, Miller glanced at Doc. "You were told to have a seat, sawbones. Do it. Carl, get in the kitchen and bring the Brickman woman and her kid out here. I don't want anyone slippin' out the back. This'll go a lot easier if we ain't interrupted."

"I thought you were in charge of this crew, Joel." Doc spoke softly, and Quinlin's face darkened.

"I am," he growled, but there was doubt in his eyes when he glanced at the gunman.

Miller stepped in front of Doc, towering above him intimidatingly. "I was hired by Art Quinlin to handle these kinds of situations, sawbones. If he or the boy were capable of the job, they'd've been done by now. I intend to do what they can't." He thrust his chin toward the table in the rear corner. "Now go on over there and have a seat, before I have Samson put you there."

At the kitchen's door, the burly African's lips peeled back in a yellow grin, and Doc grudgingly moved to comply. A few seconds later, Carl Roth ushered Hannah and Daphne into the main dining area. Miller nodded toward the table and the two women joined Doc without comment.

Brownie and his men were back within fifteen minutes. Offerman's eyes were wide with apprehension as he was shoved inside. He immediately started toward the table where Doc and the Brickmans were seated, but Miller intercepted him. Nodding toward the same table at the front of the café where the citizens' committee had sat not thirty minutes earlier, he told the liveryman to sit down.

Paul looked at Doc, but all Doc could offer was a stoic shrug.

"What do you want?" Paul demanded.

"I want you to sit down," Miller replied calmly, then nodded toward the window table a second time. "Right there, right now."

"Why?"

Doc blinked at the stinging sound of Miller's palm striking Paul's cheek. Daphne uttered a startled cry and jumped in her chair. Paul stumbled backward, more from surprise than the force of the blow, and his eyes grew even wider. At Doc's elbow, Hannah grated, "Joel, are you going to allow this to happen?"

"You stay outta this, Mrs. Brickman."

"I ain't gonna tell you again," Miller told Offerman.

Swallowing audibly, Paul backed toward the table, sitting down heavily when the backs of his calves bumped into the edge of the nearest seat. Miller pulled a second chair out and spun it around to sit with his arms folded across the back. Joel moved to the opposite side of the table, but he didn't sit down. Doc couldn't make out what was said after that, but he could sense the malevolence dripping from Miller's words, could see the fear that was twisting Offerman's expression into one of childlike simplicity. A clock hanging on the wall above the counter read a quarter of seven when Miller began questioning the liveryman. It was barely five after when he shoved to his feet. He looked across the table at Joel. Quinlin's cheeks were flushed a deeper red than Doc had ever seen, and his knuckles were pale where they clenched the grips of his nickeled revolver.

"I want to talk to 'em," Joel said thickly.

Miller motioned Brownie forward, but Joel cut him off.

"No, you stay here, Miller. I'm gonna handle this on my own. Carl, you and Samson and Goose can come with me, but I want the rest of you to sit tight until I get back."

Doc could tell Miller didn't like it. The three men Joel had singled out hesitated, as if waiting to see what he'd say, but the gunman remained silent, and after a moment's pause they shuffled forward. It was a victory of sorts for Joel, but Doc didn't think the younger man was even aware of it. Miller glared as they left the café, his jaw working furiously. Then he ordered Paul to join the others at the rear table.

Tears of humiliation streaked Offerman's cheeks as he approached the table. He came around its side and sat down without looking at them. Hannah asked if he was all right, but he refused to answer. Then she asked what had happened, and he just shook his head.

"Paul," Hannah said gently. "Talk to me." She placed a hand reassuringly atop the liveryman's forearm. "What did they want?"

The words slid from Offerman's throat like logs hauled out

of a bog, so thick and slow that Doc at first had trouble making out what he was saying.

"What do you think he wanted?"

"What did you tell him?"

Paul finally looked up. Daphne recoiled at the look of raw anguish on the liveryman's face, but Doc and Hannah kept their expressions neutral, and Hannah continued to stroke his forearm.

"Paul, tell me."

"I told 'em the truth," he answered raggedly. "Ain't that what everyone wanted?"

Hannah's grip tightened on his arm. "Where did Joel go?"

Offerman shook his head. He was trembling all over, as if chilled.

"Paul, please, what did you tell them?"

"They . . . Joel went to talk to Fred."

Hannah's shoulders sagged and Doc bit back the condemnation that rose like bile in his throat. As calmly as he could, he said, "Why, Paul?"

"What did you expect me to tell them? That Les shot himself, or that . . ." He abruptly shut up as Miller started toward them. A cold grin slashed the gunman's face as he pulled a chair around and sat down.

"He was wise to talk, Doc. That's what they all call you, ain't it? Doc?"

"It's what I am."

"If they called me what I was, I'd be Death." He laughed and glanced around the table, but neither Doc nor the Brickmans responded, and Paul seemed beyond any kind of acknowledgment. He sat as if frozen in his chair, his gaze fixed woodenly on the table in front of him. Miller's eyes narrowed, staring at Paul. "You believe me, don't you, boy?"

Paul's head bobbed dutifully, but he still didn't look up or speak.

"What about you, sawbones? Do you believe me?"

"Yeah, I believe you. I've made a career patching up what men like you have done to others."

Miller nodded curtly. "That's good. That's good you know what I can do, and will do, to get what I need."

"Including murder?"

"Whatever it takes."

"What now?" Hannah asked.

"We wait."

"For what?"

"For the kid to make up his mind."

"The Somers are good people," Doc said. "They didn't have anything to do with Les Quinlin's death."

"Good people shouldn't go against their own kind," Miller replied.

"What do you mean?" Hannah asked.

"I mean the sawbones here might not've known what kind of a back shooter Ryan was when he treated him, but the storekeeper sure as hell did when he outfitted him."

"It wasn't a back shooting," Doc said. "It was a fair fight, at least as fair as any fight can be when it's three against one."

"Sawbones, I just flat don't give a damn what kind of fight it was. Art Quinlin's boy is dead, and someone is gonna pay for it."

"Fred?"

Miller grinned and shrugged.

"Is that why Joel is so angry?" Hannah asked. "Because Fred offered a stranger an act of kindness?"

"Might could be. Or maybe it's something else. Something in a skirt."

"Peggy," Doc guessed, glancing at Hannah. "Peggy and Earl?"

"Oh, no. Joel couldn't blame Peggy for Earl's death, could he?"

Miller smiled lazily. "That the stuck-up bitch the kid keeps talkin' about?"

Although Doc's face warmed with indignation, he knew Miller was trying to bait him. "Earl was Joel's older brother. It was rumored that he and Peggy were friendly, but she didn't have anything to do with his being shot last fall."

"Who's Reece Ward?"

"You know full well who the Wards are," Hannah retorted.

Miller looked gratified for the heated response from her that he'd failed to elicit from Doc. "Yeah, I know who they are. I also know cattle rustlers and back shooters generally ride the same trails. Usually after dark."

"That's what some of the homesteaders are saying now about Art Quinlin," Hannah pointed out, drawing a laugh from Miller.

"You've got sand, Mrs. Brickman. I've always admired that in a woman." He glanced at Offerman. "It's good to know someone in this town does."

Paul didn't reply, and Hannah's lips thinned in frustration. "There are no cattle rustlers in the Ensillado, Mr. Miller, and I suspect the only back shooters are those hired by Arthur Quinlin."

"Someone shot Earl Quinlin last fall. The old man thinks it might've been the Ward boy, and that he's been nosin' around the storekeeper's back door like a randy dog. You know anything about that?"

"I know it's a filthy lie, and that only scum like you would think to repeat something so inappropriate around women and children."

Miller's face hardened. He started to look at Daphne, then forced his gaze to remain on Hannah. He glared, but she refused to look away, and after a moment Doc said, "Do you intend to make war on widows, as well, Mr. Miller?"

The gunman leaned back. "No, I reckon not, although I ain't yet decided about fat doctors." He rose abruptly, kicking his chair across the room. "Palmer, keep an eye on these three. And you . . ." He jabbed a finger at Doc. "On your feet, sawbones. We're going to pay the folks down the street a visit, see how the kid's doing with his questioning. Hoag, you're with me." He fixed the black man with a menacing stare. "And when we get over there, don't make the mistake of thinking Joel Quinlin is in charge of anything I don't want him to be. You savvy what I'm saying?"

"You ain't gonna get no trouble from me," Samson promised, then drew his revolver and motioned for Doc to stand. "Let's go, sawbones."

CHAPTER FIVE

Although the sun was already up when Reece Ward rode into the Flying W's ranch yard, there wasn't much heat in its rays. Reining over to where his pa was breaking ice in the corral's water trough, he noticed there wasn't a whole lot of warmth coming from that direction, either. Not that Reece expected any. Big Max wasn't a man to turn his back on a day's chores, and Reece knew that's what his father thought Reece had done when he rode into Larkspur yesterday, rather than stay close to home like he was supposed to.

Reece didn't figure the excuse that he'd wanted a beer at Bannerman's and something with flavor to put in his stomach besides Two-Socks' poor bunkhouse fare would hold much water for Big Max. Hector Romero, the old *vaquero* Reece had been riding with when he'd made his decision to go into town, hadn't seemed overly impressed with his reasoning, either.

"What should I tell your papa when he asks about you?" Hector had inquired after Reece told him where he was going.

"Tell him I was so starved down from Two-Socks' cooking that I fell through my ass and damn near strangled myself."

Reece had thought it a fine joke, but Hector hadn't even cracked a smile.

"One of these days it will be your papa who reaches up your ass and strangles you."

"You're just jealous you ain't got no more piss and vinegar

left in your veins. Otherwise you'd be riding into town with me."

"Bah!" Hector waved the younger man away. "Go, have your fun, *niño.* It is not me who will have to face your papa's wrath when you return."

Reece had laughed at Hector, but now, seeing the look on his pa's face, he wondered if he should have heeded the *vaquero's* warning.

Neither Hector nor Two-Socks were in sight as Reece approached the corral. He supposed it wouldn't have made any difference if they were. They all knew, and Big Max as much as any of them, the real purpose of Reece's visit to Larkspur, and that it didn't have anything to do with Ira Bannerman's Santa Fe beer or Hannah Brickman's roast beef.

"Pa," Reece greeted, drawing up some twenty yards away to eye the ice-coated axe in his father's gloved hands.

Big Max's eyes were like two slits cut into a leather mask. He was a short man—five foot seven at best—but solidly built, with a barrel chest and a square, stubborn jaw. A harbinger of his own future, Reece's ma had once told him, noting her son's similar build and intractable disposition. Reece supposed there were worse men in the Basin to be compared to. He just hoped Big Max's squint was because of the sun's glare off the recently fallen snow, and not an indication of his mood—something Reece wouldn't know for sure until his father spoke.

"I ought to whop your behind a good one, boy," Max growled; it was a definite threat of violence, though thankfully delivered without much heat.

"I'm too old to be whopped," Reece replied with more bluster than confidence.

"That ain't likely to happen in my lifetime." Max leaned his axe against a corral rail and tugged on the cuffs of his toil-blackened gloves. "You're lucky I ain't so old I've forgot what it's like to have piss and vinegar running through my veins."

Reece grinned in relief, knowing then that Hector had passed along his message, and that his pa wasn't overly upset about his son's trip into town. Then his expression sobered. "Les Quinlin was killed."

Max's head reared back in surprise. "Killed? How?"

"He was shot. Him and Tim Jackson both."

"The hell you say! Someone shot Les Quinlin and that bulldog of his?"

Reece told him what he'd seen, then heard afterward in Bannerman's. "Ira says Les thought he was a hired gun working for you," he added.

Big Max made a sound of disgust. "Damned fools."

"Who?"

"All of 'em, but Art Quinlin and them wild boys of his in particular, thinking I brought a hired gun into the Basin just because they did." He shook his head in scorn. "Hell, I can barely scrape together enough *pesos* in a month to pay Hector and Two-Socks." He glanced toward the solid log home where his wife—Reece's ma—lay with one of her debilitating headaches, and shook his head again, this time in aggravation. "As if we ain't got problems enough."

For a moment Reece wasn't sure which problem his pa was taking about—his mother's chronic headaches or the Sun's increasing aggression toward the North Rim.

Big Max's voice softened. "That's why I don't want you slipping off to see that Somers gal anymore, Reece. The Quinlins are looking for a chance to burn some powder, and you being in there by yourself only provides 'em a target."

"I'm not going to tippy-toe around the valley because of Art Quinlin."

"Nobody'd want you to, but you have to start using your head."

Reece's nostrils flared. "What one person calls using their head, another might call cowardly." He started to rein away, but his pa called him back.

"Where're you goin'?"

"I'm going to put my horse up, then catch me another. You're still wanting to gather our cows off the east range before they start calving, don't you?"

Max hesitated, staring out over the Basin. Reece followed the direction of his gaze. Even with the storm-swept sky as clear as it was, he could barely make out the distant rim of mountains to the south.

"No," Big Max said after a while. "It's too cold to be pounding a saddle all day. I reckon I should've listened to Hector. He tried to tell me it was too early to start the spring gather." He sniffed, then rubbed his nose with a gloved hand. "Tell you what, you take care of your horse, then grab a bite to eat. Two-Socks has some oatmeal left over from breakfast, and likely some beans and beef from last night. After that, go tell your mama you're home safe so she won't have to worry. Then I want you'n Two-Socks to start cutting firewood."

"Firewood! Hell, we have enough firewood now to last us into next winter."

"Good. Double that, and I'll let you take the afternoon off to go fishing."

"What about . . ."

Reece shut up. He'd started to ask what his pa had in mind for Hector, but knew Big Max would just tell him the gray-bearded *vaquero* was too old to stand on the business end of a whipsaw all day. He'd be right, too. Although Hector Romero didn't do a lot of manual labor anymore, he was probably the most valuable asset Max had on the Flying W. Even Two-Socks, thirty years younger and twice as strong, would acknowledge that.

When it came to cattle ranching in the arid West, Big Max Ward had been about as green as they came when he first brought his family into the Basin. That was several years ago, after the Apache troubles were over but before Quinlin surreptitiously constructed the Larkspur Hotel and the empty train depot in anticipation of the railroad building a spur into the valley. But if Max hadn't known much about raising livestock, he'd at least been smart enough to recognize the elderly Mexican's knowledge and skills, and to hire him and Two-Socks before he left Albuquerque with a wagon, a wife, two daughters, one son, and one hundred and fifty head of stumpy Durham cows and a pair of bulls.

Sometimes Reece thought it was his father's importation of shorthorns to the Basin that galled Art Quinlin more than their homestead. Quinlin was a Texan by birth, and his cattle all sported the long horns and gaunt frames of that sinewy breed, no matter that the meat they produced was generally dry and tough. Nothing at all like the Flying W's sturdy Eastern cattle.

Although the W was a pint-sized outfit compared with the Sun, they'd already trailed a couple of small herds to markets in Albuquerque and Santa Fe, and the reception had been good. People liked the fattier cuts of meat they got from the W's Durhams, with its richer flavor and moister texture. According to Max, it was only a matter of time before old-timers like Art Quinlin would be forced to give up their more traditional beliefs. Either that or be pushed to the side. Reece figured Art probably knew that as well.

While Big Max knocked ice off the axe head and returned it to the tool shed, Reece led his horse into the barn and stripped his gear from the animal's back. He curried it first, then turned it loose in the small corral beside the freshening pen. After forking hay into the rack and scooping chunks of ice out of the barn trough, he trudged up to the house with his fingers half-froze, his nose dripping. He slipped quietly inside, careful not to make too much noise in case his ma was still in bed. He found her sitting up in the main room instead, shutters drawn and the lamps unlit. Reece stopped at the door, watching her in the murky light. Sally Ward was a gaunt woman with pallid skin and hair already turning to silver, even though she was barely forty years old. Her expression seemed permanently pinched and her eyes were always hooded. A small flame in the stone fireplace, kindled more for heat than light, illuminated the cramped room and his mother's petite form, curled in his pa's big chair with her feet tucked up under a Navajo blanket.

"Jilly, is that you?" she whispered.

Reece's bit down gently at his lower lip. Jill was his sister, all of seventeen and married to Bob Teller, who had taken her and fifteen-year-old Jenny back to Albuquerque the previous spring. Reece thought his ma's headaches had worsened after her daughters moved away, although he knew she'd suffered from them long before they left Tennessee. And they all agreed, even Sally, that the girls were probably safer in Albuquerque than they would be in the Basin.

"Maybe they can come back someday," Big Max would tell his wife when she seemed especially despondent, but Reece didn't think either of them really believed they would. Albuquerque may not have seemed like much compared with a city of Nashville's status, but it was head, shoulders, and most of a trunk above Larkspur.

"It's me, Ma," Reece said, crossing the room and seating himself in a horsehide chair with ornately carved arms, the ends in the shape of roaring African lions.

"Reece, I'm sorry." Her apology was sincere, but she didn't look up or even open her eyes. "Where's your father?"

"He's still down by the corrals looking after the heifers."

"He said you went to Larkspur."

"I did." He pulled a small bottle of reddish-brown liquid from his pocket and leaned forward to tap her shoulder. She reached out blindly to accept it.

"Thank you," she murmured gratefully, then slipped the bottle out of sight beneath her blanket. She'd keep the laudanum hidden from her husband, who didn't believe the medicine Reece sometimes brought back from town did any good. Big Max was also convinced the opium concoction made her groggy and slow-witted, but Reece was willing to accept that as long as there was a possibility the laudanum would help ease her headaches—migraines, Dr. Shaw called them—so bad at times she could only lie writhing gently in bed, clenching the coarse sheets with white-knuckled fists until the tendons stood out in her neck. At those times Reece would have gladly sailed to the Orient himself to buy a shipload of the drug to alleviate her suffering.

Sally's voice, when she spoke again, held a hint of the light-hearted banter Reece recalled from her younger days in Tennessee, when he was still a boy and his mother hadn't spent so much of her time living in pain. "Did you talk to Peggy?"

Reece hesitated. He hadn't told his family yet of his encounter with Fred Somers after last fall's Harvest Dance. "A little," he finally admitted. "They'd just closed up when I got there."

"You should have taken her to the Paris and bought her supper. After working in Fred's store all day, it would have been a treat for her not to have to fix a meal or eat her own cooking."

Reece considered telling her about the shooting in order to change the subject, then decided against it. Maybe when she was feeling better. Besides, he could tell her thoughts had already moved on. They often flitted like this when she was feeling ill.

"I should be cooking for you and your father, instead of letting Two-Socks do it."

"Two-Socks doesn't mind."

"Don't lie to your mother," she chided.

Reece smiled. She was right about Two-Socks. He hated to cook, but he liked working for the Flying W even more, and accepted the chore without complaint whenever Sally Ward wasn't able to do it for all of them.

Standing, Reece leaned forward to gently pat the back of his mother's hand. "Can you sleep?"

She nodded and smiled, then brought the small bottle of laudanum out from under the Navajo blanket. "I'll soon be fine," she assured him.

Reece wished he knew if that were true.

More and more of late, Hal Keegan was regretting his decision to accept Art Quinlin's offer to come up from Galveston and take on the job of lawman for the Ensillado Basin. He hadn't felt that way at first. In fact, during those early, heady days of seemingly boundless authority, he'd damned near luxuriated in the position.

"I feel like a hog in fresh mud," was how he'd described it to Ira Bannerman late one night after saluting the saloonkeeper, the town, and Art Quinlin, all in the same toast.

Sure, there had been some annoyances along the way. Horses stolen or some waddie getting shot in the butt after an alcohol-fueled argument on a Saturday night hoorah, but never anything serious. At least not until Earl Quinlin got himself killed on the road south of Larkspur late last fall for not minding his own damned business. It wasn't long afterward that Hal began to notice changes coming over his old friend. Not so much a difference in personality as a deepening of what he'd already been. Not just ill-tempered, but mean, angry, and ruthless. Hal had ridden with Quinlin in Texas, and seen things then that would turn a normal man's blood to ice.

Hal remembered those days now with a heavy sense of trepidation. At that time he'd put the blame on politics. Texas, in the decade following the War of Northern Aggression, was as volatile a place as any Hal had ever known, especially to those who remained loyal to the Confederacy even after Lee's surrender. Carpetbaggers and rogues had descended on the South like swarming locusts, and there hadn't been a whole lot a true son of the Lone Star could do about it, what with the Rangers disbanded and the State Police in the pockets of wealthy Northerners.

In disgust and defeat, Art had finally packed up his family and taken it West. To the Pecos River country first, then up here to the Ensillado Basin, where he claimed he intended to make his stand.

"This is it, Keegan," Art had growled over a tumbler of bourbon not even a week before. "I own this goddamned Basin, earned it with blood and bullets, and I'm not gonna let a bunch of thievin' homesteaders start nibbling at its edges like they done in Texas."

Hal had gotten a real uneasy feeling hearing that. Staring into Art's eyes, he'd recognized the disconnection, the inwardness of vision that told him the aging rancher wasn't really there that evening. And now he'd lost another son, shot down by a hired gun right in the middle of Larkspur's single street.

There had been witnesses this time, too, and that brought an unanticipated chill to Hal's spine. In his experience, witnesses could be a problem. They had ways of popping up unexpectedly, of throwing kinks into the best-laid plans, the worst impulses. Witnesses could turn a simple incident into a complicated one; they could force a man to take a stand behind something otherwise indefensible, or dredge up a thing that would have been better left buried. Witnesses scared Hal Keegan for reasons he'd just as soon Art Quinlin never found out about.

Hal glanced at Art, who was riding toward Larkspur at a swift gallop, his buckskin kicking up sparkling showers of fresh-fallen snow. The old rancher's shoulders looked as rigid as a weld, and his jaw was thrust forward in fair imitation of a granite knob. Rage burned hotly within the man's breast; you could damn near see it, like waves of heat radiating outward from the sides of a wood-burning stove.

Hal and Art weren't riding into Larkspur alone. Others rode with them. Odell Love was there, about as useless a piece of cow patty as a man was ever likely to stumble over. In Hal's opinion, Love was a coward, to boot, although, yellow or not, he was staying right up front with them. Art had seen to that, instructing Odell in clipped terms to stay close if he valued his hide. Hal didn't doubt for a minute that Art meant what he'd said. He'd just about drawn and quartered Odell with his questioning that morning, demanding so much detail that Hal doubted if even Odell knew which was a lie and which was truth by the time Quinlin finished with him. He had to admit, though, that Art had wormed a lot more information out of Love than Hal would have thought possible. Probably more than even Odell knew he had.

Afterward they'd gone outside to round up the rest of the crew, and the first thing Art did after gathering everyone in front of the main house was to send Lou Saunders and Little George Isley down to the head of Ensillado Canyon to make sure Les's killer didn't escape the Basin that way.

"Nobody goes through that canyon unless you know who it is," Art had instructed in a voice that sounded half wild with anguish. "Savvy?"

Saunders had replied for both of them. "Yes, sir, Mr. Quinlin."

"Not a wagon or a stagecoach goes out without you two searching it top to bottom."

Lou and Little George quickly nodded their assent.

"If he tries it, we'll catch him," Lou vowed.

Art hadn't replied. He'd sat his big buckskin gelding, glaring at the two men until a light finally dawned on Little George Isley's coal-black face. "Let's git," he'd said tersely to Lou, and Saunders had immediately nodded and pulled his horse around. Art waited until they disappeared over the low ridge east of the ranch before turning back to the rest of them.

"By God, I've let the interlopers in this valley have free rein long enough," he grated. "I've turned my back on their lawlessness ever since the first outsider cut the first tree to build their sorry shacks." His voice rose. "Well, no more! We're gonna find the son of a bitch who murdered Les, and while we're doin' that, we're gonna start rootin' out every thieving homesteader and every worthless rannahand with a dozen wormy beeves that calls hisself a stockman. We're gonna clean the riff-raff outta this valley for good, and if any of you sorry sons'a bitches ain't got the craw for it, you'd best hightail it outta here now, 'cause I won't have no patience for bullshit when the fat hits the fire."

Hal didn't even bother to look around. He knew no one would dare speak up, no matter what their true feelings might be. If they wanted out, they'd bide their time and follow orders until the first opportunity to flee presented itself. Then they'd take off for the horizon and never look back. And watching Art's face, seeing the rage and pain that had twisted his features, Hal wasn't sure he'd blame them. Wasn't sure he shouldn't cut his own pin, and tell the fiery old coot *adios*.

He wouldn't, of course, and loyalty had nothing to do with it. He'd stay because Art wanted him to, expected him to, and Hal had learned a long time ago that what Art Quinlin wanted, he got. One way or another.

★ ★ ★ ★ ★

Part Two:
The Debt

★ ★ ★ ★ ★

CHAPTER SIX

And then one day Gil Ryan opened his eyes and the sky was blue again. He could see the sun shining on the pines through the low opening of the hut he'd crawled into during the height of the storm. Snow glistened in the distance, and the air was so crisp and cold he had to breathe shallowly to avoid further irritating his already tortured lungs.

For a long time he was content to just lie there quietly, staring at the rough ceiling, a jagged latticework of broken timbers and brittle limbs, covered with sod. The walls were constructed of heavier logs, mostly unchinked after being abandoned for so long, although someone had taken time to stack dry firewood in the hut's two farthest corners, and to leave a small coffee pot and a tin kettle hanging from the stubs of branches that jutted from the low walls. The shack was no more than ten feet square and barely half that high, and from the narrow trail where he'd first spotted it, looked more like a squat, squared stump than a legitimate shelter.

Gil barely recalled his ride back up into the mountainous country north of Larkspur. With his chest drawing tighter with every mile, his brow sultry with a fever that seemed to be consuming him from within, he'd pushed onward with primitive urgency. Although he hadn't been consciously aware of a destination at the time, somewhere within the deeper recesses of his mind he must have remembered this tiny log hovel that he'd passed on his way into the Basin. Even so, he hadn't been the one to find it. It was his horse that had turned off the trail as if it had known all along that this was their destination.

When the gelding finally stopped at the base of a low ridge, out of the brutal blast of wind and snow, Gil had numbly raised his head, spying the little hut partway up the slope. With the last dredges of his strength, he'd guided the sorrel toward it. He had only the vaguest recollection of stripping his gear from Rusty's back, but he remembered clearly almost sprawling across his saddle as he shoved it inside, then tossed the bridle in on top of it. He'd crawled in after it on his hands and knees. His chest was heaving for oxygen and sweat poured off his face as he roughly knocked his bedroll open. After that he'd peeled out of his snow-packed clothing to burrow naked under the layers of prickly wool, still lucid enough to realize that if he didn't shed his wet garb first, he'd surely die.

Whoever had brought the firewood inside had taken time to build a little pyramid of kindling in a fire pit in the center of the hut. From his blankets, Gil had spilled the contents of his saddlebags across the floor, then fumbled clumsily in the pre-dawn darkness until he located a packet of fresh matches. He had to focus to hang onto a green-tipped match in one hand and the striker plate with the other. Even when he had a blaze started, he nearly smothered it by adding too much wood too soon, scattering the kindling with his numb fingers and only awkwardly able to scoop it all back into a pile. But his luck held and he kept the fire going, building it carefully until it burned bright and hot, the draft from the open door taking the smoke out through a bucket-sized hole in the ceiling. Exhausted from these efforts, he'd fallen backward across his bedroll, his body trembling from cold and exertion as he dragged the blankets over his head.

After that he'd drifted hazily through a world without meaning, days that couldn't exist, others he couldn't deny. He remembered waking up one evening to find a bear sitting at the entrance to the hut, staring pensively into the flames. Gil eyed the giant bruin curiously. He could see his rifle poking from its scabbard near the bear's side, but couldn't recall where he'd put his revolver. He was wondering if he even dared move to find it when the bear asked him if he had anything to eat.

"I'm dreaming," Gil said aloud, his voice startling in the tiny shelter.

"Should I leave?" the bear asked.

Gil told him he should, then pushed up on one elbow to add more wood to the fire. Pulling his saddlebags close, he dug around inside for something to eat, but when he brought a small wedge of cheese into the light, he almost gagged at the thought of consuming it.

Another time he awoke to find the log walls shimmying on every side, and became worried that the roof might cave in. He stared for a long time, then forced himself to reach out and gingerly touch the nearest wall, frowning uncertainly at its warm stillness.

"I'm dreaming," he whispered, repeating what he'd told himself when he saw the bear. Then he amended, "No, I'm hallucinating."

That made more sense. The walls were not moving, and if there had been a bear, it surely hadn't spoken. Yet when he pulled his hand away from the logs they continued to shimmy, and later that night the bear returned, snuffling at the hut's entrance although not venturing inside or speaking, leaving Gil to ponder what was real and what was his fevered imagination.

Occasionally he dreamed of Idaho, of standing with his brother in the deep silence of an early winter storm while men moved through the gloom toward them. His brother ordered them to stop, but they only laughed. Then came the bright flowering of muzzle blasts and the mule-shoe kick of the bullet.

When he awoke, he swore he could still smell gun smoke, and his shoulder throbbed painfully.

He was aware of days passing into night, and of nights turning back into day. He drank sparingly of the codeine Somers had sent along, but did a poor job with the mustard plaster, having only the snow outside his door for water and the small kettle to melt it in. His cough worsened and his fever rose and fell but never entirely went away. Time flowed through murky corridors in which nothing seemed real. After a while he became cognizant of entities prowling near the shanty's low entrance, shadowy figures who would peer impatiently inside as if waiting for him to arrive at some sort of decision; impalpable and featureless, distinctly human, yet when he tried to focus on them they would not so much vanish as simply lean back out of sight. He thought about crawling to the door for a closer look, but something deep inside his brain told him he didn't want to know who they were, or what they waited for.

After an unknown amount of time his sweating worsened, bathing his chest and shoulders and turning his dark hair wet. It soaked into his blankets in Turin-like shapes and shades, and his cough intensified until he began hacking up gobs of phlegm that he spat into the fire pit—sometimes alive with flames, at other times dead and cold, although for the life of him he couldn't remember ever rekindling a fire.

And then one day Gil opened his eyes and the sky was blue again.

His chest hurt and his throat ached, but his mind seemed clear after its long odyssey through a world populated with talking bears and darting shadow figures. After a while he propped himself up to have a look around. The fire was down, but there were embers under the ashes. He brushed these aside, added twigs to the center of the pit, and blew gently on the coals until he had a fresh blaze ignited. Then he fell back in his blankets, another cough lurking restlessly deep inside his chest, a fresh glaze of perspiration across his brow.

His clothes lay scattered across the hut, tangled but dry, and when he felt up to the task, his need to cough brought under control by a sip of the nearly depleted codeine and a couple of tentative swallows of water from the kettle, he drew his shirt on over his head, then pushed his blankets back and slid into his trousers. He was startled by how loosely his clothes seemed to hang from his frame, and tried to remember the last time he'd eaten. He spotted the wedge of cheese lying in the dirt beside the fire, a slab of side pork next to it with one end gnawed ragged.

Staring at the meat brought back humbling memories of chewing ravenously at the raw, unsliced bacon, of dipping his face into the kettle afterward to wash the crude meal down over his tender throat, too weak to lift the small tin container to his lips. The animal-like images wormed uneasily under his skin, making him realize that he was probably more lucky to be alive than he might ever fully appreciate.

Gil didn't try to leave the hut right away. He had nowhere to go, nor enough strength to attempt it. After he dressed, he eased back into his blankets and soon drifted into a deep slumber, the reassuring flames of a fire the last thing he saw. It was dark when he awoke, but there were no bears at the door, and the walls remained still and sturdy. With a single blanket draped over his shoulder, he rekindled the fire, then nudged the chunk of side pork close to the flames. After draining the kettle of the last of its water, he pulled on his socks and boots and ventured cautiously outside. He could hear a stream nearby, but couldn't see it in the raven-colored shadows of the tall pines south of the hut. There was plenty of snow, though, and he packed the little kettle full before bringing it back inside.

The side pork was barely warmed through when he pulled it

away from the fire and sliced off a corner with his knife. The smell of the half-cooked meat awakened his appetite, turning it into something wild and demanding. He would have thought he could have devoured the whole slab in a single setting, but discovered that, even as hungry as he was, he couldn't tolerate more than a few ounces of the greasy fare, and the warm water he drank straight from the kettle afterward felt like a small anvil clunking down on his gut. When he'd eaten as much as his shrunken stomach could hold, he refilled both the kettle and the coffee pot with snow and set them by the fire to melt. Then he toed off his boots and crawled back under his blankets.

It went on like that for several days. Gil spent most of his time dozing, but forced himself to leave his bedroll on a regular basis, to venture outside into the brilliant sunlight, tentative at first, but growing steadily more confident as his strength returned. He found the stream he'd heard from the shanty on his second foray into the pines, and paused there to stare solemnly at the bear tracks in the snow along its bank. A young one, he thought, gauging its age by the smaller size of its prints, likely awakening early from winter's hibernation and on the prowl for food. He wondered if it had smelled the bacon in his shack. When he returned to the hut he searched for prints, but the spring melt had already begun and the ground around the tiny shelter, away from the trees and exposed to the sun's rays for much of the afternoon, revealed nothing.

Rusty had vanished, without even a trail in the snow under the pines to tell Gil in which direction he might have wandered. He couldn't fault the horse for seeking better pastures, or at least lower elevations where the grass wouldn't be buried so deep, but he felt bad for the loss. He'd left Idaho's high country just after Christmas and had been making his slow way south ever since. He'd passed through a few small settlements in Utah—Mormon enclaves suspicious of strangers and largely unwelcoming—but no one at all during the last few weeks. His only companion had been the lanky gelding, and he'd nearly talked the sorrel's ears off in his loneliness.

As Gil's strength returned he began to roam farther afield, exploring the deeper forest across the creek, and especially the bare ridge behind the hut. Although his cough lingered long after the codeine was gone, the whiskey Fred Somers had sent along, mixed with honey and dried lemon peel, then warmed by the evening fire, served as a viable substitute.

Several days after venturing outside for the first time, Gil finally slid his Winchester from its scabbard with the intent of putting fresh meat in the pot. He'd heard an elk's bugle the night before, and recalled an aspen-ringed meadow that he'd spotted earlier from the top of the ridge, its south-facing slope free of snow.

It was still dark when Gil left the hut, but his belly was already rumbling with thoughts of fresh meat sizzling over a low flame, accompanied by the last of the coffee Fred had sent along. The voracious hunger that had speared his guts in the days after waking from his fever had largely abated, but a smaller, though no less intense, appetite continued to hound him. His increasing vitality was demanding more sustenance, even as it ate steadily into the supplies he'd brought with him from Larkspur.

The morning was cool but clear, the faint gurgle of melting snow competing with the morning trilling of birds and the gentle hum of a southerly breeze as dawn spread its pale light over the mountains. It was a forty-five-minute hike to the meadow. Gil covered the last quarter of a mile below the crest of the ridge, out of sight of any grazing ungulates. Expecting elk, if he saw anything at all, he was mildly surprised but just as satisfied when he spotted a mule deer browsing within a fringe of aspens at the meadow's lower rim.

Easing forward on his stomach, Gil studied the grazing mulely for several minutes. Every once in a while he'd let his gaze sweep the surrounding terrain. He'd once shot a bighorn sheep high in the Sawtooths, only to stumble upon a stalking mountain lion when he climbed up the side of the peak to butcher it; he didn't intend to make the same mistake twice.

Satisfied that he was alone and that the deer wasn't being stalked by another, Gil flipped up the tang peep sight on the Winchester's wrist and adjusted the staff to 300 yards. Although anticipating a clean kill, he took his time snugging the rifle's smooth walnut stock to his cheek, breathing shallowly as he brought the slim silver blade of the front sight into the small aperture at the rear. Satisfied with the circular image framed within the tiny orifice, he squeezed the trigger, and the Winchester's hefty .45-75 charge shoved back firmly on his shoulder. The morning breeze quickly whisked away the gray veil of powder smoke to reveal the small deer on its side at the far end of the meadow, unmoving.

Gil waited a few minutes, watching for any sign of an intruder. Not really expecting anything out of the norm, he was startled when a long, coppery face appeared from the fringe of aspens on his left. He watched in disbelief as the animal stepped out of the trees. Then, pushing to his feet with a small laugh, he called, "Rusty, you clown. Where have you been hiding?"

With the old man in such a foul mood, Odell Love was determined to stay as far out of sight as possible. That was why he'd reined his dun mare to the rear of the crew that morning, listening with his eyes averted, shoulders hunched, as Art Quinlin angrily roweled his men for their inability to locate Les's murderer.

"Where the hell *is* he?" the old man thundered for the third time since beginning his tirade nearly twenty minutes earlier, as if volume alone could pry the answer out of the heavens; sure as hell, no one on the Sun's crew seemed to have any idea where Gil Ryan had gotten to.

Odell thought it likely that Ryan had slipped out of the Basin to the south before the old man could get his men down to Ensillado Canyon to cut him off. He was likely somewhere far below even now, enjoying what was left of the desert spring before full summer arrived to show him the error of his midwinter assumption that there was anything wrong with a little snow and ice.

The knowledge that Ryan had come south to escape the harsh winters of the Sawtooth Mountains was something else the old man had squeezed out of Larkspur's fat doctor, although it had taken quite a bit of effort to do so. Odell still felt queasy when he recalled Shaw's agonizing screams, or the sounds of shattering glass and broken lumber as they tore through Fred Somers's store like jackals. Art refused to believe that Ryan had escaped. He was basing this conviction on the word of a Mexican station keeper named Ramirez, who ran a road house and stage stop near the head of the canyon; that plus a lack of hoofprints in the snow leading down through the Ensillado.

"That son of a bitch is up here," Quinlin avowed to anyone who might listen, and no one Odell knew was going to argue the point with him. Art was convinced Ryan was either holed up on his own or hiding out with someone's help, and just the thought of some nose-picking homesteader pulling such a stunt on Sun range was enough to fry in the old man's gut like a plateful of Inez Ramirez's *chili colorado*.

"Any damned fool knows you can't cross the Saddleback in winter," Art kept insisting, despite Shaw and Somers both swearing that Ryan had entered the valley from the north.

Although Odell, like most of the Basin's residents, had always assumed a midwinter crossing was impossible, he had to admit he didn't have any proof that it couldn't be done. It was simply one of those accepted facts that no one questioned. Art had called the doc a liar straight to his face when he said it was true, and Shaw had shaken his head in disgust at the rancher's refusal to believe it was at least conceivable. That was before the old man turned serious about prying out all the information the sawbones had on Ryan. Before Shaw started screaming so loud it seemed likely to bring the clouds tumbling out of the sky for all the noise he was making.

Right now, Art had a barrier of men and guns thrown across the head of the canyon that nobody could pass without the say-so of a Sun rider.

"You cork that canyon like it's the last bottle of whiskey in the Basin," was the old man's order. "If that son of a bitch gets through, I'll flay the hides off every damned one of you."

Standing there in the snow on the day following Les's death, his face as red as a boil, eyes bulging like they were about to pop out of his skull, the boys had all believed him, too. From that morning on, no one entered or left the Basin without the Sun's blessing. Not even the Ensillado Stagecoach Company, which owned the road and the stage station at the head of the gorge.

That had been . . . what? Nearly three weeks ago, Odell mused, and not a sign of the drifter since. But the old man wouldn't quit, and that crazy gun-toter of his, Clint Miller, wouldn't let him. Miller was keeping both Quinlins fired up with his talk of conspiracies among the homesteaders and small ranchers, and hinted regularly that the citizens of Larkspur were probably in on it, too. The way it was starting to feel, Odell was afraid the entire Basin was about ready to explode in violence. Art's next words seemed to confirm it.

"Boys, I'm tired of buttin' my head into brick walls and solid rock. It's time we took the fight to them."

Odell figured he knew who Art was talking about, too. Next

to the Sun, the largest rancher in the valley was Max Ward and his Flying W, up under the North Rim. Although the W was small beans compared with Quinlin's spread, it was big enough to prod the old man's ire every time he saw one of Ward's stubby Durham cows pushing in among his longhorns.

Then Art Quinlin's voice lowered menacingly, and the gleam in his eyes steadied. "Mount up, boys. We're riding north."

Chapter Seven

The snow had nearly disappeared from the ridge above the hut when Gil decided it was time to move on. Green was spilling out all over, and the elk and deer were already grazing slowly upward, toward ever higher elevations.

Although in no hurry to leave, he was out of just about everything except for the meat he'd shot himself, and he was craving something more satisfying. Coffee and bread, with salt for flavor, and maybe a good cigar now that his lungs felt clear again.

Gil took his time straightening up the camp. He replaced the chinking between the logs in the walls and replenished the firewood he'd used during his time there. He even built a pyramid of kindling for the hut's next occupant, who might need a quick fire and shelter against the elements just as desperately as Gil had when he'd fallen inside, almost out of his head with fever. Then one morning right as dawn was flowing down off the higher peaks in the east, he saddled Rusty and bid the little shanty goodbye. After his long illness he didn't know what day it was. He wasn't even sure of the month, but there was a penetrating warmth in the air that told him winter had finally relinquished its hold over the land, and that it was time to be on his way.

Without a blizzard hammering at him, it was an easy ride south out of the mountains. Gil followed the Saddleback trail down off the north rim into the Ensillado Basin, then across the broad sage plain toward the sprawling grove of cottonwoods where Larkspur had taken root. With so much greenery surrounding the town, he knew there had to be a plentiful source of water somewhere within the trees. The rest of the Basin was mostly flat and nearly treeless save for along some of the streams, good cattle country but no place to try to stake out a town or a homestead.

Bringing his mount to a halt at the northern edge of the town, Gil studied the row of businesses that made up the east side of Larkspur's single thoroughfare. Then his gaze shifted to the widely spaced trio of empty structures across the street, scattered like discarded ambitions, and a frown creased his brow. The town's cockeyed alignment had seemed odd the last time he'd come through. Today it struck him as vaguely sinister, as if the core of whatever rift separated these two sections of the hamlet ran deep and sharp.

Gil turned his attention to Bannerman's. Except for the seemingly abandoned hotel north of the depot, the saloon was probably the largest structure in town. He tried to recall how the community had appeared the first time he'd seen it, but found those memories all but buried beneath the haze of his fever. His clearest recollections were of the doctor who had examined him and the codeine that had soothed both his raw throat and the lung-scouring coughs that had nearly clubbed him from his saddle. He did remember the saloon, though. That and the men who'd left it to accost him in the street. Although their startled expressions from the impact of the Hopkins and Allen's slugs were never far from his thoughts, the encounter itself, wrapped in gathering dusk and swirling snow, seemed distant and not quite real, like the talking bear and the hut's shimmying walls.

Grinding his teeth, Gil tore his eyes away from the street, staring into the trees behind the row of businesses until he spotted the doc's low adobe house with its bright blue trim.

Remembering the physician's kindly manner during his examination, as well as his concern in the street afterward, brought a sense of welcome to Gil's mind, and he reined the sorrel in that direction.

Although pockets of snow had lingered in the deep forest under the North Rim, the vegetation here was lush with spring, the leafed-out cottonwoods creating a dappled shade under which the town's residential section seemed to doze in the late-afternoon warmth. Wood smoke rose lazily from the chimney above the physician's house, and a fat mare with gray whiskers lay in the tall pasture grass in the rear. The complacent purr of roosting hens from a nearby coop brought back memories of Gil's boyhood home, nearly twenty years in the past.

Dismounting, he looped his reins through the ring of an iron hitching post in front of the doctor's house, then removed his hat and self-consciously ran his fingers through his long, unruly hair. A curtain moved at one of the front windows as Gil approached, then fell gently back into place. He felt a stirring uneasiness as he knocked, but tried to remain outwardly calm as he stood there with his hat in hand. The door swung open and the doctor's wife—he couldn't remember her name now, or if the physician had even mentioned it to him—stood before him with a stiff, almost defiant manner. Worried eyes traveled up and down Gil's lanky frame as if searching for either injury or infirmity. Then she gasped and took a step backward, one hand flying to her throat as if it had been cut.

"Mr. Ryan?"

"Yes, ma'am," Gil replied, his voice still faintly raspy. "I hope I didn't frighten you. I was wondering if your husband was in, and if I could talk to him."

"Yes, of course." Her gaze darted past him, toward the street. Then she grabbed his sleeve and pulled him inside. "William," she called over her shoulder and swiftly closed the door.

Gil was caught off guard by the woman's unusual reaction, but he didn't have time to ponder her motives before the stocky figure of the physician appeared at the door to his office. The doc's eyes widened with instant recognition, and he quickly stepped forward. Although Gil noticed the heavy bandage covering the older man's left hand from wrist to fingertips, he didn't mention it.

Doc glanced at his wife and she nodded.

"I'll put his horse in Snowball's shed," she said, grabbing a shawl off one of the pegs driven into the adobe wall next to the door and hurrying outside.

"Let's go into my office," Doc said. "Were you seen?"

"By who?"

"Anyone."

Gil shrugged. "Maybe. There were a few people on the street when I rode in. Why?"

Doc considered the question for a moment, then motioned toward the back room. "Come on in, we need to talk." He turned away without waiting to see if Gil would follow. In his office he patted the examination table with his good hand. "Sit down here and take off your shirt and vest."

"I'm not sick anymore."

"Not like you were," Doc agreed, "but if I'm not mistaken, you're still congested. I imagine you're coughing fairly regularly, too."

Gil started to unbutton his vest. Nodding toward the physician's injured hand, he said, "Who looks after the doctor when the doctor's hurt?"

"Alma has assisted at my side for many years. She's quite capable of most procedures, including resetting broken bones when necessary."

Gil hung his vest and shirt on a rack. After a pause, he

115

unbuckled his gun belt and placed it on the floor below his shirt.

"We hadn't heard from you in so long we were beginning to think you'd made it out of the Basin."

"Is someone saying I didn't?"

"Art Quinlin is convinced you haven't. He believes one of the local homesteaders has been hiding you." Doc gave him a searching look. "If that's true, I don't want to hear about it."

Gil considered the physician's words as he watched the older man fit the stethoscope around his neck. His movements were awkward with just the use of his right hand.

"How have you been faring, Mr. Ryan?"

"I'm still kicking."

"How about your cough?"

"It's hanging on. Matter of fact, I was hoping you might have some more codeine I could buy, or maybe I can get some from Somers."

"Then I guess you haven't been hiding out at one of the smaller ranches."

"No, I've been up in the mountains to the north."

"To the north?" Doc nodded thoughtfully. "That's why they didn't find you."

"How seriously have they been looking?"

"Seriously enough that you shouldn't have come back."

"I told you before I wouldn't leave with people thinking I'm a killer on the dodge."

"I'd hoped you might change your mind."

"What I did was in self-defense," Gil replied doggedly.

"Art Quinlin doesn't care. He wants you dead."

"There's nothing I can do about that, but I won't run. I'll be damned if I'll run."

"You'll likely be killed if you stay."

"Maybe."

Doc's brows arched. "You seem considerably more confident than you did the last time you were here."

"I barely remember the last time I was here."

"You may wish you'd forgotten it completely," Doc stated glumly.

"There's a jail across the street. I don't remember if you mentioned a lawman."

"I might have. Hal Keegan wears a badge and calls himself a sheriff, but it wasn't an elected position."

"How'd he get the job?"

Doc hesitated, then shook his head. "It's a long story, Mr. Ryan. Right now you need to be quiet so I can listen to your lungs." He fit the stethoscope's tips into his ears, and for the next several minutes they went through the same routine as before, Gil taking a series of deep breaths as Doc slid the cool steel bell over his chest and back; he tapped lightly at Gil's ribs as if listening for an echo, then peered into his eyes and mouth and ears. When he was finished, he removed the stethoscope from around his neck and returned it to his desk. Gil heard the front door open and close, and a couple of seconds later Alma appeared at the entrance to the examination room, toting Gil's heavy Winchester rifle and the cartridge belt he'd left tied to his saddle.

"Your horse is stabled out back with our mare," she said without any hint of embarrassment at Gil's bare chest. "I gave him some oats, and there's hay and plenty of fresh water if he wants it. I left your tack in the shed, but thought I ought to bring your rifle inside."

"Set it in the corner," Doc said, noticing Gil's puzzled expression and seemingly wanting to intercept any questions before he could ask them. "If there's any dinner left over, I suspect our young friend here could put it to good use."

Alma smiled. "There's plenty," she assured him, then added

117

over her shoulder as she turned away. "I'll fix a plate."

"Make it a full one," Doc called after her. He took Gil's shirt off the rack and handed it over. "Go ahead and get dressed. I can give you a small bottle of codeine to tide you over, but the Basin is currently in short supply of medicine."

Gil held the shirt in both hands. "What's going on, Doc?"

"Who said anything was going on?"

"I do, and I'm thinking it's more than just a rancher looking for the man who shot his son and one of his drovers."

Doc gave him a wry glance. "Isn't that enough . . . for you?"

"You tell me."

Sighing, Doc said, "All right, there is more to it, a lot more. But before we get into the details, why don't we start putting some meat back on your bones. We can discuss Art Quinlin and the Basin's problems after you've eaten."

Although a part of Gil wanted the information immediately, there was a larger part of him that had been smelling Alma Shaw's cooking since he entered the house, and the prospect of sampling some of it now had set his mouth to watering. He slid off the table and quietly pulled on his shirt and vest. Without much enthusiasm, he offered: "I could eat somewhere else if my being here might cause you any trouble."

"I think it'd be best if you stayed out of sight until you know what you're up against," Doc replied. He rummaged through his medicine cabinet until he located a small bottle of codeine, then handed it over. "I'd use that sparingly, since I don't know when we'll get another shipment."

Gil nodded and slipped the bottle inside his vest pocket, then followed the physician back through the parlor to the dining room on the opposite side of the house. Although the Shaws had already eaten, there seemed to be plenty of leftovers. Alma was setting a platter of still-warm roast beef and potatoes down between bowls of fried green beans, stewed apples, and pickled beets. Thick slices of bread sat on a cutting board to one side, along with a wooden crock of butter with *Schwartz Dairy* burned into the side.

Having subsisted on trail fare for so long, the aroma of home cooking was about to buckle Gil's knees. As he stood at the dining room's entrance eyeing the clean linens and spotless dinnerware, he became keenly aware of his own shabby appearance. The frayed and dirty clothing and thick beard, hair falling over his collar in back, halfway to his shoulder blades. The sole of his right boot was starting to separate at the welt, and both were badly in need of a good saddle soaping. He'd left Idaho a relatively wealthy and well-dressed man, and crawled out of the Big Sandy three months later nearly a pauper. His time in the hut below the Ensillado's North Rim had done nothing to improve either fate or circumstance.

"Please, have a seat, Mr. Ryan," Alma said graciously, pouring freshly brewed coffee into a thick white china mug.

"I think our guest is feeling a little self-conscious about his dress," Doc observed.

"Nonsense," Alma replied. "He looks no different than any decent man who has just come in off the trail." She smiled and added, "William and I have lived in our share of hovels, Mr. Ryan. We're both aware of how the elements can affect a person's attire, but clothes can't mask a man's true character. Please, sit down." She raised the coffee pot a few inches in her hand. "Do you drink coffee?"

"Yes, ma'am, whenever I can."

"You're going to like Alma's coffee," Doc assured him. "She adds a pinch of cinnamon to the brew."

"I can smell it."

Doc pointed to a seat where his wife had already laid out a plate and silverware, then moved around the other side of the table and took a chair behind the coffee she'd already poured.

Alma filled a second cup for Gil, then returned to the kitchen.

"You'd best dig in, Mr. Ryan, before it gets cold."

"You can call me Gil."

"Very well. You can call me William, or Will. But if you want to call me what everyone else does, it'll just be Doc." He nodded toward the platter of meat and potatoes. "You don't strike me as a shy man, Gil. Larkspur may be lacking a number of amenities at the moment, but food isn't one of them. Go on and put something in that stomach of yours, before it rattles loose. I've been listening to it growl ever since you showed up."

Gil smiled and nodded and dug in, while Doc leaned back in his chair with a faraway look in his eyes and sipped contentedly at his coffee. As hungry as he was, it didn't take long to polish off double helpings of everything, and he had to restrain himself from thirds. Noticing Gil's hesitation as he pushed his plate away, Doc grinned knowingly.

"You sure you've had enough?"

"Yes, sir, I believe I have."

"Watching you eat puts me in mind of when I rode through the Black Hills with Crook in Seventy-six, chasing the Sioux."

Gil looked up with sudden interest. "You were with Crook during his Starvation March?"

"I was, and if I never eat horse meat again, I'll die a happy man."

"I'd imagine so," Gil said, impressed. General George Crook's Starvation March in the weeks following Custer's defeat on the little Bighorn was the thing of legends.

"I know what hunger, real hunger, feels like, and to appreciate a fine meal when one is presented," Doc continued. He nodded toward the meat platter. "We have plenty, if you'd like some more."

"I'd better not. My belly wants it, but my head is telling me to go easy. I reckon I'll listen to my head, now that the edge has been taken off my hunger."

"Some more coffee, then?"

"Sounds good."

Doc pushed his chair back. The sound of its legs scraping across the floor acted like a summons for his wife, who appeared from the kitchen before Doc could fully rise. Her glance took in Gil's empty dinnerware, swabbed clean with slices of bread.

"How about some pie to go with your coffee, Mr. Ryan?" she asked.

"Maybe later," Doc replied for him. "Gil and I have some business to discuss in the other room, although we'd appreciate more coffee. And would you mind bringing us a couple of my good cigars?" He looked at Gil. "I'm assuming you smoke."

"Not on a regular basis, but I've always enjoyed a good cigar. In fact, I've been craving one lately."

"I'll bring them," Alma promised before returning to the kitchen.

Gil followed Shaw into the parlor and paused uncertainly in the middle of the room. As with the rest of the house, the furniture here looked clean and in good repair. He wasn't sure where to sit until Doc motioned him toward an oak settee covered with a fine, blue cotton print.

"I've had patients in here dripping everything from blood to mud," he told Gil. "A little mountain dirt won't hurt anything."

Although Gil wasn't sure how Alma would feel about that, he didn't argue. While he made himself as comfortable as an outdoorsman could astride such an unyielding contraption as a settee, Doc eased into a matching chair of the same flowery pattern across the room. Noticing a violin case tucked behind his host's seat, Gil recalled his first visit to the physician's home, the tortured notes that had emanated from the residence that evening. Nodding toward Doc's bandaged hand, he said, "I hope that's temporary, and that you'll be adding fresh rosin to your bow before too much longer."

Doc's genial expression abruptly sagged.

"Aw, hell, Doc, don't listen to me. I've been holed up for so long I've nearly forgotten how to talk to anything that doesn't have four legs and a tail."

"No, there was nothing untoward in your remark. It's just an uncomfortable subject. It does bring up what I've been wanting to talk to you about, though."

He stopped speaking when Alma arrived carrying a tray laden with two freshly poured mugs of her good cinnamon-flavored coffee and a pair of long golden-brown cigars. She set the tray on a table next to her husband, brought Gil his cup and a cigar, then silently exited the room.

"What's going on, Doc?" Gil asked when she'd gone. His gaze dropped to the physician's maimed left hand. "Does that have anything to do with me?"

"Other than that the source of Larkspur's problems is the same as yours, no."

"You mean Quinlin?"

"I do."

"And the fact that I killed his son?"

"There's that."

"What else?"

"The whole morass that Art Quinlin's ambitions have dragged all of us into, I suppose. It's true there are people in Larkspur who say Les's death was the catalyst for everything that's happened since, but they're just deluding themselves. Our problems with Art go back years, long before you ever left Idaho."

"But I'm still the outsider who killed his boy."

"In self-defense."

"Yeah, but Quinlin isn't going to care about that, is he?"

Doc smiled wryly. "You're using my own arguments against me now. I ought to resent that."

"Tell me what's going on," Gil said quietly.

Doc paused as if to gather his thoughts, then he began to speak. He started slowly, as if sorting carefully through each revelation for coherence, but as time went on, his words came more swiftly, the story unfolding with an incisive detail that held nothing back, yet betrayed none of the emotion Gil detected in the physician's eyes—the anger and sorrow and helpless frustration for the injustices he and the town had endured over the years. When he finished, he looked away and shook his head. "It's not something Alma and I anticipated when we retired here. One man's unbridled greed, and not even for wealth, mind you, but for power. The ability to crush and control."

"He wants his own kingdom."

"Exactly." Doc chuckled. "I wonder if he's even realized that yet?"

Gil didn't reply. He'd witnessed enough blind corruption in the mining districts of Idaho and Montana to no longer care what motivated the kind of lust Shaw had just described. As far as he was concerned, it wasn't necessary to understand evil to know that it needed to be stomped out, and as quickly and thoroughly as possible, before it spread. What he didn't understand was why a town, even a small one like Larkspur, continued to tolerate men like Art Quinlin and his toughs.

"Why haven't you stopped him?"

Doc looked up in surprise. "Is it that simple?" Then he shook his head. "No, don't answer that. The problem isn't yours, Gil, it's ours. I only told you what I did so that you'd understand why you can't stay."

"Because if I do, it'll make things worse for Larkspur?"

"Because you'll be risking your neck every minute you're

here, and your death wouldn't accomplish a damned thing. It would be a waste of my skills as a physician, not to mention a loss of good medicine."

"I haven't changed my mind, Doc."

"It's an honorable stance, though hardly practical."

"Practical isn't always what's right."

Doc seemed genuinely puzzled by Gil's refusal to flee. "What in the world will you accomplish by staying?"

"I don't know that I'd accomplish anything, but I won't run. I'll face the law and whatever it thinks is appropriate, but I'm not a murderer, and I'm not going to act like one."

"Quinlin has a dozen men riding for him, Gil, and none of them are drovers."

"Meaning they're gunmen?"

"At least one of them has that reputation. The others are ruffians, at best."

"Who has the reputation?"

"A man named Clint Miller. Have . . ." He stopped and his eyes narrowed. "I was going to ask if you've heard of him, but judging from your reaction, I'd say you have."

"I've heard of him." Gil forced his fingers to relax their grip on his coffee cup. He set it on the floor next to the settee.

"What have you heard?" Doc asked curiously.

"That he's a killer for hire." He jutted his chin toward the physician's hand. "Is he the one who did that?"

Silence greeted Gil's question. For a minute he wondered if Doc would respond at all. Then he said, "Miller was there, with Art. They wanted information. At first I wouldn't tell them anything, but after Miller slammed a hammer down on top of my hand, I told them what I knew. Luckily for you, that wasn't much."

Gil sat in silence as Doc's words churned through his mind. Then his eyes strayed to the violin case and understanding dawned. Doc must have seen it and realized what he was thinking.

"I guess it was my misfortune that Art remembered that I was trying to learn to play the violin."

"Is that why he broke your hand, so that you couldn't play?"

"That was the goal, although I suspect I'll eventually regain most of the use of my fingers. Maybe not with the same dexterity I once had, but enough to play for my own pleasure." He chuckled. "I doubt if many people around Larkspur will notice the difference."

"I'm not sure I could joke about it like that."

A thoughtful expression came over Doc's face. "I wasn't there when Les and the others challenged you that night, but Ira Bannerman was. He says there wasn't a trace of fear in your reaction to either Les Quinlin or Tim Jackson, and that you barely acknowledged Odell Love at all. He said it was like you'd already dismissed him as a threat."

"There was fear," Gil assured him. "I was just too eared down by fever to show it."

"I'm not trying to dismiss your perception of what happened, but when I got there a few minutes afterward, I didn't see any outward sign of anxiety. Even as ill as you were, you'd just stood your ground against three hardened strangers, yet you seemed completely in control of yourself. That's not a common reaction."

Although Gil didn't try to refute the doctor's opinion, he didn't agree with it. In his experience, fear was a funny thing, controllable one time, wild and intractable the next. Sometimes a man was just thrown into a situation where he had to put his head down and shove forward, no matter how harrowing the task. That didn't mean he wasn't rabbit-scared on the inside. Not unless he was either drunk or a fool—or maybe burning up with fever.

"You seem proficient with firearms," Doc went on. "Since you don't strike me as a gunman, I wondered if you've ever been a lawman."

"No," Gil replied quickly, bluntly.

"Yet you handled yourself extremely well. Several of us remarked on it."

Gil's eyes narrowed. "You've got a bad itch about something, Doc. Why don't you go ahead and scratch it?"

"All right. Larkspur needs a sheriff, someone who'll represent the town and the Basin until the position can be filled legitimately, by election."

"What about . . . what was his name? Keegan?"

"Hal Keegan is no lawman, Gil. At best, he can be counted on to turn the other way when trouble presents itself."

"I think I've asked before how he got the job."

"He showed up a little over a year ago, after the citizens' committee put an ad in several newspapers around the Southwest. We were looking for a lawman, but Keegan wasn't our choice. It was Quinlin who brought him in, then gave him the keys to the jail. He wears a badge, but it's Art he answers to. He has a room at the Sun where he stays more often than he does in Larkspur." He raised his uninjured hand as if to stave off questions. "We've sent for a United States Marshal, if that's what you were going to ask. He replied a few weeks later and told us there wasn't anything he could do about it."

"Doesn't sound like much of a marshal."

"I don't think most people outside the Basin consider us much of a priority. Larkspur isn't even incorporated yet."

"Then you don't have the authority to hire a sheriff."

Doc's brows rose in amusement. "Now, I'd call that a fairly astute observation for someone who doesn't claim any familiarity with a badge."

Gil looked away. Memories rose like flotsam. He pushed them

back under. He had enough to think about in the present without reliving the past. "I'd like to help, Doc, but . . ." His words trailed off.

"You can't, or won't?"

"That's about it."

"But you won't leave?"

"No, sir."

"For God's sake, man, if you're going to stay and fight, then do it legally, with a badge."

"A badge doesn't make a man's actions right. Hal Keegan ought to've convinced you of that."

Doc took a deep breath and leaned back in his chair. "You didn't ask about the codeine."

Gil touched the outside of the pocket where the small bottle was nestled. "What do you mean?"

"I said earlier there wasn't much medicine left in the Basin, but you didn't ask why."

"All right, I'll ask it now. Why?"

"Do you remember Fred Somers?"

"Sure, I remember him. I hope to talk to him again."

"I'm afraid that isn't going to be possible. Fred was killed."

Gil straightened slowly. "What happened?"

Doc lifted the bandaged hand off his lap. "Art Quinlin knew I was trying to learn the violin. This was his way of reminding me what happens to men who cross him. Sadly, I was the one who got off easy that day. You hadn't killed Les when I treated you for pneumonia, but you had when Fred outfitted you later that evening."

There was a roaring in Gil's ears like that first night in Larkspur, with his sinuses packed from congestion and his body raging with fever. Doc's expression was subdued as he continued.

"It's not much comfort to those of us who knew him, but Art

insists he didn't want Fred to die. Keegan called it an accident, and refused to do anything about it."

Gil shook his head slowly, in disbelief. Then, remembering Fred's daughter, he asked, "What about the girl? Was she hurt?"

There was a hint of acid in Doc's reply. "You mean other than having to watch as Quinlin's thugs beat her father senseless? No, they didn't hurt her. Not physically. They did wreck the store, though. They shattered most of the glass bottles containing medicine, and tossed pills into the snow by the handful. Peggy is still trying to reorder what she needs, but supplies are always slow to reach Larkspur."

Gil cursed softly and pushed to his feet.

"Those are the kind of men you'll be dealing with if you stay, and . . . damnit, I want you to stay, Gil. I want you to be mad enough to stay."

"And fight?"

"With a badge, yes. Without that, you'll just be another hard case looking for revenge."

Leaving his coffee untouched, the cigar unlit, Gil walked into the office to retrieve his rifle and cartridge belt. He was buckling the Hopkins and Allen around his waist when he returned. Doc was still seated. He didn't look up as Gil entered the parlor, and there wasn't much ardor in his voice when he spoke.

"You're welcome to spend the night here if you'd like."

"I reckon I've caused you enough trouble, Doc, but thanks. Tell your wife she's a good cook, and that it was an honor to sit at her table."

Doc nodded and stood, his movements lethargic, almost mechanical. "I will," he promised, following Gil to the door. "If you change your mind about leaving, you should know that Quinlin has men stationed at the head of Ensillado Canyon. If you want to go out that way, you'll have to find a way around them. Or go back north, the way you came in."

"I'm not going anywhere."

"I know." Doc pulled the door open. "I'm a member of Larkspur's citizens' committee. It's currently an *ad hoc* board without any real legal standing, but it's the only government we have right now. If you change your mind about that badge, come see me and I'll call a meeting. We'll make the position as legal as possible."

Gil glanced to where Doc's cased violin leaned against the adobe wall beside the physician's empty chair and unconsciously rolled his left shoulder, feeling the tightness of the flesh over the old bullet wound, the deep ache beneath it.

Softly, Doc said, "Gil?"

Chapter Eight

It was still dark that morning when Art Quinlin split his men into two groups. Most likely out of spite, he sent Odell east along the base of the North Rim with Clint Miller, Brownie Hillman, Carl Roth, and Goose Carter, while he took the rest of his crew on up into the piney hills toward the Saddleback.

For Odell, the old man's decision to place him with Miller wasn't much of a surprise. Everyone knew how he felt about the cold-eyed killer, and that alone would have been enough for Art to send him along with the gunman. Sure as hell it had nothing to do with Odell's skills as a pistoleer, nor any desire on his part to avenge the deaths of Les Quinlin or Tim Jackson. As far as Odell was concerned, dying had been their own damned faults. If they'd minded their business like any smart man would have, they'd likely still be alive.

With Art and his crew out of sight, Miller led his men into the foothills. Odell hung back until the others had passed, then fell in at the rear of the column. They were on the scout for a small farm owned by a couple of Norwegian brothers named Martinsen, immigrants barely a year into their new country and already hock-deep in trouble. Thinking of the Martinsens made Odell wonder if they were even aware of the sorrow heading their way. He knew from Ira Bannerman that the two had only a limited grasp of the English language. That and a deeply ingrained distrust of anything to do with Art Quinlin's Sun

Ranch, thanks to an encounter with Les and Joel the previous fall.

The Martinsens had been on their way home from Larkspur when the Quinlin boys spotted them. Their names were Anders and Edvin, and being poor and armed accordingly—just a muzzle-loading shotgun and an old pinfire revolver between them—they hadn't put up much resistance. Odell considered their decision not to fight a wise one. He'd been along that day, and knew the Quinlins were looking for some kind of mischief to amuse themselves with. Of course, a lot of people around the Basin claimed Joel and Les were always on the hunt for deviltry, and Odell wouldn't have argued the point.

Being cut from a different strip of leather than the Quinlins, Odell had been relieved when Joel finally told the Martinsens to get out of his way. He'd also told them to pack their belongings as soon as they got home, and to abandon the valley before the first snowfall because, as he'd claimed, *All hell's gonna break loose around here come spring.*

Standing alongside their harnessed mules and small wagon, dusty, scuffed, and bleeding from a number of minor cuts put there by Lester's quirt, the Martinsens had listened intently, but Odell didn't think they understood a third of what he said. He hadn't tried to explain it to them, either. Not with Joel and Les sitting their mounts nearby, beaming the universally broad and triumphant grins of fools, drunks, and bullies everywhere.

Around the Quinlins, Odell had found it prudent to keep his mouth shut and his eyes averted, although he kind of wished now that he'd made an effort to seek the Martinsens out afterward. They probably wouldn't have listened to him, but maybe he'd feel less guilty about what was likely going to happen later that day.

Odell was still thinking about the last time he'd seen the Martinsens when Clint brought his party to a halt and ordered

Odell forward.

"What the hell are you doing way back there, anyway?" he demanded. "You ain't scared of a couple of half-witted farm boys, are you?"

"I don't know as I'd call 'em halfwits," Odell replied, nudging his mare up alongside Miller's gray.

"You ever hear 'em talk?" Miller demanded. "They sound like a couple of squawking monkeys."

Odell shrugged but let it slide. If he got cross-wise of the old man or one of the Quinlin boys—well, there was only Joel left now, stashed safely away at the Sun where the old man wouldn't be as likely to lose his last precious offspring—Odell risked having his ass raked over a bed of hot coals. Getting on the wrong side of Clint Miller would more likely garner him a bullet in the back, followed afterward by a half-hearted excuse from the gunman that Odell had stepped in front of his revolver just as he pulled the trigger. Odell doubted if Art would consider it much of a loss, either.

"You've been to their place before, ain't you, Love?"

"The Martinsens?"

Miller's expression loosened in exasperation. "Who the hell do you think I'm talking about?"

"It's hard to know sometimes," Odell snapped back, then instinctively hunched his shoulders waiting for the response, but Miller only laughed.

"Take the lead," he said. "Get a move on, too. It's gonna be light soon."

"I don't know where their ranch is."

"You've got a better idea than anyone else here in this bunch. Take the lead, damnit."

Wordlessly, Odell guided his mare into the deeper forest skirting the North Rim's lower slopes. The sky was just beginning to lighten when they came to a narrow wagon road winding through the timber. Twenty minutes later they crested a grassy ridge and hauled up. Below them lay a narrow green valley. A creek tumbled down its center and a small herd of shorthorns— not even a dozen head—grazed on the tall grass growing along its banks. Birds sang in the trees, and off in the distance a mule deer, a doe, nibbled daintily at the abundant forage. It was such an idyllic scene it nearly twisted Odell's gut in a knot to think about why they were here.

Miller reined in at his side, the others bunching up close behind. They stared silently across the valley at a small cabin perched on a piece of flat ground above the creek. Smoke rose from the chimney like raveling yarn and chickens pecked in the dirt near the front door. There was no barn nor any other kind of outbuilding, but a pair of dug-outs had been cored into the earth below the cabin, and a corral behind it held a pair of bay mules, standing hipshot in the first warming rays of the sun.

"That the place?" Miller asked.

"I think so."

"You *think*?"

"It looks like their mules."

"It *looks* like their mules, but you ain't sure?"

"I ain't never been here before, so I couldn't rightly say," Odell replied irritably, "but if you're worried it's the wrong place, we can ride on by."

Miller gave him a curious glance. "You ain't growing a spine all of a sudden, are you, Love?"

"No, I mean . . . I kind'a know those boys, and they ain't hurtin' no one."

"They're stealing Sun cattle when they have their own right there in front of them," Miller returned flatly.

"Even if they are, it'd be no more than a cow once in a while to eat, so they can save their own for breeding. It ain't like they're driving 'em off in bunches."

"It's still stealing, and I was hired to put a stop to it." Miller twisted in the saddle. "You boys back me up and do what I say, understand?"

"Sure," Brownie agreed, and Goose Carter quickly nodded. Only Carl Roth denied Miller the satisfaction of a reply, although his refusal and the hard return of his stare said a bundle.

"Let's go," Miller said, jabbing his spurs into the gray's sides.

They kept their horses to a walk and their guns holstered, but there was no mistaking the tension that rippled galvanically through their ranks. They were still about sixty yards away when one of the Martinsens came around the cabin's far side and spotted them. He immediately sprinted for the front door. Miller yanked his revolver and snapped off a hurried round, his bullet peeling bark off the cabin's front wall a couple of feet above Martinsen's slouch hat.

"Head for cover, boys," Miller shouted, spurring his mount toward the low ground in front of one of the dugouts.

Brownie, Carl, and Goose quickly scattered amid a flurry of their own wild shooting and incoherent yells. Only Odell held back, caught in the paralysis of the moment and not sure which way to turn. It was Miller, already dismounted and ducking below the front wall of the nearest dugout, who shouted for Odell to start moving his hind end before he had it shot off.

"Over here," Miller bellowed, and Odell, startled out of his bewilderment, dug his heels into the dun's ribs and raced for the dugout.

Expecting to be shot off his horse at any moment, Odell was as surprised as anyone when he jumped to the ground unpunctured. He gave the dun a slap on the rump to scare her out of the line of fire, then dived into the hollowed-out trough of earth that was the dugout's entrance. Bellying down next to Miller, he peered cautiously over the top of the dugout. From here he had a clear view of the cabin's front and east side. The door was closed and the two windows that he could see were shuttered.

"Why'd you shoot?"

The gunman gave him a withering look. "That's what we're here for, ain't it?"

"I thought we were here to see if they were rustling any of Quinlin's cows."

"They ain't dumb enough to keep stolen livestock on their property, but we already know they've been rustling."

Odell leaned back. "How?"

"Because Quinlin says they are. Now shut up and let me think."

"Call to 'em," Odell suggested. "See if they'll surrender."

"Damnit, Love, I told you to shut your trap." Miller shook his head as if in exasperation, but after a couple of minutes he raised up and called out, "You Martinsens, can you hear me?"

The reply from the cabin was heavily accented and hard to follow. "*Ja*, you vant vhat?"

"Damned monkeys," Miller grumbled, then shouted, "I want you out here where we can see you, hands in the sky."

"*Nei*, I tink ve stay. You go now, leaf us be alone."

Miller glanced at Odell. "Some smart idea you had there, Love."

Odell shrugged and Miller turned back to the cabin.

"Listen, if you boys don't haul your butts outta there real quick, we're gonna start pouring lead inside," Miller shouted. "Is that what you want?"

"Ve vant for you to go avay."

From the far side of the cabin, Brownie yelled, "We ain't going nowhere until you jackasses walk out here with empty hands."

"Shut up, Hillman," Miller roared. "Goddamnit, I'm in charge here."

Laughter floated down from the hill behind the cabin—Roth's, Odell thought—and Miller muttered darkly to himself. After a long pause, he shouted: "Martinsens! You boys have two minutes to talk it over. If you ain't come out by then, we're gonna start shooting."

His ultimatum made, Miller turned away from the cabin and punched the empty cartridge from his Colt. After replacing it with a live round, he snapped the loading gate closed, then looked up worriedly. "Quinlin wants 'em hung. Says it sends a stronger message to the others than bullets. I don't know how he's gonna take it if we have to shoot 'em."

Miller's concern for what the old man wanted didn't surprise Odell nearly as much as the gunman's willingness to share his doubts aloud. He eyed the big man warily. Ever since Miller's arrival at the Sun, he'd acted like he didn't give a damn what anyone thought. Not even Art Quinlin.

The seconds slogged into minutes, the minutes into a quarter of an hour, until Miller finally swore and squirmed over to where he could see the cabin past the dugout's corner. "Time's up, boys," he yelled. "Show yourself or we're coming in."

"*Ja,* you come on in," one of the brothers returned. "Ve vill vait right here for you, no?"

Miller cursed, then raised his voice for the others to hear. "Open up, boys. Let 'em know we're here."

Grimly, Odell thumbed his revolver's hammer back to full cock. The others had already starting shooting, although there didn't seem to be much enthusiasm for it. The firing was sporadic, and the only damage to the cabin was splintered shutters and chipped bark. They kept up a halfhearted fusillade for a couple of minutes, then tapered off. As far as Odell could tell, the Martinsen brothers had yet to return a shot.

"Give it up," Miller shouted into the ear-ringing silence. "Goddamnit, get out here or we'll burn you out."

"*Ja*, I tink the grass is pretty green for to burn, don't you?"

"Bastards," Miller spoke softly.

"He's right, though," Odell said. "You'd have to pour kerosene all the way from here to the cabin, and even then I doubt if it'd catch."

"When I want your advice, Love, I'll let you know," Miller retorted.

Odell eased back on his haunches, curious to see what the gunman would try next. What he eventually ordered made Odell feel half sick.

"Brownie, Goose, can either of you see their mules?"

"Yeah, two mules and a Guernsey milk cow," Brownie hollered back.

"Kill 'em," Miller ordered.

"Hey, hold on," Odell protested.

Miller whirled toward him, glaring fire. "You keep your mouth pinned, Love."

"The hell! There ain't no call to shoot their livestock."

A shot barked dully from the timber and one of the mules squealed loudly and went down. It thrashed for a moment, then lay still. "That's one, you sons of bitches," Brownie shouted. "You want me to shoot the others, too?"

"What about it, Martinsens?" Miller called. "You want us to kill . . ."

The front door slammed open without warning and the two brothers burst into the open. Anders came first with the shotgun. He skidded to a halt in the yard to fire toward the dugout where Odell and Miller were crouched. The heavy lead shot whistled angrily overhead. Edvin darted around the side of the cabin toward the Guernsey and the surviving mule, screaming and firing his revolver as he ran.

"Don't shoot!" Odell cried, knowing the brothers' weapons would soon be shot dry, but he was too late. Thinking about it later, he supposed it had been too late the moment Art Quinlin ordered them north. Anders managed to fire his second barrel into the trees behind the cabin, then he spun wildly on his heels as a bullet from Carl Roth's rifle slammed into his chest. Edvin didn't even empty his revolver before a bullet sent him sprawling. His gun bounced free and disappeared into the tall grass.

"Damnit, quit shooting," Odell hollered, jumping onto the dugout's roof and waving his arms for the others to cease fire. He didn't hear Miller behind him, didn't even know he was there until the gunman's pistol was jammed solidly into his back.

"Shut up, Love! Shut the hell up, or I swear I'll pull the trigger."

Odell froze with his hands still above his head. Slowly, he lowered them to his sides. Miller pulled his gun away and stepped around him. The others were just coming out of hiding, converging on the cabin where Anders lay motionless and Edvin writhed painfully. Lightheaded and nauseated, Odell followed Miller.

Brownie reached Edvin first. He stood above him with his pistol aimed at the Norwegian's head. For a moment Odell thought he was going to kill him outright. Then Brownie glanced at Miller. "What do you wanna do with him?"

"We're gonna do what Quinlin told us to do," Miller replied. "We're gonna hang the cattle-stealing sons of bitches."

"*Both* of them?" Bownie exclaimed.

"Ain't you hurt him enough?"

Miller gave Odell a sour look. "Love, you've acted like you've been scared shitless to open your mouth ever since I first met you. Now you can't seem to keep it shut." He turned to Goose. "Go find a couple of ropes. Brownie, open the gate on the corral so their stock can get out. Me and Carl and loudmouth here," he tipped his head toward Odell, "are gonna search this place top to bottom until we find proof of rustling."

"What if we don't?" Odell asked dully.

Miller chuckled low in his throat. "Oh, we will, Love, don't fret yourself over that. If we can't find what we need on the property, I have evidence in my saddlebags we can use. Just get it in your head that one way or another, we're gonna ride outta here with proof that the Martinsens were stealing Sun cattle."

Gil entered quietly, then paused to look around. The store appeared as he remembered it, narrow aisles and the shelves stacked high with merchandise. No physical evidence remained of the destruction that had taken place here, yet he sensed . . . something, and without conscious thought he allowed his arm to swing back and brush the Hopkins and Allen's grips.

Peggy Somers emerged from the back room. She approached behind the counter. It was where he'd seen her on his last visit, Gil recalled, coolly remote and thinking he was another of Quinlin's gunmen.

"May I help you?" she asked.

"Yes, ma'am." Gil removed his hat and Peggy's face kind of scrunched up as she studied him. Recognition struggled just below the surface.

"Do . . . are you . . . ?" Her expression turned suddenly to stone. "Are you looking for the Sun?"

Gil smiled in spite of his unease. "No, ma'am, but you've asked me that before."

"I know you, don't I?"

"Only barely. I'm Gil Ryan. I came through . . ." He stopped at her startled gasp. Her eyes darted toward the front door as if expecting . . . what? A savior? Satan? "I'm sorry," he continued. "Doc Shaw told me about your father."

Her eyes misted and she looked away. Almost briskly, she said, "We thought you'd made it out of the Basin."

"I went north instead."

"To the Ward place?"

He vaguely recalled the name—Max Ward—but that was all. "No, ma'am, just a shack up in the mountains. Probably some hunter's camp. It wasn't much more than a cave, but there was plenty of firewood and all the snow a man could ask for to melt for drinking water."

"Why did you come back?"

"Because of what happened the last time I was here, the shooting and my not being able to talk to the law about it." She made a face when Gil mentioned the law, and he added, "Doc told me about Keegan, too."

"Did he tell you Art Quinlin is still searching the Basin like a madman, looking for you?"

"Yes."

"They say that when Art heard about the killing, his first order of business, before he even rode into Larkspur to see his son, was to send a group of men to the head of Ensillado Canyon to make sure you didn't escape. They're still down there. They search every wagon and rider that comes in or goes out."

"He sounds determined."

"He's insane," she replied. "Only death will stop him now."

"What if he were brought to justice?"

"There's no justice in the Ensillado Basin, Mr. Ryan, and Art Quinlin owns the mockery that Hal Keegan calls the law."

"There's a U. S. Marshal's office in Albuquerque," he reminded her.

"And who would take him there?" She laughed, the sound as brittle as cracking glass in the still, dusky air. "Dr. Shaw's sent for a marshal, but the one who showed up last year only reprimanded us for bringing him all the way up here without just cause. I don't expect any better this time."

Gil frowned thoughtfully. "Are you saying Doc's sent for another marshal?"

"He wrote to the Marshal's office a couple of weeks ago, but we don't know if his letter made it through. We aren't sure how closely Quinlin's men are searching the outbound stagecoaches, and we daren't ask for fear of making the situation worse." Her jaw tightened and her lip trembled, and she looked away.

"Are you all right?" he asked gently.

"Of course I'm all right. We've learned to toughen ourselves where the Sun is concerned."

Although Gil felt sympathy for the woman's pain, he didn't say anything or attempt to comfort her. She'd need her anger for a while yet, he thought.

"I'd like to buy some clothes and a better pair of boots," he told her. "I'll need a razor and soap, a toothbrush, baking soda, a few things like that. I was hoping I might also be able to rent a room. Doc said last time I was here that you had some above your store."

"I can sell you what you need, but I won't rent you a room. It wouldn't be proper." She hesitated, then added, "You can't stay here, Mr. Ryan. In Larkspur, I mean. You know that, don't you?"

"Because of Quinlin?"

"He has informants in town. Maybe not on his payroll, but men who'd like to curry favor with him."

She came around the end of the counter and led him to where the men's clothing was stacked on floor-to-ceiling shelves. Gil picked out a new wardrobe, keeping only his hat and gun belt, then carried the merchandise to the counter where she tallied the bill. He paid her from his dwindling pile of funds.

"Shall I wrap these for you?" she asked.

"No, no need." He pulled the stack of clothing closer, then hesitated. "If someone could get Art Quinlin and his boy to trial, would you stand witness against them?"

"Mr. Ryan, it would take an army to drag the Quinlins to trial now, and while I hope I'm wrong, I don't really expect the Marshal's office to send anyone up here. Not after what happened the last time. Besides, what would my chances be if Quinlin was arrested?"

"It's just a question, Miss Somers."

"Then the answer is yes." She returned his stare evenly, her eyes as hard as German flint. "I would do everything in my power to take the witness stand against Art Quinlin and his gang."

Gil nodded and scooped his purchases under his arm. "Thank you, ma'am." He touched the tip of his hat brim. "Maybe I'll see you again, before I leave the Basin."

Peggy Somers didn't reply, but Gil was aware of her puzzled gaze following him to the door. She was curious about what he meant about getting the Quinlins to trial. Truth be told, so was he.

CHAPTER NINE

Max Ward carefully tore a page from the daily calendar hanging on the kitchen wall and placed it in the hutch where it could be used later for notes or figures, or to start the morning fire when there was no space left for scribbling. At the table, Reece studied the back of his father's balding head and wondered what was churning inside of it.

What he was hoping was that Big Max would give the okay to start the spring roundup today. After nearly a month of cutting, hauling, and stacking firewood, Reece was bone-deep weary of the whole affair. Not just the gut-busting labor of wrestling heavy logs and stumps into position for the saw, but the unrelenting monotony of it, the same chore day after day until he thought he'd go *loco* from boredom. He hadn't been back to Larkspur since the last heavy snowfall, which he suspected was what his father'd had in mind all along, keeping him confined to the Flying W and away from whatever trouble might be brewing down below.

Reece glanced across the table to where Two-Socks was brooding over a third cup of his ma's good coffee. If the burly Welshman was thinking about anything, Reece couldn't tell it from his expression. Two-Socks—it was the name he'd given them in Albuquerque when Big Max hired him and Hector Romero to drive their first herd of shorthorns into the Basin, and the only one he'd ever answered to since—was a stocky slab of a man with a weathered face and a heavy, coal-black mustache. His hair was dark and curly, his brows as shaggy as a pair of winter remounts. He was a good worker, though. Big Max wouldn't have kept him on the payroll if he hadn't been. Reece's biggest complaint was that he was so slow and deliberate in everything he did, not even prone to talking if a grunt could get his idea across. Even Hector Romero could hold a better conversation than Two-Socks, and about half of what Hector said would come out in Mex once he worked up a good head of steam.

Reece's gaze shuttled from Two-Socks to Hector, then back to his pa, who was still staring at the calendar as if searching for an answer to whatever he was deliberating over in the paper's coarse weave. While his pa glared at the calendar, his ma came away from the stove with the coffeepot gripped tightly in one white-knuckled fist, its handle wrapped with a piece of sacking to keep it from burning her palm. Sally Ward's normally pale complexion was flushed from the heat and exertion of cooking breakfast, and Reece's brows furrowed in concern. Big Max had offered to have him and Reece eat in the bunkhouse with the hired men that morning, but Sally insisted he was being foolish.

"I'm fine," she'd assured them both, while Reece kindled a fire in the box and his pa pulled on his heavy coat, buttoning it slowly as he studied his wife in the lamp's amber glow.

"If you're sure," he'd finally relented, and his ma had given him a gentle shove toward the door.

"See to your chores, the both of you," she'd ordered. "When you're done, come back in for flapjacks and bacon. Bring Hector and Two-Socks with you. They're probably as tired of beans and beef as you two are."

Big Max had nodded uncertainly, and Reece had given his mother a peck on the cheek before following his pa outside. They'd both commented on their way to the barn that she looked a lot better that morning.

"A little sunshine is what's done it," Big Max declared, and although Reece wasn't as sure, he had to admit that the laudanum he'd brought back from Larkspur last month hadn't seemed to do her much good. She was out of the medicine now, and even though she hadn't said anything, he decided he'd try to get away as soon as he could to pick up another bottle. It was six hours to Larkspur by saddle and another six coming back, a long night's ride under the best of conditions, although not as difficult as it had been the last time he'd gone in, bulling on home afterward in the face of a howling blizzard, the promise of violence riding the trail behind him.

Les and Tim's deaths seemed like ancient history now. Like the stories Hector told about the Apaches who used to roam these mountains, before Art Quinlin and others like him had forced them into the harsher climates lower down, where the army finally succeeded in rounding them up and depositing them on reservations. Those who weren't sent to prison in far-off Florida.

Two-Socks softly cleared his throat, and Reece blinked and brought his thoughts back to the family's cozy kitchen. It had been early that morning when his mother insisted she felt fine. By the time the men finished their chores and trooped inside, her condition had worsened noticeably. Her cheeks looked wan and her hand trembled as she circled the table pouring coffee. Neither of the Ward men made mention of it. They didn't want to embarrass her in front of the others. Hector had also noticed but politely kept his mouth shut, and Two-Socks—well, Reece was never certain what that taciturn individual noticed or didn't notice. For the time being, he was keeping his attention focused on the food in front of him, and barely managed a thank you when Sally refilled his coffee cup for the fourth time.

Turning away from the calendar, Big Max pegged his son with a troubled look. "You've been itching to let go of that whipsaw ever since I put you on it. I reckon it's time." His eyes shifted to the hired men sitting on the opposite side of the table. "We'll start bringing the herd in today. Let's take our time and try not to chouse 'em too much, but I want it done." He was watching Hector now, waiting for the elderly Mexican's input. When it didn't come, he said, "Well, what about it, Romero? Am I jumping the gun again?"

Hector leaned back in his chair and pulled out the makings for a cigarette. "No, I do not think so," he replied in his careful but heavily accented English. "Is early yet, but if we do not push too hard." He shrugged.

"The calves, you mean?"

"*Si*, the little ones that have only recently been born. They do not yet have the strength in their legs for a hard drive, and maybe a few of the older cows have not yet had their babies. It would not be wise to get too *ambicioso*, but if we take our time, maybe no so bad, eh?"

"*Ambicioso?*"

"Ambitious," Reece translated. Although he hadn't spent nearly as much time with the older Mexican as his pa, he'd been quicker to pick up the language.

"*Si*, ambitious," Hector agreed. He tore a sheet from his little bible of smoking papers, then dropped the packet on the table beside his coffee cup.

Big Max nodded thoughtfully and glanced covertly to where his wife stood at the cutting board next to the stove, kneading dough for that evening's bread. Reece knew his pa was as concerned about her as he was. She was the reason he wanted to get the spring roundup under way, to get all the newborns branded and the young bulls castrated, then drive the whole lot up into the high country for the summer. Once they had that task behind them, Max was determined to take his wife to Albuquerque to see their daughters. They were especially anxious to find out how Jilly was faring. She was in a family way, according to her Christmas letter, expecting in June, and she was hoping her mother could be with her when the time came.

Sally wanted to be there, and so did Max, although for different reasons. He was naturally worried about Jilly, but Reece knew he was even more fearful for his wife. He wanted to get her out of the mountains as soon as he could, down where the air was warm and dry, and where his daughters could offer him the kind of assurances a son couldn't.

"Let's go," Big Max said abruptly. "We'll start on the east range and work our way home today, kind of get an idea of where they are, then we'll dig in hard tomorrow, maybe take along some extra food and blankets so we won't have to come back if we're too far out at sundown."

The men nodded and stood and began their shuffle toward the door.

"I'll fix some biscuits and bacon for today," Sally said, moving away from the cutting board with her pale hands powdered with flour. "Tomorrow I'll have something more substantial to take along, in case you have to be away overnight."

Max gently touched her elbow. "You rest if you need it, Sally. We'll manage just fine on cold beef today, and Two-Socks can put some grub together for tomorrow. We won't need much."

"Nonsense, you'll be famished after a hard day in the saddle. I'll be fine, and if I start to feel weak, I'll lay down."

"See that you do," Max replied gruffly, then stepped self-consciously around so that his back was to the others when he leaned forward to give her a goodbye kiss.

Sally smiled, watching her son and husband pull on their coats. With a motion from Max, they all filed outside. Hector and Two-Socks were in the lead, the two Ward men a few paces behind. They hadn't covered more than a few yards when a shot rang out from the trees to the south.

Max howled and cursed and went down hard on one knee, his thigh just below the hem of his coat on the right side splattered with blood. Hector dropped instinctively into a crouch and slapped the hip where his Colt normally rode. Only Two-Socks reacted decisively, taking off in a loping run for the bunkhouse where the hired men kept their guns. Hector ran beside him, keeping low to the ground and making surprisingly good time for someone with so much gray in his beard.

Caught by surprise, Reece remained where he was, staring dumbly toward the dark wall of pines where a tuft of gun smoke hung like a ragged cotton boll. Big Max roared and pushed forward with his good leg. He swung one of his powerful arms like a sweep, catching his son solidly behind the knees and collapsing him to the ground.

Reece landed hard on his back and the air exploded from his lungs; his head rapped the earth solidly enough to rattle his senses, and the sky danced a crazy jig. He could hear his pa hollering and his ma screaming and more shots blasting out of the trees, but there was no one in sight. It was if the forest itself had taken up arms against them. Powder smoke blossomed from half a dozen locations, and the sod around them jumped like ticks where lead plowed into dirt.

It was several seconds before the world slowed enough for Reece to roll onto his stomach and hustle over to where his ma was hauling on Big Max's broad frame, dragging him toward the house in desperate, backward lunges. Reece scooted in on the other side and practically picked his father up with one arm around his waist, the other gripping the older man's wrist tight over his own shoulder.

"Get the door," he yelled for his ma, and she ran back to the house and flung it wide, then stepped out of the way as Reece dragged his father inside. When she slammed the door closed behind them, it sounded loud enough to shatter glass.

"Lord love a cross-eyed duck," Max grated as Reece dumped him in a chair at the kitchen table. Motioning toward the front room with his free hand, the one that wasn't pressed tight against the hole in his leg, he said, "Grab the rifles, boy. Hurry!"

Big Max didn't need to add that last part. Reece had already darted into the other room. He yanked the gun cabinet door open and snatched a pair of long guns out of the rack, then returned to the kitchen with his pa's Winchester and a box of .44 center-fires in one hand, his own Whitney-Kennedy in the other. He leaned the Winchester against his father's chair, then broke open the box of cartridges with a sharp, downward blow, scattering ammunition across the table.

"Watch yourself, Reece," Big Max said in a kind of breathless tone that spoke of serious pain.

"I will," Reece replied, shoving .44-40 cartridges past the Whitney-Kennedy's loading gate.

Gunfire was still pouring out of the trees, but it seemed wild and uncoordinated, as if the solid log walls of the house and barn and bunkhouse were targets enough, rather than the glass windows that would have allowed their bullets inside.

"Where's Hector and Two-Socks?" Big Max rasped.

Sally came into the kitchen from the back room with her sewing kit and a roll of clean bandages. She began laying her tools out on the table, casting quick, worried glances at the oozing hole in her husband's leg. Her movements were cool and methodical, though, and her color had returned somewhat.

"I can't see them, but someone's in the bunkhouse," Reece replied to his father's question.

"Good, they've got their guns."

Generally the men of the W didn't carry their firearms around the ranch, strapping on their handguns only when they were heading out to the range or going into town. They carried their rifles even less frequently. Maybe for hunting in the fall or if they were having trouble with a mountain lion or a grizzly bear killing calves. They always kept them loaded and handy, though, even in the bunkhouse, because you never knew when you might need one in a hurry.

"What do you see?" Max asked.

"I can't see anything except smoke."

"Smoke!" Big Max echoed, and Sally looked up in alarm.

"Gun smoke," Reece amended. "It looks like there might be five or six of them out there, but they're staying back in the trees. I can't tell who they are."

Max exhaled loudly and closed his eyes. "That'll work as much to our advantage as theirs. What we can't see from here, they likely can't see from there."

Reece glanced toward the bunkhouse. Hector was standing with his back to the inside wall next to one of the windows. When he had Reece's eye, he made a sign Reece interpreted as asking if they were okay. Reece nodded that they were, and Hector signaled that he and Two-Socks were also uninjured. Then he eased away from the window, out of sight.

"If they try to surround us, we won't be able to hold them off," Reece said worriedly.

"I doubt they'll try that," Max replied, bracing himself as Sally began trimming the bloody fabric away from his wound.

"Who do you figure it is?" Reece asked, listening to his pa sucking wind and stifling grunts at the table behind him. The sound of his ma's scissors as she cut into the heavy wool trousers reminded him of a rat gnawing through a burlap feed sack to reach the grain inside.

"Who do you think it is?"

"The Sun?"

"Gotta be," Max agreed. "It ain't likely the old man'll spread his crew too thin, either. They were probably trying to work in closer when we came outside and surprised 'em."

"Why'd they . . ." Reece shut up at his father's sharp yelp.

"Jesus, woman," Max breathed. Sally apologized, but continued to probe at the now exposed crater in her husband's thigh. She didn't even look up, so intent was she on examining the wound.

"If they don't surround us, they'll rush us," Reece said, then bit his lip in regret. He didn't want Big Max thinking he was afraid, or that he wouldn't hold up his end of a fight if the Sun's crew made a charge.

"I don't think so," his pa hissed.

Reece cast a hurried glance. Big Max was still in his chair by the table, gripping the edges of the seat with both hands while sweat rivered off his brows.

"Are you all right, Pa?"

"Yeah, fine as a snake's whisker."

"The bullet's still in there, and it's near the bone," Sally said, continuing to peer into the wound. "I can feel it, but I can't get a grip on it."

"Lord, woman, *I* can feel it. Quit poking at it."

She raised her eyes with concern. "That bullet has to come out, Max."

"I know, but not now. You keep grubbing for it and I'm gonna keel over, and I can't do that until we've got that hoary old devil out there on the run."

"What do you want me to do, Pa?"

"I want you to keep your head down for the time being. The shooting's easing off. Quinlin's probably trying to decide what he wants to do next. We need to be ready for whatever he tries."

"You figure maybe he'll give up and leave?"

"That ain't likely, at least not for a while." Max smiled and patted his wife's arm. "Let's wrap this leg, Sally-girl, so I ain't sitting here bleeding when Quinlin makes his move."

Sally didn't reply, even though Reece could tell that she didn't agree. Big Max needed to be put to bed and old Doc Shaw sent for, but she knew better than to argue with him.

Reece stayed close to the door where he could keep an eye on both the timber and the bunkhouse, although from time to time he would make a quick pass through the rest of the house to check the windows, in case his pa was wrong about Quinlin sending some of his men around back. From time to time one of the W hands would snap off a round from the bunkhouse, or the men in the timber would fire toward them, but for the most part it seemed like everyone was content to hunker down and not make a target of themselves. Eventually the shooting stopped altogether, and as silence and a thin film of dissipating gun smoke spread across the ranch yard, Max heaved out of his chair and gimped across the kitchen to the door. He cracked it open and put his face to the gap.

"Quinlin!" he bellowed. "Art Quinlin."

There was no answer. Max cursed, then glanced sheepishly toward his wife. Pretending she hadn't heard, Sally gathered her supplies and carried them into the back room.

"Quinlin, talk to me."

There was a reply this time, although the voice belonged to neither Art nor Joel. "You were given fair warning last fall, Ward. Squatters ain't welcome in the Basin."

"We ain't squatters, you son of a bitch."

"We're going to burn you out, Ward, unless you swear you'll pack up and move on today."

"We ain't going nowhere. I told your boss that last year. I ain't changed my mind."

The shooting started again, heavier this time, the bullets coming closer. Max jerked his head back and closed the door, then stepped away from its thinner wood. The men in the trees kept up a steady fusillade, causing bark to fly and lead to whine.

After several minutes, Max grimly instructed Reece to stay where he was. Carrying his Winchester in both hands, Max slipped outside and hobbled over to a waist-high stack of firewood in an awkward crouch. Bullets thudded into the woodpile, kicking a few of the top pieces clear of the rick. Then Hector and Two-Socks started shooting rapidly from the bunkhouse, drawing fire away from their boss.

Taking a deep breath, Reece ducked through the door to join his pa at the woodpile. He half expected Max to raise hell about it, but he didn't. Finding a niche within the stack, he made an opening for the Whitney-Kennedy's barrel and started firing back. It was the first time in his life that he'd ever shot at anyone, or been shot at for that matter, but it wasn't as intimidating as he'd thought it might be. It helped, he supposed, that he couldn't see who he was shooting at. He did notice that he didn't have any urge to be a hero, and that he was content to stay where he was, ducking his head every few minutes when a bullet kicked up a shower of flying kindling and cottonwood splinters.

It went on like that for a couple of hours, and it was the damnedest battle Reece could have imagined. He shot through two full boxes of .44-40s and, as far as he could tell, never came close to hitting anyone. His pa and Hector and Two-Socks kept up a similar sniping, apparently with the same results, judging from the number of guns that were returning fire. After a while Reece actually began to feel impatient with the whole affair. He half-wished whoever was in charge out there would order his men to attack, but they never did. By midmorning the shooting tapered off once more. Reece heard a horse snort and squeal the way they sometimes did when crowded or otherwise disturbed. Then the silence returned, deeper than before and vaguely ominous.

"What's happening now?" he asked.

"I don't know."

"Then what do we do?"

"We wait."

"How long?"

"As long as it takes," Big Max replied, but Reece noticed he was no longer watching the timber. He was scanning the slope above the bunkhouse. Reece looked, too, and a couple of minutes later Hector Romero stood up and waved his sombrero slowly over his head.

"How'd he get up there?" Reece asked as the elderly Mexican begin his careful descent.

"I reckon that's it," Max grunted, ignoring his son's question as he pushed stiffly to his feet. His face turned pale when he put too much weight on his injured leg, and he sat down heavily on top of the bullet-churned woodpile, breathing hard.

"Are you all right, Pa?"

"Yeah, fine."

Reece glanced toward the bunkhouse. Two-Socks was standing in the doorway with his Winchester in hand, its muzzle sloping toward the ground. "So it's over?"

"They couldn't afford to hang around all day," Max explained. "Sooner or later someone would have heard the shooting and passed the word along the Rim. By this time tomorrow, we'd have likely had a dozen men up here helping us."

If we could have held out that long, Reece reflected. Yet the more he thought about it, the more convinced he became that they could have—even against Quinlin's hard cases. His first gunfight had been a surprise in more ways than one.

Reece was still thinking about the battle when he heard wood slide off the top of the stack behind him. His mother screamed as she burst out the kitchen door, and Reece's scalp crawled. Big Max lay at his feet, fresh blood pouring from the reopened wound in his thigh.

★ ★ ★ ★ ★

PART THREE:
WAR

★ ★ ★ ★ ★

CHAPTER TEN

Gil's mood was low as he exited the mercantile with his purchases tucked under one arm. He made his way down the street to a narrow plank building with a barber's pole bolted in brackets to the front wall; a sign in the window promised hot baths at twenty cents per half-hour.

He went inside and gave the barber his instructions, and when he left the chair thirty minutes later he looked like a new man. His hair had been clipped and his beard sheared to bare hide. Only his mustache and neatly trimmed sideburns remained, the former curling down slightly on both sides of his mouth, the latter ending at a point level with the hinge of his jaw. An hour after leaving the barber's chair he stepped out of the steaming bathing room behind the shop *feeling* like a new man, freshly bathed and decked out in clean clothes from top to bottom. He'd kept only his stained and trail-worn hat, and if he'd had the money he might have considered a new one of those, but his funds were starting to dwindle, the bulk of his finances still somewhere along the Big Sandy with his packhorse and the rest of his gear.

The barber wasn't around when Gil exited the bathing room, so he paid the woman sweeping up around the chair and left the shop just as the sun was setting behind the distant range of mountains. He turned north toward a tiny restaurant with an ambitious title and went inside. Although he'd enjoyed a hearty meal at the doc's place only a few hours earlier, he was already hungry again, his mouth watering at the aromas emanating from the café.

He was surprised to find Doc Shaw and the barber inside, sitting at the table closest to the front window with the saloonkeeper and another man he didn't know. Gil nodded to Doc but didn't stop. He took a seat at a table near the back wall and dropped his hat on the chair at his side. It was growing cool outside, but the restaurant was small and homey and comfortably warm. Gil's gaze lingered on a painting above the rear counter, a street scene from a kind of city he'd never visited, nor ever expected to. Then a teenage girl with copper-colored hair and a bridge of freckles across her nose appeared from the kitchen. She was smiling brightly as she approached his table, and Gil wondered if he'd ever feel that young and optimistic again.

"What can I get you?" the girl asked.

"What kind of pies do you have?"

"Raisin and huckleberry for pies, and Ma just took a peach cobbler out of the oven that's still warm."

"Your ma a good cook?"

"Best in the Basin," the youngster replied, and Gil grinned and ordered a slab of peach cobbler and coffee.

"You want cream on that cobbler?"

"Deep enough to wade in," Gil said, and her smile grew even larger.

"Be right back," she promised.

Gil was aware of the men at the front table talking in low voices. Once or twice he thought he heard his name mentioned, along with Quinlin's, but he tried not to pay too much attention, and the girl was back sooner than expected with his order. After that, he didn't need a reason to ignore the townsmen hunched earnestly over their coffees at the front of the room.

He made short work of the cobbler, and told the girl—

Daphne, her name was—that he wholeheartedly agreed with her assessment of her mother's baking.

"Real good," he repeated, then admitted solemnly, "Of course, I haven't sampled everyone's cooking yet."

Daphne's laughter seemed to light up the room, and she immediately carried his compliment back to the kitchen to share with her mother.

Gil was still working on his second cup of coffee when an older woman in a gravy-stained apron appeared from the kitchen with another pot. She was tall and solid without being heavy, her hair like a fresh dusting of rust on new metal, her eyes a penetrating blue. A smear of flour was chevroned across one sleeve, and there was a darkening of sweat under each arm. She came straight to Gil's table and asked if he'd like a refill.

"Fresh-brewed and on the house," she added. "My daughter told me what you said about the cobbler. That kind of appreciation earns rewards in my kitchen."

Smiling, Gil pushed his cup closer. The woman filled it, then hesitated briefly before sitting down opposite him. She set the coffee pot to the side of the table, out of the way. "My name is Hannah Brickman. I've been told you're Gil Ryan?"

"Folks mostly call me Gil."

"I saw you on the street that night with Lester Quinlin and Tim Jackson, but I don't think I would've recognized you if Doc hadn't told me you were back."

"Word travels fast."

"It always does in a small town, and you can't get much smaller than Larkspur. Besides, a stranger in the Basin is naturally going to draw attention, no matter who he is. You won't need to worry about Quinlin, though. At least not yet. It'll take awhile for word to reach the Sun."

"You make a good cobbler, Mrs. Brickman. I'm looking forward to breakfast, unless you'd rather I not come around."

She snorted and jerked her head back as if catching a whiff of something foul. "Because of that overblown botfly called Art Quinlin? Not hardly, Mr. Ryan."

"My friends call me Gil," he reminded her.

"All right, Gil. My friends generally show up for breakfast between six and eight in the morning, although I'll serve a hungry man any time he knocks at my door." She winked. "As long as he doesn't make a habit of it." She propped an elbow on the table. "It isn't any of my business, but I was wondering if you intended to stay and fight, like Doc thinks you might."

"I'm not looking for a fight so much as to clear my name."

"You know that's not likely?"

"You sound like Doc. Do you feel the same way about the Quinlins?"

"I suspect most of us do, and those who say they don't are generally lying, although I'll admit Art Quinlin has put a real scare on this town, and it's taking a toll."

"What about you?"

Her cheek twitched in agitation. "I'd be a fool if I didn't worry about it. I'm a widow with a daughter just turned fourteen and looking at boys in a way that makes me feel almighty old all of a sudden. But I'd hate more to give in to Art Quinlin's intimidations and think I was gaining anything from it. Especially safety." She sighed and shook her head. "Look, I'm not going up against Art Quinlin by myself, but if you do . . . well, know that you can depend on me to help in any way I can."

"Would you stand witness against him?"

"Hell yes, and pardon my enthusiasm."

Gil smiled. "You know, this is about the best peach cobbler I've ever wrapped my tongue around, Mrs. Brickman. I do admire your skills in the kitchen."

She chuckled. "My friends call me Hannah, and that cobbler's on the house, too. Just don't get used to it. A gal has to make a living, and compliments don't put firewood on my back porch or flour in my pies." She stood and picked up the coffee pot. "You be real careful, Gil Ryan."

He started to reply, but Hannah held up her hand to stop him. Glancing to where the townsmen were gathered around the front table, she said, "Are you galoots going to sit there all evening trying to screw up your courage to talk to this man?"

Only Doc seem unembarrassed by her mild admonition. Leaning back in his chair, he said, "We were waiting for you to soften him up, Hannah."

"I don't believe there's much soft in this boy, Doc. For all our sakes, I hope I'm right. Now come on over here and make your offer."

Doc pushed up from his chair and ambled across the room, his silhouette softened by the diminishing twilight coming through the window behind him. After a pause, the others rose and followed him. Approaching Gil's table with an almost apologetic look, Doc said, "I wonder if we might join you."

Gil motioned toward an empty chair and told him to sit down, then moved his hat off the chair at his side and hung it from the ear of his own chair while the others arranged themselves around the table.

"Gil, I'd like for you to meet the rest of Larkspur's *ad hoc* citizens' committee," Doc said, then made the introductions. There was Roger Greene, whose barbershop Gil had just come from, and Henry Fisher who ran the carpenter shop next to it, plus Ira Bannerman, whom Gil remembered from his last visit.

"Fred Somers is no longer with us, of course, and we decided against asking a sixth member to join us," Doc added.

"Paul Offerman," Ira elaborated. "He's the liveryman. I'd say Quinlin's bunch put the fear of the hammer in that boy, but good."

"The hammer?"

Ira tipped his head toward Doc's broken hand, and Gil nodded.

"It's a hell of a weapon, and just about as deadly as a pistol to a man determined to use it as such," the bartender said, then glanced at Doc and shook his head. "Was it my bones they busted, I'd be sore for vengeance."

"Justice will be my revenge," Doc replied.

"We ought to get to the point," Henry Fisher interjected stiffly, and Gil glanced at Doc.

"You have something to say?"

"I think you know what we're going to ask." Doc's words sounded oddly awkward and uncertain, and he paused to rub thoughtfully at his chin. "I wanted to talk to the committee first, and they're mostly behind me."

"Mostly?" Gil glanced around the table. Greene and Fisher stared back almost hostilely; Bannerman sniffed and shrugged. "But not Offerman?"

Doc curled the fingers of his good hand into a fist. "At this point I doubt if Paul would support anything that might upset the Quinlins, which was why we didn't invite him, but, damnit, we're trying to start a government here, and we need to keep things as simple as possible until we're on our feet."

"Aw, hell, what the doc means is that we ain't got no more legal authority up here than Art Quinlin does," Ira butted in. "We're looking for justice, Ryan. Real justice, and not what some mob can carry out in the dark. If a man wants to settle down in the Basin, he ought not have to ask the old man for permission, nor worry about back-shooters and night riders."

"Maybe it wouldn't be strictly legal," Henry added tentatively, "but since there's no law up here anyway . . ."

"All right," Gil said.

An uncertain silence greeted his words. Then Henry blurted,

"All right? You mean, you'll do it?"

"As long as I can do it my way."

"Just what way is that?" Ira asked.

"That we make it as legal as possible under the circumstances. Signatures and statements of support from everyone at this table, and as many other citizens as we can find who'll stand with us."

"That won't be many," Roger muttered, then scowled at Doc's chastising stare. "It won't," he insisted, then made a quick motion toward Gil. "Folks aren't going to put their neck on the block for a stranger, Doc. No offense, Ryan, but where the hell did you come from, anyway? And why would you want to wear a badge for Larkspur?"

"I guess we've all been wondering about that," Henry agreed.

"Fact is, we don't know anything about you," Roger continued. "Doc says you came down from Idaho, but that's a long ride for no apparent reason. Especially in the middle of winter."

Gil didn't respond. Although he felt vaguely angered by their suspicion, he couldn't blame them for it. Considering the situation the town was finding itself in, there were a lot more reasons to distrust a stranger than accept him at his word.

"Sometimes we have to make decisions without all the facts," Doc said quietly. "We've seen the way Gil handled himself against Les and Tim, and I've had a number of conversations with him now. I trust him. I think we all can."

"Well, talk's real cheap, Doc," Roger said. "I don't doubt your trust in this fella, but what happens if he folds when Quinlin comes hellin' into town with his whole crew? We'd all be sitting here like turkeys in a cage."

Gil stirred and the others grew silent. "Doc, Peggy Somers said you wrote to the Marshal's office in Albuquerque."

"I did. Unfortunately, I don't know if my letter made it past Quinlin's men."

"I'd say if you haven't heard from Quinlin by now, it likely did. If you explained what's been happening, the Marshal's office will be duty-bound to send someone up here to look into it, whether they think it's legitimate or not. The trick is going to be having witnesses who'll testify against Quinlin and his men when the marshal or his deputy gets here."

"That didn't work the last time," Henry reminded them.

"The people we were depending on for witnesses were from the outlying homesteads," Doc told Gil. "Most of them are immigrants who can barely speak English. They're isolated, poorly armed, and probably scared half to death. I'm afraid we counted too much on their willingness to stand up to Quinlin's hard cases."

"Max Ward might do it," Ira said.

"He might," Doc agreed. "He's the biggest rancher along the North Rim, although hardly powerful enough to stand up to the Sun alone."

"We won't need Ward," Gil said quietly. "We'll have enough witnesses right here in Larkspur." He was looking at Doc now. "You, for one, and Peggy Somers said she'd testify against the men who killed her father." He glanced across the table at Ira. "You were there when Les Quinlin and Tim Jackson braced me on the street. I'll need your testimony, too."

"Mine!" Ira rocked back in his chair as if someone had dumped a hatful of snakes in the middle of the table. "Hell, Ryan, I'll support you any way I can, but if I testify against the Sun, my business'll be ashes 'fore Art Quinlin ever sees the inside of a jail cell."

"Damnit," Doc said in exasperation. "Are we always going to be afraid to stand up to that man?"

"Easy, gents," Henry said in alarm. He held the fingers of his left hand up off the table as if to stop a rolling ball. "I'm sure we can find a way around . . ."

"No, there's no other way," Gil interrupted. He was looking at Doc, while his anger toward the others grew. "Bannerman's out. What about you? Will you take the stand against Quinlin and his men?"

"Absolutely."

"Look, I ain't no coward . . ." Ira began, but Gil cut him off with a sharp gesture.

"I need men I can count on. If anyone else here isn't willing to stand up to Quinlin, to fight him if it comes to that, then they need to leave right now."

"By God, ain't no man gonna talk to me that way," Ira blustered, but when he saw the fury in Gil's eyes he suddenly backed down. His hands were shaking with rage as he pushed to his feet. "You're makin' a mistake putting your trust in this man, Doc. He'll be worse than Quinlin before it's over."

"I don't think so," said a voice from the kitchen, and they turned as one to see Hannah Brickman standing behind the counter. She had a washcloth in one hand, the other cocked in a fist on her hip. She nodded toward the door. "Go on, Ira. Coffee and pie's on the house tonight."

The saloonkeeper's mouth gaped, but no words came. Gil turned to Henry Fisher and Roger Greene and repeated his question. "Will you fight?" A heavy silence followed, and Gil nodded curtly. "Then go home, and stay out of the way."

Fisher and Greene exchanged hesitant glances; it was Hannah who made the decision for them. "Go on, boys," she said gently. "No one's judging you."

Shoving to their feet in a mixture of anger and humiliation, the three members of Larkspur's provisional citizens' committee left the café. When they were gone, Hannah turned to Gil.

"I'll fight, I've already told you that. I've got a shotgun in the kitchen and a pistol in my bedside table, and I know how to use them. I'll testify, too, although I wasn't there when Fred was killed or when Doc got his hand busted. But I'll tell you this, too, Mr. Ryan. You can't trample folks' pride like you did to those three men tonight. We've had enough of that dirty wash from Art Quinlin and his bunch. Folks won't put up with it from a stranger."

"I have to know who'll stand with me and who won't," Gil replied stubbornly, yet he couldn't deny that the tone of Hannah's words burned as much as her accusation. It wasn't lost on him that she'd called him *Mister*, too, instead of Gil.

"No one'll stand with you if you push them away," she said. "You tell him, Doc, else this war'll be lost before it's begun." Then she turned her back to them and pushed roughly through the door to the kitchen. A few seconds later, the sounds of slamming kettles and pans rang from the other room.

"She right, you know," Doc said gently.

"I have to know who I can count on," Gil repeated, but there wasn't nearly as much heat in his reply as there had been earlier.

Doc was silent a moment, then he glanced at Gil's shoulder. "How'd you get shot?"

"That has nothing to do with it."

"Henry had a legitimate concern when he asked about your past. I suppose I was in such a hurry to talk you into staying, maybe finishing what was already started . . ."

Doc stopped and looked away, and Gil took that opportunity to slowly roll his left shoulder, testing its stiffness in the warm air of the café. In his mind he saw men coming toward them through a curtain of falling snow, saw a blossoming muzzle flash and heard his brother's ragged cry. Then his jaw tightened and he shoved his chair back and stood. Doc's head jerked around in surprise.

"Where's Keegan?" Gil asked.

"Hal? He was in the saloon about thirty minutes ago. Why?"

"And the Quinlins?"

"They say Joel's at the ranch, keeping his head down. I don't know where Art is."

Gil put his hat on and started for the door.

"Where are you going?" Doc called after him.

Gil paused and half-turned, his expression grim. "I'm going to go get my badge."

Doc's eyes widened. "There's only one that I know of, and that's pinned to Keegan's shirt."

"Then that's the one I'll take," Gil said, heading for the door.

CHAPTER ELEVEN

Odell Love's shoulders were slumped with something more than fatigue as he followed Clint Miller down off the Saddleback that night. It had been a damned sad day, he reflected, and testimony to just how far he'd allowed himself to sink since the old man had turned lobo.

At one time Odell considered himself an honorable man. A coward, perhaps, and maybe not all that sharp when it came to ranching, but not a killer or bushwhacker. In the last twenty-four hours he'd become both. Well, a bushwhacker for sure. He wasn't as certain about being an assassin, although with the way things had played out that afternoon, he figured the odds were in favor of it.

The prospect of having taken a human life weighed on him like sacks of horseshoes draped bandoleer-fashion across his chest. He didn't often think of his mother, way back East and likely long dead, but if she were still alive, he hoped she never heard of what had occurred that day along the Ensillado's North Rim, and of his part in it.

No one was speaking as they wound single file through the pines. Brownie Hillman, Carl Roth, and Goose Carter rode behind him, every one of them jaded down to nubs. All except for Miller, who sat his tall gray horse up front like a general leading his troops home after a victorious battle. The problem, Odell reflected, was that there hadn't been much of a fight. Just a couple of scared Norwegians and, later, a florid-faced German named Seifert, with a large belly and worn-out clothing, working at a crop of collards just starting to push their heads above the gravelly surface of his garden.

Seifert had given them the most trouble. He'd been a crack shot, and not shy at all about using his Winchester to its best advantage. As at the Martinsen place, Odell had tried not to get involved, but when the lead started flying close enough for him to hear the buzz, he'd fired back. It was with his second shot that the heavy-set German dropped to one knee, then stumbled awkwardly inside his cabin with one hand clamped tightly over his ample stomach.

Afterward, Roth and Hillman had both claimed the killing shot. Odell had kept his mouth shut and hoped that one of them was right. Seifert had three other bullets in his body by the time the fighting was finished, but Odell was afraid it was the stomach wound that finally brought the big man down.

Three dead on their first day, and no telling what kind of carnage the old man and his crew had inflicted on their swing through the pines along the North Rim. There were families up there, Odell knew, women and children, and his blood chilled at the possibilities.

The dun mare stumbled in the darkness under the trees, jerking Odell out of his morbid ruminations. He looked around as if awakening from a deep slumber. The sky was frosted with starlight, and the glow of the soon-to-rise moon was a luminous dome on the eastern horizon. Although his view was largely hemmed in by towering pines, he'd occasionally catch a glimpse of the Basin to the south. Once he thought he saw the distant lights of Larkspur, but only for a second. Then they plunged back into the trees and the view was snuffed like a candle next to a slamming door.

It was several hours after sunset when they spotted the flames of a good-sized campfire through the trees and veered in that direction. Thirty minutes later they came to a bivouac in a small meadow. Odell thought they might have arrived undetected, but they'd barely entered the firelight's fringe when several men appeared out of the surrounding forest with cocked rifles.

"You looking to get shot, Miller?" Art Quinlin inquired from where he lay comfortably before the fire, propped against his saddle.

"It'd been these boys of yours who would've swallowed lead," Miller replied coolly, stepping down and tossing his reins to one of Quinlin's newer men. The guy told Miller to go to hell, but Art laughed and said, "Take care of his horse, Louie."

While Louie grudgingly led Miller's gray into the trees, Odell guided his own mount away from the fire, grateful to be shed of both Miller and the old man. If he thought he could have kept on riding and gotten away, he'd have done so, but he knew he was in too deep now. They all were.

Odell picketed his horse on good grass close to a stream tumbling down off the Saddleback, then returned to the fire with his cup, plate, and a spoon. Quinlin had ordered a packhorse to be brought along when the outfit left the Sun two days before, carrying a plentiful supply of grub, cooking utensils, and extra ammunition. The spicy odor of sausage and refried beans wafted invitingly through the camp. Odell knew the meat hadn't come from the Sun. No true cattleman would raise hogs or sheep, not even for the table, was the old man's opinion, which meant the pork must have been plundered from one of the homesteads they'd raided. From the looks of things, Quinlin's boys had done quite a bit of plundering that day. Odell recognized at least one new hat among the old man's crew, and Louie Saunders was wearing a better pair of boots than he'd left the ranch with.

Bending over the kettle, Odell helped himself to a plateful of meat and beans. Hard crackers lay scattered across a piece of canvas close to the flames, and he took a couple of those as well, plus coffee from a graniteware pot hanging from a tripod. Then he took his food and moved back out of the light. A few minutes later, Doug Hayes came over to sit with him.

"Miller said you boys had a good day," Hayes began tentatively.

"It wasn't no damned hunting trip."

Hayes was quiet a moment, then he growled and shook his head. "The hell it wasn't."

Odell decided he couldn't argue the point, so he didn't try. Having had nothing to eat all day, nor the appetite to pilfer anything earlier from either the Martinsen or Seifert cabins, he wolfed his supper down in heaping spoonfuls. When he was finished, he set his plate aside and belched contentedly.

"There's more coffee," Hayes said without much enthusiasm.

"I think I'll stay out of the old man's sight for a spell."

"That's smart thinking. Wish I'd done the same before throwing in with this ragtag outfit."

Doug Hayes had wandered into the Sun late last winter, a gaunt man with unshorn hair and a scraggly beard. He'd been out of work, out of money, and damn near out of the seat of his worn trousers when he showed up, having lost his entire poke bucking the tiger in an Albuquerque saloon several months earlier. He'd been riding the grub line ever since, and had been damned glad to accept Quinlin's offer of a job. He hadn't balked when the old man told him they'd be dealing harshly with horse thieves and cattle rustlers come spring, either. Of course, that was before he discovered the lax standards Quinlin was using in his determination of who in the Basin was a thief and who wasn't. Although Odell didn't consider anyone on the Sun to be a friend anymore, he kind of figured Doug Hayes and Louie Saunders came closest to sharing his feelings toward Art Quinlin's ambitions.

"What happened out there?" Odell asked after a couple of minutes, and that was when Hayes told him about the men they'd killed that day, the cabins and barns they'd burned, the crops they'd trampled beneath their horses' hooves.

"A damned sorry business is what it was," he declared after relating the day's activities in hushed tones. "I'm just thankful there weren't no kids nor women hurt."

"What about the Ward place?"

Hayes chuckled caustically. "We hit the W right after first light, but that was a nut the old man couldn't crack. We hammered at it until midmorning or so, then went looking for something easier to shoot at."

"Farmers?"

"Poorly armed ones, too."

"They're the easiest kind," Odell agreed dolefully. "Goddamn it, we've got ourselves corked up in a pickle barrel, Doug, and no way to kick free. Not unless we want to get crosswise of the old man, and I ain't keen on that. As prickly as he's been of late, we'd likely get our asses shot off if we tried."

Hayes was quiet for a long time. Then, after a furtive glance into the darkness behind them, he said, "There could be a few who's thinking about doing a little kicking."

"What do you mean?"

"I ain't saying certain-sure, but I wouldn't be surprised if our numbers didn't thin out pretty soon."

"Who?"

"I said I ain't saying, and I ain't. I just wouldn't be too surprised, is all."

"Are you one of them?"

After a pause, Hayes shook his head. "I reckon not. I don't condone what we're doing up here, but the old man gave those settlers their leave last fall. It ain't his fault they didn't take it."

"It's their homes, Doug."

"They likely see it that way, and I wouldn't argue with them, but I'm sure as hell not going to brace Quinlin over it, either. If he says they're rustling Sun cows, that's gonna have to be good enough."

Odell wanted to reply, but Hayes pushed to his feet before he could get his thoughts corralled.

"You're right about one thing," Hayes said in lowered tones. "The old man feels like his back is to the wall, and he won't be pushed no more. It ain't no secret he doesn't like you, either. You get crossways to him, Odell, and he'll shoot you dead."

Hayes's words stung. It was bad enough knowing how the old man felt toward him, but having someone else voice it so openly made it even worse.

"I don't know what he's got against me," he replied.

"Hell, I do. I figured it out the morning after Les was killed, seeing the way the old man watched you on the ride into town. You've been around just about from the beginning, Odell. You saw the old man the way he used to be, and you've told some of the rest of us about it, too. Now you're seeing him the way he is, and it's eating at him something fierce. He wouldn't tell you that, and the others'd probably call me crazy if I tried to explain it, but that's what it is. I'd bet my saddle on it. You remind the old man of what he used to be before his wife died and all his plans for the Basin got shot to shit, and now you won't go away. All the other old hands did, but you stayed, and I figure that bothers him, too."

"Jesus," Odell breathed. "I'm damned if I stay and damned if I go."

"You might be damned if you stay, but you'll be dead if you try to go. It's too late for you, Odell. Some of the others might sneak away and the old man'll probably let 'em, but if you try it, he'll chase you to the far side of hell to bring you back." He shook his head with what seemed like genuine sadness, then abruptly thrust his hand forward. Odell took it uncertainly. Hayes's grip was firm as he pumped Odell's arm. "I wish you luck," he said quietly, then chuckled without humor. "Hell, I wish us all luck. We'll likely need it before tomorrow's over with."

Gil paused on the boardwalk in front of the Paris Café to breathe deeply of the crisp night air. His lungs twitched threateningly, but the codeine he'd taken at Doc's office earlier was still working and kept the cough at bay. He stared at the sky, cloudless, carpeted with stars, then turned toward Bannerman's. The heels of his boots thumped hollowly atop the wooden planks of the walk, an ominous pulse flowing along the deserted street.

Light spilled out over the tops of the saloon's batwings, carrying with it the lazy murmur of conversation and the easy laughter of men relaxing after a long day at work. Halting just shy of the doors, Gil slid the Hopkins and Allen from its crossdraw holster to make sure it was fully loaded, and that the cylinder spun freely. Then he returned the revolver to his holster and pushed through the swinging doors.

The saloon was smaller than it looked from the street. Shabbier, too. A narrow room with wallpaper curling at the seams, one corner of its pressed-tin ceiling stained with rust from an old leak. Gil counted half a dozen tables down the right-hand side of the room, but there were no gaming devices, no faro layout or chuck-a-luck cage, not even a pool table.

The bar ran halfway down the left side of the room. A stubby man in an age-grayed apron stood behind it. A trio of customers leaned against the near side, and a couple of others—laborers from their dress—were playing cards at the table nearest the front door. Ira Bannerman, Roger Greene, and Henry Fisher were sulking at one of the middle tables with an uncorked bottle of whiskey sitting between them. Uncarpeted stairs rising along the south wall reminded Gil that he still didn't have a room for the night. Not unless there was a bunk in the jail he could use.

After a moment's scrutiny, the bartender moved away from the men he'd been talking with and ambled in Gil's direction. "What'll you have, friend?"

"Whiskey'll do." Gil met the bartender at the end of the rail. "Old Overholt, if you have it."

"Sure, we've got a couple of bottles of that."

While the bartender went to fetch his drink, Gil propped himself against the counter and eyed the trio of men halfway down its length. Hal Keegan wasn't hard to pick out. He was a stocky man with thick black hair and a full mustache, his face puffy from too much booze. He wore a revolver on his right side, although with his shirttails pulled loose of his baggy trousers and nearly covering the grips, Gil couldn't identify the make. A badge was pinned high on his chest above his shirt pocket, a star with five balled points, one of them bent slightly inward. They exchanged a long look, and when Gil didn't avert his eyes, the sheriff pushed away from the bar and sauntered toward him.

"Passing through, stranger?"

"I was."

Keegan came to a halt about ten feet away. The saloon had grown unnaturally quiet, as if the small crowd could already sense the tension between the two men. Bannerman and his friends were watching, their eyes as bright as rats' in the lamplight. One of the saloon's batwings eased open behind Gil, but he didn't look around. He could see Doc's reflection in the back bar's side mirror, slipping in and to one side with his medical bag in hand. Keegan's brows crinkled when he spotted it.

"Somebody sick, Doc?" the lawman asked.

"I came in for a drink."

"I've never known you to drink here. Figured you did your carousin' in private." He chuckled loudly, but quit when no one else joined him. His gaze returned to Gil and his frown deepened. "What's your name, friend?"

"Gil Ryan."

Keegan stared dubiously for a moment, then swallowed audibly. "Then I reckon you won't be needing that drink, will you? Nick," he said to the bartender, "put that cork back in the bottle. Me'n Ryan's gonna take a little walk over to the jail."

"Go ahead and bring the bottle, Nick," Gil said. "The sheriff and I have some business to discuss."

Keegan's expression abruptly changed. "No, by God, you put that bottle away, Nick, or I'll use it for target practice."

"Bring the bottle, Nick, then step clear," Gil said mildly.

Keegan's face fairly glowed. "Mr., just who the hell do you think you are?"

"I've already told you my name." Gil slid his fingers lightly over the Hopkins and Allen's grips. "I hear your boss is looking for me."

Doubt returned to Keegan's eyes. He glanced uncertainly toward Doc. Licking tentatively at his lower lip, he said, "Enough of this nonsense. You're under arrest, Ryan. Now pull your pistol and let it drop."

"I reckon not."

"You . . ." He looked at the Hopkins and Allen. "I am duty-bound to take you in."

"No, you aren't," Gil replied calmly. "You've been removed from office, and I'll need your badge." He moved closer, and Keegan took a step back.

"Mr., ain't nobody taking my badge without Art Quinlin's say-so."

"I'm taking it," Gil said. "Unpin it and put it on the bar."

176

Keegan put his hand on his revolver, but Gil could tell he was afraid to draw it. He was too unsure of himself and of whom he was facing, and was no doubt remembering how quickly Tim and Les had died. His hesitation was the advantage Gil had been waiting for. Stepping swiftly forward, he whipped the Hopkins and Allen from its holster and slammed it down hard on top of the sheriff's right shoulder. Keegan's face paled and he grunted and half fell against the bar, grabbing its edge with his good hand at the last minute to prevent himself from collapsing.

"Son of a bitch," he hissed, his eyes rolling in their sockets.

Gil slid a nickeled Frontier Model Colt from the lawman's gun belt, then stepped back out of easy reach. After returning the Hopkins and Allen to its holster, he flipped the Colt's loading gate open and ejected the live rounds one by one onto the floor. Then he set the empty gun on the bar and slid it toward Nick.

"Hang onto that," he told the barman. "Hal might want it back when he leaves the Basin." He smiled thinly. "In a day or so. He's going to be spending some time at the jail until I can round up his boss and a couple of others."

Nick glanced uncertainly toward the table where Ira Bannerman sat with his mouth slightly agape. Then he scooped the Colt off the bar and placed it on a shelf under the counter. "Yes, sir, Mr. Ryan. It'll be right here when you get back, along with that shot of Old Overholt if you still want it. My treat."

Gil didn't respond to the bartender's offer. He grabbed Keegan by the arm—his good one—and pulled him away from the bar. Keegan was still woozy and Gil had to half drag him out of Bannerman's and across the street to the stone jail. The front door was closed but unlocked. Gil pushed it open and hauled his prisoner inside.

The office was embarrassingly bare in the thin light shining in from across the street. Just a desk and swivel chair and a squatty stove layered with dust that sat in the corner like a fat sentry. A second door behind the desk stood open to reveal the shadowy image of bars. Gil propped Keegan against the wall while he dug a match from his vest pocket and touched it to the wick of a small globe lamp bracketed to the wall. He grabbed a set of keys off the desk, then propelled his prisoner through the door to the cells. There were two of them, both iron-strapped and cramped, still a little chilly from winter. He deposited Keegan in the cell farthest from the door and let him flop down on the iron bunk. Doc had followed them across the street, and when Gil felt confident Keegan wasn't going to cause any trouble, he stepped aside to allow the physician to enter.

Watching as Doc bent over his charge, Gil felt an odd flaring of excitement. He'd been feeling morose all afternoon, ever since learning of Fred Somers's death and Doc's busted hand, but that had changed in the Paris Café. Changed because of Doc's frustration with the other members of the citizens' committee and their reluctance to challenge Art Quinlin's hold over the Basin.

The same way Gavin had been unable to summon support from the miners in the Sawtooths of Idaho.

The thought occurred to him without its usual bitterness, even when he recalled his brother's helplessness against the hired thugs brought in by the big mines. Brought in to take by force what they couldn't steal through more conventional means. Now Gavin was dead and a killer had gone free, and Gil had been laid up for weeks in a dirt-roofed shack waiting for his shoulder to mend, impatient to ride out after the man who'd killed his only remaining family.

Coming south, Gil hadn't expected to become involved in someone else's war. His only goal had been to find Gavin's killer, his only clue an overheard conversation in a crowded saloon.

"Headin' south toward desert country is what they say. Gonna kill some rustlers."

"Do the same to them that he done to Gavin Ryan . . ."

Gil stirred and his gaze hardened. "You about finished, Doc?"

Shaw nodded and closed his bag. He left the cell and Gil shut the door and turned the lock. Doc handed him the badge he'd taken off Keegan's shirt, and the two men returned to the front room.

"He going to be okay?" Gil tossed the keys on top of the desk, then pinned the badge to his own shirt.

"He should be. That shoulder is going to be sore for a couple of weeks, but there's no serious damage." He set his medical bag on the chair, then drew a cigar from an inside pocket of his jacket. Peeling the band off carefully, he said, "That was a pretty neat trick you pulled back there. I've heard it called buffaloing in some places."

"I've heard it called that, too."

"There was a lawman down in Tombstone who was pretty good at that. Generally used it to tame drunkards." He looked up speculatively. "Keegan wasn't drunk."

"Keegan wasn't expecting it, either. That makes a difference."

"Still, it's a slick move. I've never known a man who didn't have some experience behind a badge to pull it off so smoothly." He lit the cigar from the top of the lamp's chimney, his face ruddy in the glow, then stepped back to examine its cherry tip. "You still haven't told me what you did in Idaho."

After a pause, Gil said, "Come with me. I want to show you something."

They walked outside and Gil jutted his chin toward the North Rim, a solid black mass against the star-lit sky. About halfway up its side was a spot of color, like a daisy bobbing gently in a breeze. A second light gleamed several miles east of the first, although dimmer, as if dying or filtered by trees.

"I noticed them on the way over," Gil said quietly.

Doc eyed the twin orbs for a long moment, then sighed. "So it's begun."

"Quinlin?"

"That would be my guess. I don't know exactly where the different homesteads are up there, but those sure aren't camp-fires."

"No, they're too big for that."

Doc's voice turned soft with reflection. "I remember riding with Crook in Arizona, chasing Apaches. One night just before an engagement, we were hiding in the dark, watching their fires in the distance. This feels kind of like that, knowing the enemy is close by and that hell is about to break loose."

"Hannah Brickman said Quinlin was keeping his boy close to home. What about Art? Would he stay behind, too, let others do his blood work?"

"I doubt it. Art would want to be there to gloat as he ran families from their homes, or burned down their barns and cabins."

"Do me a favor, Doc. Find someone to keep an eye on Kee-gan until I get back, will you?"

"Where are you going?"

"I'm going after Joel Quinlin. If he's at the Sun by himself, this might be my best chance to get a halter on him, bring him in before the others show up."

Doc smiled. "All right. There are a couple of men I think might help us, and if they won't, I will."

"Do what you have to." He handed the set of keys to Doc, then swung off the veranda and started across the street.

"Gil."

He stopped and turned. "Yeah?"

"Just . . . thanks."

Gil nodded and continued on his way. He knew Doc thought he was doing this for Larkspur, but he wasn't. Not all the way, at least. Maybe someday he'd share the full story with the Shaws, and Hannah Brickman, too, if she was interested, but not tonight. He had a long ride ahead of him, and glancing once more at the fires burning along the North Rim, he thought time was probably running out.

CHAPTER TWELVE

It was nearly midnight before Doc finished the assignments he'd accepted from the Basin's new lawman. For deputies he chose Arnie Hale, Russ Kendrick, Vern Greer, and Warren Bishop, four of the town's earliest residents.

Russ owned the Basin's only leather shop, and Warren was a blacksmith. Although both men had contracts with Paul Offerman to handle any repairs or horseshoeing that might be needed by the Ensillado Stagecoach Company, neither worked directly for the livery's owner. Vern was employed by Larkspur Feed and Supply, and even though that was a Quinlin outfit at its core, there was no affection between Vern and the Sun faction, nor between him and Lloyd Thompson, who ran the business for Art. Arnie Hale was a woodhawk, supplying rough lumber and firewood for those in Larkspur who didn't, or couldn't, bring in their own.

In Doc's opinion, Arnie Hale was probably the most competent of the lot. He would also be the most reliable if Art showed up before Gil could return with Joel. Arnie and Russ Kendrick were at the jail now; Doc would send Warren Bishop and Vern Greer over at dawn to relieve them.

Standing on the veranda outside the jail, Doc breathed deeply of the cool night air. The yellow glow of the fires on the Rim had died away, but he thought he could still make out their locations, as if it were the *memories* of the fires that continued to smolder in his mind.

Heels thumped the wooden planks, and Doc glanced over his shoulder. Arnie Hale approached. He was a big man, solid and strong, his hands scarred from all the nips and bites of the heavy saws he used to rip firewood into manageable, stove-length pieces. He was carrying a six-shooter at his waist and had a double-barreled shotgun in his right hand, its muzzles sloping toward the ground.

"Doc," Arnie greeted kindly. "Ain't you up kind'a late?"

"I'd be too wound up to sleep even if I was home."

Arnie scanned the distant Rim, then turned south toward the Sun. "You reckon he can do it?"

"I think so."

"I hope so. Quinlin's gonna spill a lotta blood in this town if he don't pull it off just right."

"He'll do it," Doc insisted.

"Yeah, well, I reckon it's gonna be a long night thinkin' about it."

"The night's already half over," Doc reminded him. He pulled a pocket watch from his vest and studied the dial as best he could in the light from the jail's open front door. "It's past midnight now." He closed the lid and returned the watch to his pocket. "Do you and Russ need anything?"

"Naw, we'll be fine. You ought to go get yourself some shut-eye, though. Morning's gonna be here before you know it." He started to add something else, then closed his mouth and frowned.

Doc looked toward the street but didn't see anything out of the norm. "What is it?"

"A wagon, I believe." He moved past Doc, down off the veranda and partway into the street. "Hear it?"

He did then, the rattle of the running gear and the shuffling clop of trotting hooves. Picking up his medical bag, he stepped down beside Arnie.

"Coming in from the north," Arnie murmured, his head cocked toward the approaching team.

"Stay here," Doc ordered tersely. "Get inside and lock the door."

"Lock it?"

Doubt marked the big man's face, and Doc wondered if he, if any of them, truly understood what they were risking in standing up to the Sun. He felt a moment's affinity for the burly woodhawk, and hoped he hadn't influenced the man into something that might get him killed.

"Go on," Doc said. "It could be some of Quinlin's men."

"What about you?"

"I'll be fine," he assured him, then walked away with quick strides.

Spotting the wagon as it turned off the North Rim Road toward his own home, Doc quickened his pace. He got there just as the driver was jumping down from the rig. A light had been left on in the house, and a second light appeared at the parlor window a few seconds later. Then the door opened and Alma stepped partway outside.

"Who's there?" she demanded, the lamp held high in one hand, a snub-nosed pocket revolver half hidden by her skirt in the other.

"It's Reece Ward, Mrs. Shaw," the driver hailed. "My pa's been shot."

"Oh, dear," Alma exclaimed. She set the revolver on the lamp table next to the front door, then hurried outside with her light. She jerked to a stop when she saw a figure moving toward them through the trees.

"It's me, Alma," Doc called.

"Thank heavens," she breathed, then continued swiftly toward the wagon.

There were two people in back. Doc recognized Big Max

Ward laid out on a mattress and covered to his chest with several heavy wool blankets. His wife, Sally, sat with her legs tucked under her, Max's head cradled on her lap.

"Please, Dr. Shaw," she said. "He's been shot in the leg."

Doc leaned over the side of the small spring wagon as Sally pulled the blankets away. Alma came in close with the lamp. Doc's eyes narrowed in the poor light. Max was unconscious, his face far too pale for an outdoorsman. A blood-soaked bandage was wrapped tightly around his thigh, bright red and sopping wet.

"It won't stop bleeding," Sally explained. "I've slowed it down, but I can't get it to quit. I was worried bringing him in would aggravate the wound, but I was more afraid of how long it might take Reece to bring you back, especially if you had a bad case here and couldn't leave."

"That's all right, Sally." Doc was holding his palm to Max's forehead, feeling the fever within. "We need to move him inside where I'll have more room and better light. Reece, we're going to slide your pa out the back of the rig. I want you on one side and I'll take the other. We'll hold hands and make a seat your father can ride in. Sally, I want you to follow behind us and help balance him. Alma, show us where to go."

"I'll be right here," she promised, raising the lamp high.

Clasped hands made a poor sling, but it was quick, and it got Max inside without wasted effort or reinjuring the wound, and that was all Doc wanted. It worried him that the rancher had lost so much blood; it frightened him even more when, as they were moving sideways through the door, Reece mentioned that his pa had been shot that morning.

"It was Quinlin's bunch," the younger man added grimly. "They kept us pinned down half the morning."

"So he's been bleeding . . ." Doc glanced at Sally ". . . how long would you say?"

"Since right after breakfast. All day and half the night, I guess."

Doc nodded but didn't speak again until they had Ward inside the examining room and laid out on the table. "Help me cut this bandage off his leg," Doc said to Sally as Alma lowered the overhead light with its polished tin reflectors.

"I'm going back, Ma," Reece said, and Sally whirled with a panicky look on her face.

"Reece, you'll do no such thing."

"I have to. If they come back, Hector and Two-Socks'll need me."

"Hector and Two-Socks will be fine. They're grown men and have been on their own for years." She looked pleadingly at Doc. "Tell him, Dr. Shaw. Tell him there's nothing he can accomplish by going back tonight."

"Your mother's right, Reece. Whatever's happened up there is long past."

"What if they're hurt, or pinned down and waiting for help?"

"What if they aren't?" Doc asked pragmatically.

"Reece, listen to him. Quinlin's men are long gone, and Hector and Two-Socks are probably fine. Besides, Quinlin's argument isn't with our hired men, it's with your father and . . . and you. Don't go, not alone. You don't know what you'd be riding into."

"Reece," Doc said quietly. "I have to look after your father, but if you want to help fight the Quinlins, then stay here in Larkspur. Hal Keegan is in jail, and we've got a man riding down to the Sun tonight to arrest Joel."

Confusion crossed the younger man's face. "Somebody's gone to arrest Joel?"

Doc nodded as he accepted a pair of heavy shears from his wife. He kept his eyes on the task at hand as he began cutting the cloth away from the wound, but continued to address the younger man. "Art Quinlin is going to be coming into town as soon as he finds out what's happened. A lot of people around here probably won't stand against him, but some of us will." He looked up. "We could use your help right here in Larkspur, son."

Reece stared uncertainly at his mother.

"Please," she said softly. "You wouldn't be able to accomplish much alone, but with others you'd at least stand a chance."

Doc knew the younger man was wavering, but he could no longer be a part of the debate. Max Ward's wound had been revealed, the raw flesh laid open before him. It had been bad from the start, then made worse by someone digging for the bullet, followed by the long trip down off the Rim by wagon.

"Alma," he said without looking up. "Let's get ready for surgery. The bullet's too close to the femoral artery to risk probing for it with forceps. I'm going to have to open the wound further so that I can see what I'm doing." He met Sally's eyes across the table. "I could use your help, but not if you're in too much pain. Do you need some laudanum?"

"No, I'll be all right. Maybe when this is over and I'm sure Max is safe."

Doc nodded and glanced at Reece. "Unharness your team and put the horses in our pasture, then go over to the jail and tell Arnie Hale I sent you. Tell him we're going to need all the help we can get before this is over, then do what he says." He paused a moment, studying the younger man's face. "Reece? Do you hear me?"

The younger man nodded. "Yeah, I hear you." He glanced one last time at his father, then turned and left the room.

It was an easy ride south from Larkspur. The night was cool without being uncomfortable, and there was enough light from the moon and stars to show him the road. Gil alternated Rusty between a walk and a slow jog, a pace the sorrel didn't have any trouble maintaining.

It was shortly after dawn when he arrived at the junction of the Ensillado and Little Ensillado rivers. Jacob Watland's stage station sat on the east side of the larger river, across from the mouth of the smaller stream. Gil slowed as he approached the collection of low log structures, but saw only harness stock in the company corral. His belly rumbled at some faint aroma, and on a whim he reined toward the roadhouse.

A tall blond man in bibbed overalls and a slouch hat appeared at the barn's side entrance as Gil rode up. He carried a rifle in his right hand with an air of casualness Gil didn't believe for a second. Reining up in the middle of the yard and careful to keep both hands in plain sight, he called, "Howdy, friend."

The tall man nodded cautiously, offering nothing.

"I was passing through and thought I smelled breakfast cooking."

"Is awful good nose you got there," Watland replied in a voice heavily accented by his native Norwegian.

"I've been eating skimpy in recent weeks. It's sharpened my sniffer where food is concerned." After a pause, he added, "I'd be willing to pay, if you're willing to sell."

"*Ja*, maybe, if you can pay."

"I can pay."

Watland nodded and pulled the side door closed behind him. "Come into the house. I will have Kari fix an extra plate."

Gil rode over to a hitching rail and stepped down. He loosened Rusty's cinch but kept the bit in the sorrel's mouth in case he had to leave in a hurry. Jacob waited for him at the door, still nonchalantly holding the long gun in his right hand.

Gil removed his hat as he stepped inside. He'd been half worried he might be walking into a trap, but relaxed when he spotted Watland's plump wife standing at the stove, yellow hair frizzled from the heat, half moons of perspiration darkening her blouse under each arm. The sound of frying meat seemed loud in the low-ceilinged room, and the smells set Gil's mouth to watering.

Jacob leaned his rifle against the front wall and Gil felt better after that, too, although he didn't completely lower his guard even then. He'd learned his lesson in Idaho, and didn't intend to repeat the mistake here.

Kari looked up questioningly, then spoke to her husband in a language Gil couldn't follow. Jacob replied in kind, and Kari nodded and smiled.

"*Sitte ned,*" she said pleasantly, motioning toward a bench flanking one side of a long harvest table.

"Sit down," Jacob translated, hanging his hat on a wall peg. "Some coffee you would like?"

"I could drink about a gallon of it," Gil admitted, drawing the hint of a smile from Jacob. He spoke quietly to his wife and she brought a couple of cups and a pot over from the stove.

"You are going south?" Jacob inquired, taking a seat opposite Gil.

"I'm looking for the Sun," Gil replied, and Watland's expression immediately drew taut. He started to rise, then settled back. His eyes darted to the rifle leaning against the wall behind Gil. At the stove, Kari watched their interaction with concern. She could sense her husband's sudden wariness, but didn't understand the language well enough to tell what was behind it.

"Doc sent me," Gil added quietly.

"Dr. Shaw?"

Gil nodded, then moved the lapel of his vest aside to reveal Keegan's badge, pinned to his shirt. "I'm working for the citizens' committee."

Jacob glanced briefly at the badge, then raised his eyes to Gil's. "And Keegan?"

"Locked up."

"In his own jail?" There was that hint of a smile again, like a distant flash barely caught from the corner of a man's eyes.

"No, in the town's jail. The citizens' committee intends to take Larkspur back from Quinlin. The Basin, too."

"And you they hired to do this thing? For money?"

"No."

Doc had spoken briefly about a salary, but Gil refused to consider it.

I'm not a gunman, he'd told the physician in sharper tones than the inquiry warranted, then forced his voice down a notch. *I've got my own reasons, Doc. Just . . . don't ask me what they are.*

He said basically the same thing to Jacob Watland, and the Norwegian nodded. "You are the one they look for, *nei?* The one who killed young Lester and the man named Jackson."

"It was self-defense," Gil said deliberately, watching the other man's face.

"Sure, is what the Doctor say, too, but the others, Arthur and his men, they say differently, no?"

"I say differently," Gil replied firmly.

"So you go to the Sun to tell them this?"

"I'm going to the Sun to arrest Joel Quinlin, if he's there."

"*Ja,* Joel is there is what I have heard. He and a Mexican who looks after the stock."

"A gunman?"

"Porfirio? *Nei.* He is old and his hands are bent." He made a motion that Gil took to mean the Mexican's fingers were crippled, perhaps with arthritis. "He does not much care for the man Arthur has become, but he has nowhere to go. Like the skinny one, I think."

"The skinny one?"

"Odell Love."

Gil remembered the name. He remembered the man, too,

the thin face and pointed nose, eyes as black as a ferret's. Or a weasel's.

"Is Odell at the Sun?"

Jacob shrugged. "Maybe. Who can say? The last I heard, from the men going south to guard the canyon, there is only Joel and Porfirio at the ranch."

Gil felt strangely relieved with this new information. No one in Larkspur had mentioned a Mexican puncher with crippled hands, so it was good to know Joel wouldn't be alone. It was also good to know that this Porfirio apparently didn't think much of Art Quinlin's ways, although that wasn't something Gil was going to count on.

The conversation shifted after that, and avoided any further mention of the Sun or the troubles plaguing the Basin. Gil was running out of things to ask about when Kari finally set out a hearty breakfast of eggs, flapjacks, and fried potatoes. Gil filled his plate and cleaned it off, then filled it a second time—six eggs altogether, a dozen 'jacks, and probably half a pound of potatoes loaded with onions and pieces of bacon. Kari, watching him swab out his plate the second time with a chunk of flapjack, looked at Jacob and giggled. The two held a brief discussion, then Jacob looked at Gil and smiled.

"She says for one so skinny, you eat like a bear. I told her what you said about smelling her cooking from the road, and coming in to ask for breakfast."

"Tell her it was good," Gil replied. "I could probably clean off a third plate, but I won't."

"Is probably a good thing that you don't. The coach from the south is soon to be here, and we would want a little for our guests."

Jacob grinned and Gil smiled and stood. He dug a fifty-cent piece from his vest pocket and dropped it on the table. While Kari cleared off the dishes, Jacob followed Gil outside.

"You know the way to the Sun?"

"West along the Little Ensillado is what Doc said."

"*Ja*. You can follow the road, or go south and follow the edge of the trees."

Gil glanced toward the deep pine forest several miles to the southwest.

"The Sun's buildings, they are nearly in the trees, and . . ." Jacob shrugged. "Is possible Arthur has a man watching the road, *nei*?"

"It's possible," Gil agreed, tightening the sorrel's cinch. "I'm obliged for your kindness, Mr. Watland."

"A little food for half a dollar is not so much kindness as business, I think."

Gil swung a leg over the cantle and settled into his seat. The sorrel tossed its head, eager to be off, but Jacob had moved close and was holding the nearside rein near the bit's lower shank.

"Listen, something maybe you should know before you ride into the Sun. Arthur, he is mean and will kill without conscience, but he *thinks*. The boys, and only Joel remains now, they were not always so quick to think, you know?"

"Like Les?"

"*Ja*, like Lester. A thought comes into their mind and immediately they have to act upon it. Arthur would give a matter some thinking, but not the boys. Not Joel."

Jacob let go of the rein and stepped back, and Gil touched the sorrel's ribs with his heels. A bridge spanned the Ensillado below where the smaller river joined it. Rusty's hooves thudded loudly on the planks, even above the wild rush of the water below, the spring melt in full swing. As he was leaving the main road to the south, the crack of a whip broke the cool stillness of the morning, and he reined in to watch the northbound stage as it rolled into view. It was a four-horse hitch, the teams' flanks muddy as they snorted and fought the bit. Worn out by the wet conditions of the road and tired of the pull, Gil thought. Rusty wasn't having a problem with the footing, but he wasn't hauling a stagecoach over the soft spring soil, either.

Gil watched curiously as the driver swung his team toward Watland's station. There was just the linesman up top, no messenger riding shotgun, telling him there likely wasn't anything of value onboard to attract road agents. He counted four passengers as the stage rolled past, a slim man with a pencil-thin mustache and a sharp business suit, an older couple who appeared to be traveling together, and a pudgy man in what looked like a shabby ensemble of green, black, and yellow plaid. None of them had the look of killers, although the man in the business suit stared back with an intensity that raised the hair across the back of Gil's neck. He waited until the coach came to a stop, then reined once more toward the Sun.

Deciding to follow Watland's subtle advice, Gil guided Rusty toward the distant pines, crowning a line of gently rolling hills that formed the southern rim of the Basin. It took nearly an hour to reach them, but there was a trail near the top, and the route proved smooth and fairly straight after that.

It was well past midmorning when Gil came in sight of the Quinlin ranch, sprawled across a low, flat knob just north of the pines. It was the biggest spread he'd seen in a long time. The main house sat at the knoll's highest point. Constructed of white-washed adobe, a red tiled roof, and heavy doors, it reminded him more of a fortress than a home. The rest of the buildings—bunkhouse, stables, tack shed, smokehouse, and a wagon barn with a trio of wooden tongues poking out from its shadowy interior—were fanned out below the main house like a skirt of wood and mud.

Leaning forward, Gil rested an arm across the tall horn of his saddle. He was impressed with what he could see of the place, and recalled something Doc had said the night before, about how the Sun had been one of the finest outfits in the territory until Art's wife died unexpectedly and his efforts to bring a railroad into the Basin had fallen through.

Maybe it all happened too close together, Doc had mused. *Losing his wife and his dreams just seemed to take something out of that old man. We all noticed it.*

It was possible, Gil supposed, but he wasn't as inclined as Doc to give Art Quinlin the benefit of the doubt. In his experience, a man was what he was, no matter what kind of veneer he used to hide himself from others. Sooner or later the gloss would wear off and a person's true character would seep though.

Gil was still admiring the ranch when a shot rang out from the buildings, and he swore and reined back into the trees. Dropping to the ground, he yanked the Winchester from its scabbard and returned to the edge of the forest. As he did, another shot echoed up from below. A cloud of powder smoke rose above the rear of the stables, followed by a lusty whoop. Seconds later, four more rounds were fired in swift succession, and Gil exhaled loudly and walked back to where he'd left his horse.

"Sounds like target practice," he told the sorrel, and Rusty flicked an ear as if in agreement.

Gil returned the rifle to its scabbard, then stepped into the saddle and rode back to the edge of the trees. He waited there until he heard another shot, then heeled Rusty into the open.

Tense though he was, Gil didn't rush, and by the time he came even with the stables, whoever was shooting was down to his last round. Easing his mount past the corner, he spied a tall young man with dark hair settling the front sight of a long-barreled Colt on a skillet hanging from the lower branch of a piñon tree about twenty yards away. An elderly Mexican wearing range clothes and a weary expression stood a few feet behind him. The Mexican's expression looked as dull as a slab of beef, but the kid with the Colt had a wide grin plastered across his face as he took aim. The older man saw Gil immediately. The kid didn't, and squeezed off his shot as Gil rode up. Dust exploded beneath the piñon, but the skillet didn't move.

"Did ya see that," the younger man shouted. "I damned near plugged it center."

"It didn't look that close to me," Gil remarked loudly, before the older man could reply. The kid whirled with a startled curse, the revolver thrust uselessly before him.

"It's empty, in case you weren't keeping track." Gil halted far enough back to keep an eye on both men. A box of .45s sat on the ground at the kid's feet. He started to reach for it, but Gil spoke sharp and the kid backed off.

"Who the hell are you?"

"Who are you?" Gil countered.

"I'm Joel Quinlin." He made a motion that included several of the nearest buildings. "This is my place."

"No, not yet," Gil replied dryly. He moved the lapel of his vest back to reveal the badge. "You're under arrest, Joel. Primarily for the murder of Fred Somers and the assault on Doc Shaw, but from what I've heard, we'll be adding more charges as time goes on."

"Huh? Like hell." He turned to the older man. "Porfirio, go get Pa."

"You stay where you are, Porfirio," Gil said, although the older Mexican hadn't made any effort to do Joel's bidding.

"Mr., you don't give the orders around here," Joel snarled.

"I think maybe he does," Porfirio said, edging away from the kid.

"If my gun wasn't empty . . ." Joel didn't finish the threat.

"That's the problem, isn't it? Yours is empty, and mine . . ." Gil slid the Hopkins and Allen from its holster and pointed it loosely in the kid's direction, the implication clear enough for even a thick-skulled thug like Joel Quinlin. "Porfirio, does this boy have a horse?"

"*Sí,* a nice little palomino."

"If I told you to put a saddle on it, would you do that without hunting up a gun or trying to cause trouble?"

A smile cleaved the older man's face. "*Sí,* with pleasure."

"You son of a bitch," Joel growled.

"*Sí,*" the older man agreed, laughing.

Porfirio took off after the palomino, and Gil let the Hopkins and Allen's muzzle bob a couple of times. "Put your gun down, Joel. You won't need it where you're going."

"This is a thirty-dollar gun, mister. I ain't gonna just lay it in the dirt."

"It'll clean up. Now go ahead and put it down, then drop your gun belt on top of it. I'm not going to tell you again."

Joel resisted long enough to call Gil a few choice names, then stooped and laid the Colt down gently on a clump of grass. He unbuckled his gun belt and placed that next to the revolver. Gil motioned toward the stables and they started in that direction. Gil stayed in the saddle, keeping Rusty close behind the younger man in case he decided to make a run for it. Porfirio met them at the stable's wide double doors, leading a flashy golden horse with a cream-colored mane and tail. Gil whistled appreciatively as the palomino was led into the light, and Porfirio turned the stallion sideways for a better view.

"A fine California stud," the Mexican said. "My papa used to ride one when he lived on a *rancho* outside of San Diego. Then he came east and the Apaches stole it."

"Likely your papa stole it first," Joel muttered.

Noticing the Mexican's dark scowl, Gil suddenly felt better about trusting him to stay out of the way. "I want you to take root here after we're gone," he told the elderly man. "Let Art

Quinlin find out on his own what happened to his boy."

Joel graced Gil with an disdainful look. "Porfirio rides for the Sun, not some Albuquerque lawdog. He'll go after Pa as soon as your back is turned."

"I don't think so," Porfirio replied, handing Joel the palomino's reins. "Not today." He rubbed his hips tenderly. "I am too sore today to go looking for your papa in the mountains. Maybe tomorrow, eh?"

"God*damnit,*" Joel raged.

"Easy, son," Gil cautioned. "You'll be old and sore yourself someday."

"That ain't likely," Joel grumbled. He jerked the palomino's head around and reached for the stirrup. He was just swinging a leg over the cantle when Gil urged his horse alongside. Putting a hand against the younger man's chest, he shoved as hard as he could. Joel flew backward off his mount, squawking like a whorehouse parrot. The palomino spooked, but Porfirio caught him before he could take off.

"What the hell'd you do that for?" Joel demanded from the ground.

"Keep an easy hand on that horse's bit, or I'll make you walk to Larkspur."

"Goddamnit . . ." Joel began, but Gil cut him off.

"No more cussing, and no more complaining. From now on you keep a civil tongue, or I'll by God yank it through your nose and tie it in a knot. Now get on your horse."

Joel's eyes blazed, but he kept his mouth shut and his opinions to himself as he climbed to his feet and took the reins from Porfirio. When he was mounted, Gil nodded toward the road leading away from the ranch. "Don't think you can outrun me, either. Your palomino may be faster than my sorrel, but he won't be faster than a bullet from my pistol, and I'm a more than fair shot." Looking at Porfirio, he said, *"Gracias, amigo."*

Porfirio smiled. "*De nada,* my friend, but watch this one, eh. He is wily, like the fox."

"I'll watch him," Gil promised. "I'm going to keep my eye on this boy's hind side like it was a skillet hung in a tree for target practice."

Joel gave him a dark look, but Gil jutted his chin toward the lane and told him to lead out.

The ranch road led toward the Little Ensillado, in the valley below the bench where the buildings sat. At the bottom of the slope they came to the outfit's official entrance, a high cross-beam resting over two stout logs planted firmly in the ground. It was for looks only. There was no fence to either side of the entrance, but there was a large wheel hanging from the center of the crossbeam. Gil ordered Joel to halt while he took a closer look. It was a ship's wheel, as Doc had mentioned, fully five feet across and modified to look, vaguely, like a full sun. Its resemblance to the outfit's brand was unmistakable, although time and the salty air of the Texas coast had eaten away at the iconic symbol. It was flaking with rust and badly corroded at its outer tips, eaten almost all the way through in a couple of places. Adding insult to injury were the white lumps and striations of bird crap—a sad commentary on what the ranch had become, Gil thought with an unexpected touch of melancholy.

"What the hell you looking at?" Joel demanded.

"Just looking," Gil replied, pulling his gaze away from the rusted sun. "Wondering what kind of a man I'm dealing with."

"If you're meaning my pa, you're gonna find out real quick. Soon as he hears what you've done, he's gonna bring the boys after you like a pack of wolves."

"I don't doubt it," Gil replied soberly, then lifted his reins. "Let's ride, son. It's a long way to Larkspur, and we're running short on time."

CHAPTER THIRTEEN

Warren Bishop and Vern Greer showed up shortly after six o'clock that morning. Russ Kendrick met them at the door, yanking it open to usher them inside.

"Where the hell have you been?" Russ demanded. "You were supposed to be here at dawn."

"Doc said six," Vern countered. "Besides, what difference does it make?"

"It makes plenty of difference to me. I gotta get to work."

"Wait," Warren said, jerking to a stop. He was looking at Reece, leaning against the rear wall. "What's he doing here?"

"Doc sent him over," Russ replied.

"Why?"

"Help keep an eye on Keegan, I guess."

"To make sure he doesn't escape," Reece interjected, aggravated that Bishop had asked the others, and not him.

"His pa was shot yesterday," Russ explained.

"Shot!" Warren and Vern exchanged uneasy glances.

"By Quinlin's men," Reece added.

"We don't know that for sure," Arnie reminded him. He had been reclining comfortably in the office's only chair, his legs crossed at the ankles. Now he rose and came around the desk. Catching Russ's eye, he tipped his head toward the door. "Come on, big talker. Let's get out of here." He paused in front of Greer and Bishop. "We'll be back about six tonight to take over."

199

"Not me," Russ stated firmly. "One night's lost sleep is enough."

"This is bullshit, anyway," Warren said. "I don't know why we're letting ourselves get roped into putting our necks on the block when no one else in town would do it."

"We're doing it so Sheriff Ryan can arrest Joel Quinlin," Reece said, pushing away from the wall in mild alarm.

"Sheriff Ryan?" Warren snorted. "Anyone here know anything about him? Hell, has anyone here even *talked* to him? I know I ain't. For all we know, he could be riding for Quinlin."

"That ain't likely," Arnie said. "Don't forget it was Ryan who shot Lester. Besides, Doc trusts him. I reckon that's good enough for me."

"Well, it ain't for me," Warren replied.

"Naw, Arnie's right, boys," Vern said. "I ain't keen on being here, either, but Quinlin crossed the line when he killed Fred and busted Doc's hand."

"Wouldn't've happened if they'd minded their own business," Russ said.

"Ain't none of that matters now," Arnie said. "Doc asked us to keep a lid on Keegan, and that's what we'll do." He walked outside, and after a moment's hesitation, Russ picked up his hat and shotgun and followed. Vern looked at Reece. "You might as well go, too, kid."

"No, I'll stay," Reece replied. He didn't add that he had nowhere to go. He hadn't talked to Peggy since her father's brutal murder, and wouldn't have known what to say to her. Nor did he want to go back to Doc's place to see how his pa was faring. The sense of helplessness he'd felt yesterday on the drive down off the Rim was too fresh in his mind. At least here at the jail there was purpose, a feeling of control, no matter how illusionary that might be.

Vern shrugged. "Suit yourself," he said, then walked over to the door that separated the office from the cells. He poked his head inside, but Reece could tell from the snores coming from within that Keegan was still asleep.

"That boy's dead to the world," Vern observed humorously.

"Likely all the booze he had at Bannerman's before they arrested him," Warren replied. He took the chair Arnie had vacated, and Reece returned to his place against the wall. Nobody spoke, which suited Reece. Hannah Brickman showed up about an hour later toting a deep skillet filled with scrambled eggs, beef, and refried beans. She seemed surprised to see Reece.

"I've got plates and forks, and Daphne will be over soon with coffee and cups." She glanced apologetically at Reece. "I'll have her fetch some extra utensils for you."

"He can go back to the café and eat," Warren said. "Me'n Vern don't need him."

"You'd be welcome to if you'd like," she told Reece. "You could have your choice from the morning menu."

"No, ma'am, but thank you. I'll stay here."

"All right. I'll send Daphne back with an extra plate and fork."

She set the skillet and dinnerware on top of the desk and moved out of the way. Vern didn't need an invitation, and immediately began heaping breakfast onto a plate. Warren held back a moment to glare at Reece, then stepped in line. Reece watched silently, with a prickling sense of disquiet. He didn't know Warren Bishop very well, but he could tell the man was annoyed by his presence. More so than seemed warranted, he thought.

Hannah left as soon as Bishop began filling his plate, promising to be back at noon with their midday meal. Reece watched her cross the street to the café. A few minutes later, Daphne came out carrying a large coffee pot in one hand and a woven basket in the other. When she brought them inside, Reece saw that Hannah hadn't forgotten him. Amid the cups and spoons and sealed containers of cream and sugar was an extra plate and fork. Daphne smiled and made sure Reece knew the utensils were for him, then said she had to get back to help her mother roll out the dough for a fresh batch of pies.

"Dried cherries," she informed them. "We'll bring you a slice when they're done." Then she slipped out the door and was gone.

Reece filled his cup but ignored the cream and sugar. He'd been drinking his coffee black since he was twelve.

Bishop and Greer finished their meals in under a minute, then scooped more food onto their plates. Greer asked Reece if he wanted some, but Reece shook his head. Warren scowled and ate faster. Reece wondered if some of the breakfast was supposed to be for Keegan, but the prisoner was still asleep when Warren and Vern finished off the skillet. Leaving their dirty dishes on top of the desk, they took their coffee outside and rolled cigarettes. Reece could hear them talking through the open door but couldn't make out what they were saying. Warren seemed angry about something, and Reece had the impression it was because of him. Vern wasn't saying much, but Reece noticed he was starting to act uncomfortable, as if whatever Warren was harping at was starting to sit heavy on top of his breakfast.

After a while Reece took his coffee into the back room to watch Keegan sleep, just to get away from the insistent murmur of Warren's voice. When he grew tired of that, he returned to the office and took a seat behind the desk. With the morning sun hitting the jail full on, the room soon grew warm, and it wasn't long before he began to feel the effects of the last twenty-four hours. He didn't think he dozed, but when he jerked his head up to the sound of angry voices in the street, it took him a moment to remember where he was, and why.

He grabbed his rifle from the corner and hurried outside. A small crowd had gathered in front of the jail. Reece recognized a few of them, including the bulk of Larkspur's citizens' committee—Ira Bannerman, Henry Fisher, and Roger Greene. Lloyd Thompson, who managed the feed store, was there, along with Paul Offerman, who was standing at the forefront of the throng with a double-barreled shotgun clutched threateningly in both hands. The other eight or ten men were unknown to Reece. He'd seen them around town but had never talked to them; he didn't know their names.

Warren and Vern were standing in the street facing the mob with their backs to the jail, but it was Offerman who was doing most of the talking. He shut up when he saw Reece.

"Who's that?"

"That's Reece Ward," Vern said. "You know him, Big Max's boy."

Offerman cursed, then waved a hand as if urging someone out of the way of a stampede. "Move aside. This ain't your concern."

"I'm not going anywhere," Reece said.

Offerman looked at Warren. "What the hell, Bishop?"

Warren shrugged and came back to stand at Reece's side. Vern Greer moved in the opposite direction, circling wide around the crowd to get out of the way. Paul Offerman took a couple of steps forward, and Reece worked the Whitney-Kennedy's lever.

"You stay where you are, Mr. Offerman."

"Boy, don't bite off more than you can chew."

"What do you want, anyway?"

"We want Keegan."

"Why?"

"That's the citizens' committee's business, not yours."

"Uh-uh," Reece said, moving his finger to the rifle's trigger.

"Keegan's staying locked up until Doc Shaw says to turn him loose or Sheriff Ryan gets back."

"*Sheriff* Ryan! Hell, Ryan ain't no lawman, boy. If Doc told you he was, his crock is full."

"This ain't none of your affair, Reece," Ira Bannerman said kindly. "This is town business, and it's done been settled by vote."

Reece shook his head. "Doc says to keep Keegan locked up, and that's . . ." He abruptly closed his mouth, his spine stiffening as the muzzle of Warren Bishop's revolver pressed firmly into his ribs.

"Don't be a fool, kid," Warren told him.

"You're part of this?"

"We're all part of it."

"This ain't right," Reece protested.

"Right or wrong don't apply today," Warren said, increasing the pressure on Reece's ribs. He slipped the revolver from the younger man's holster. "Put the rifle down."

Reece had no choice but to comply. The Whitney-Kennedy's butt struck the veranda's plank deck with a hollow thud. On the street the tension seemed to drain out of the mob. They shuffled closer, spreading out as they did. All except for Vern Greer, who backed off a couple of paces, then turned to scurry across the street toward the Paris Café.

Bounding up the steps, Offerman snatched the rifle from Reece's grasp and took it inside. The rest of the mob swarmed after him, crowding into the jail until only Reece and Warren were left outside. Reece wished he had a key to the front door. If he could have gotten Warren inside with the others, he could have swung it shut and corralled the whole bunch.

It took only minutes for the mob to hustle Keegan outside. Reece wanted to laugh at the frightened expression on the ex-lawman's face. He obviously didn't know what the townsmen had in store for him, and he was fearing the worse. When the crowd had cleared out, Warren took Reece inside and locked him in the front cell.

"Don't worry, kid. Someone'll be along soon to let you out."

Grasping the bars, Reece said, "You know this is wrong."

"Likely it is, but I gotta do what the town wants."

Reece shook the bars. "Don't let them do this. You know it's just going to hurt us all in the end."

Warren's eyes dropped to the floor and he slowly shook his head. "I know, but that's down the road, and it's today that's got my scalp crawling." Then he turned away, tossing the keys on the desk as he headed for the door.

"Bishop."

"Just let it go, kid," Warren said, and quietly pulled the door closed.

Gil knew something was wrong as soon as he rode into town. It was late afternoon, but the street was deserted. There wasn't a soul to be seen, not even a horse hitched to one of the street-side rails. His gut tightened as he slid the Winchester from its scabbard and laid it across his saddlebows. Joel continued down the middle of the street as if he intended to ride straight through town, until Gil called for him to head for the jail.

Joel glanced over his shoulder with a broad grin. "My pa's gonna skin you real slow, Ryan. Gonna make you scream with every inch of hide he peels off your bones."

Gil didn't reply, but he was glad they'd finally reached their destination. Periodically on the ride in, Joel had called back some threat of retribution that he or his father would mete out. Being skinned alive wasn't the worst of the fates Joel had promised, but Gil wasn't overly worried.

They hauled up in front of the jail and dismounted. The front door was closed but unlatched, and Joel watched curiously as Gil shoved it open with his foot. He still hadn't picked up that something was out of whack. Gil prodded him inside, then closed and latched the door. "In there," he said, gesturing toward the back room.

Gil locked Joel in the forward cell, then walked down the short aisle to check on the second one. He wasn't surprised to find it empty. Returning to the office, he hung the keys on a peg, then glanced around the room. There were dirty dishes on top of the desk, along with an empty skillet and a nearly empty pot of cold coffee. Keeping the Winchester with him, he returned to the front door. Although anxious to know what had happened, he wasn't going to leave Joel unattended. Not until he found out what had become of Hal Keegan.

He was still staring at the deserted street when he spotted Shaw leaving the trees north of the business block, from the direction of his house and office.

"They turned him loose," Doc blurted as soon as he entered the jail.

"Who turned him loose?"

"Most of the citizens' committee, some of the townspeople."

"What happened to the men you had watching him?"

"What did you expect them to do, shoot their own neighbors?"

"Yeah, if that's what it took!"

"It doesn't work that way, Ryan. Not in a town like Larkspur."

Gil cursed and fire sparked in Doc's eyes. Then it was over, and they both sagged backward.

"What happened?" Gil asked after a moment.

"I was wrong about one of the men I chose." Doc paused, then began telling the story as he'd heard it from Vern Greer and Reece Ward. He included the attack on the Flying W and Big Max Ward's bullet wound, then shook his head in resignation. "They just let him go, Gil. Stood there and watched him ride off."

"Which way?" Gil asked, although he had a pretty good idea of the direction Keegan would choose.

"North," Doc confirmed. "Probably looking for Art and his men."

Gil sighed and leaned his rifle against the wall. "How's Ward?"

"Max? He stands a good chance if infection doesn't set in. It was a bad one, though. Took me most of last night and part of this morning to extract the bullet and stop the bleeding."

"Did he say who shot him?"

"Max is still unconscious, but Reece and Sally are convinced it was Quinlin. They admit they didn't see him, and that whoever was calling back and forth with Max didn't sound like Art."

"How long has Keegan been gone?"

"They cut him loose early this morning, so I'd guess right around ten hours by now."

Gil swore softly, then pulled the door open and went outside. Doc followed him.

"Where is everyone?"

"They're staying low, although I don't know why. Quinlin probably won't be in until later tonight or sometime tomorrow."

After a long silence, Gil said, "Can you ride?"

Doc appeared startled by the question. "A horse? I've ridden hundreds of miles on horseback, chasing Sioux and Apaches. Or do you mean since I've gotten old and fat?"

"I mean if we pulled out now and rode hard, could you keep up?"

A slow smile crept across the physician's face. "Yeah, I think I could. What do you have in mind?"

Gil glanced deliberately at Doc's bandaged hand.

"I can use it . . . some. Enough to saddle my own horse, or

fire a weapon if it comes to that."

"Can you leave Max Ward?"

Doc nodded. "Alma and Sally can look after him."

"Go get your medical bag and some extra clothes. Bring a coat and a heavy bedroll, too, then round up a couple of good horses."

"Two?"

"I'm going to ask Peggy Somers if she'll come with us. We can use her testimony in Albuquerque . . . if we make it that far."

"We'll make it."

Gil didn't reply. He was staring across the street at the saloon, where a man in a gray derby had appeared at the batwing doors. The derbied man was standing partially in shadow, and was watching the jail intently. Gil was pretty sure it was the same man with the intense stare that he'd seen coming into Watland's on the northbound stage that morning. "Who is that?" he asked Doc.

"I've never seen him."

Gil told him about the stage and the four people he'd seen inside.

"Uh-huh. Ed and Wilma Davidson and Edgar Peabody were the others. The Davidsons have been in Santa Fe on some kind of legal business, and Peabody's a clothing peddler who passes through every couple of months to take orders. I'd heard there was a stranger, too, but I never got a name."

"Where's he been all day, do you know?"

"I don't. Frankly, I haven't even thought about him."

Gil decided to let the matter drop, although he was still curious. Turning to Doc, he said, "Go on and get your stuff. I want to be on our way as soon as possible."

Shaw nodded and took off, and Gil closed the door. Joel started complaining as soon as he heard the latch slide home.

"Ryan! Goddamnit, Ryan, I'm hungry. I ain't et all day. If you're the lawdog around here now, it's your job to bring me . . ."

Gil went to the door between the cells and quietly pulled it shut, sending the kid off in a new direction, lamenting the cell's dimness and poor bedding, the coolness of the stone walls that had held frost only a few weeks before. The door didn't mute him completely, but it did soften the intrusion into Gil's thoughts.

Time seemed to drag while he waited for Doc, and the heat inside the front office began to grow oppressive. Gil went to the front door and stood with his shoulder propped against the jamb. Joel eventually quieted down, although from time to time he would kick the cell door hard enough for Gil to feel the vibration through the floorboards.

Later on, a couple of wagons trailed in from the north. At first Gil thought they might be freighters, even though he didn't know where they would be coming from if the Saddleback was still snowed-in. The wagons veered off into the trees before reaching the business district, and Gil watched as they went into camp. When he saw that there were women and children with them, he realized they weren't freighters but homesteaders on their way out of the valley, and he turned his eyes to the distant bulk of the North Rim. He wondered where Art Quinlin was now, and what kind of trouble he was causing the settlers still up there. He was just about ready to step inside when Hannah Brickman appeared from the alley beside the mercantile. She approached the jail in quick, determined strides, and Gil left the veranda to meet her.

"Mrs. . . . Hannah," he greeted, reaching up to remove his hat.

She nodded curtly and said his name, then waved toward his head. "Put that thing back on. It's too hot for that kind of nonsense." She didn't waste any time getting to the point. "Peggy Somers is missing."

"Fred's daughter? Are you sure?"

"Sure enough to start feeling scared. Edgar Peabody came into the café a while ago and said he's been waiting for her since noon. Peabody's a drummer who . . ."

"Doc told me," Gil interrupted.

"Okay. Well, Peabody's been waiting at Ira's all afternoon, figuring Peggy was laying low upstairs because of all the trouble that's brewing. I guess he kept going back to check, and this last time he went all the way through the store. He says he found broken glass on the floor in back, and the rear door was hanging wide open. He didn't go upstairs, but came to fetch me in case she was ill. I was going to check on her when I saw you." She glanced at Joel's mount. "I see you found him."

"He's inside."

"Good. Maybe we can get this one to trial, but right now I'm more worried about . . ." Her words trailed of when she saw Doc riding down the street on a tall bay, an already saddled roan trailing behind him on a short lead.

"Are you two going somewhere?" she asked quietly.

"We were going to Albuquerque. I wanted Peggy to come with us and testify about what Quinlin's men did to her pa. With depositions from her and Doc, I was hoping to convince a judge to issue warrants for Art and the rest of his men."

She gave him a searching look. "Are you a lawman, Gil?"

"I wish people would quit asking me that."

She waited a moment, giving him a chance to explain, then said, "I suspect Peggy will go with you, assuming she's able."

Doc rode up with a broad grin splashed across his face. He was riding one of Offerman's rental horses, a stocky bay rigged out with a good McCellan saddle, the kind the physician had likely pounded for years in the army. His gear was attached military-style, everything neat and tidy and handy to reach. A Sharps Business rifle rode in a boot off the bay's right side, its butt slanted back past the horse's hip.

Doc had replaced his town garb with a clean but worn and sun-faded field uniform, right down to the medical insignias on the collar and captain's bars on the shoulders. It looked tight, especially across the stomach, but functional, as did the Army model Colt holstered at his hip.

"Hannah," Doc greeted, touching the brim of his campaign hat.

"Doc, you look as shiny as a Fourth of July parade."

Doc smiled, but Hannah didn't give him time to reply.

"I think Peggy's missing, Doc, and I fear the worst."

"Peggy! Have you checked the store?"

"Not yet, but Peabody searched the lower level and she wasn't there. He thought there might have been a struggle, but he wasn't sure. I was just heading over when I saw Gil."

"Did Peabody call for her?" Doc asked, stepping down from his saddle.

"Said he did. Said he stood at the bottom of the stairs and hollered several times, but she didn't answer."

"Maybe I'd better go, too," Doc said worriedly. He hitched the bay next to Gil's sorrel and brought his medical bag down from behind the cantle.

"Hannah, I need someone to watch Joel," Gil said. "Can you do it?"

"Is he locked up?"

"He is, but I don't want anyone busting him out while I'm gone."

Hannah smiled thinly. "You got a shotgun I can borrow?"

"Would a rifle do?"

"Fine as flint. Where's it at?"

"Inside." He hesitated, then added, "Don't let anyone in, not even a member of the citizens' committee."

"Nobody's coming in, especially not a member of the citizens' committee," she assured him, and Gil didn't have any doubt that she meant it.

Gil and Doc went in through the mercantile's front door and stopped to look and listen. The store was as dark as Gil remembered it from past visits, but the silence seemed ominous. He called her name, softly at first, then raised his voice. "Miss Somers?"

"Peggy!" Doc added loudly. "It's Dr. Shaw."

There was no answer. Gil went to the counter to peer over the top, then straightened and shook his head.

"Let's look upstairs."

Gil started down the aisle next to the counter, Doc hard on his heels. They entered the back room where Fred had been working on Gil's first visit. Floor-to-ceiling shelves sparsely filled with a variety of bottles, flasks, and pasteboard boxes took up three sides of the pharmacy, and an apothecary's desk, set against the east wall, was cluttered with brass scales, measuring spoons, trays, and tiny vials. There was broken glass on the floor in front of the desk, and Doc picked up one of the larger shards. He sniffed the glass, then made a face.

"What is it?"

"Laudanum."

The hairs across the back of Gil's neck rose. He moved to the rear door and peered outside. There was a small, doorless barn, a clothes line stretched between a couple of wooden posts, and a privy partially hidden behind a row of lilacs not yet in bloom. Gil instinctively headed toward the barn. He stopped at the entrance, then knelt to run his fingers lightly over a horseshoe-shaped trough pressed into the damp soil.

"What did you find?" Doc asked.

"Tracks." Gil stood and peered inside. "Did the Somers own a horse?"

"Not in years."

Gil traced the line of tracks leading away from the barn. They were headed north, and from the angle it looked like they were trying to leave town the back way. Turning away from the trail, Gil entered the barn's dark entrance. The smell of old hay and long-dried manure lingered, and his lungs twitched warningly. He was still carrying the small bottle of codeine that Doc had given him in his vest pocket, but left it where it was. It took only seconds to assure that the single stall and adjoining hay bin were empty, but there were more prints in the dust. At least two horses had been recently tied to iron rings bolted to the walls, but they hadn't remained long. The ground where they'd stood wasn't packed enough to account for more than a ten- or fifteen-minute wait.

When Gil went back outside, Doc was standing in the yard, staring through the trees to where the settlers from the North Rim had gone into camp. "I have a bad feeling about this," he said quietly.

"Come on," Gil replied, tapping the older man lightly on the arm. "Let's check upstairs."

Neither man spoke as they re-entered the store and made their way up a set of narrow stairs along the south wall. Gil hesitated on top, his muscles taut as a drum's head. "Which way?" he asked.

"The four rooms Fred used to rent out are at the front. He and Peggy shared the rear portion of the upstairs." He nodded toward a closed door on their right that would take them into a room overlooking the rear yard. "That's Peggy's," he said, then took a reluctant step toward it. Gil was at his shoulder as he twisted the knob and shoved the door open. He cursed softly when he saw the room, then grimly followed Doc inside.

Chapter Fourteen

It didn't surprise Odell one whit when Doug Hayes proved to be correct in his prediction that the Sun's crew was about to shrink, but it must have caught the old man completely off guard. He was raging like a madman, turning the misty morning air blue with obscenities. Scrambling out of his blankets, Odell learned that Lou Saunders and Goose Carter had sloped overnight, no doubt heading for more distant pastures, someplace where they weren't as likely to catch a bullet in the back as one from the front. What did surprise Odell, though, and saddened him, too, was that Doug had gone with them; he hadn't expected that.

Three men deserted, and Art Quinlin was as mad as hell. Yet when Miller asked if he wanted to send anyone after them, the old man's anger had unaccountably leveled off. Glaring at Odell for no apparent reason, he'd growled, "No, we've still got work to do up here. I'll find 'em, though. Find 'em, then skin the little cowards alive."

Odell swallowed hard, recalling Doug's words from the night before.

"It ain't no secret he doesn't like you, either. You get crossways to him, Odell, and he'll shoot you dead."

The way the old man was anymore, Odell didn't figure it would take much to get crossways. He just wished Doug had been a little more open about his plans. Odell might have considered tagging along if the option had been presented, although he suspected Art's dislike of him had likely carried some weight in their decision not to ask.

You remind the old man of what he used to be before his wife died and all his plans for the Basin got shot to shit, and now you won't go away. All the other old hands did, but you stayed, and I figure that bothers him.

They ate in the saddle, a wanting breakfast of jerky, hard crackers, and canteen water. No one spoke much. Even Miller was keeping his distance from the boss that morning. Nor did the old man split them into two groups as he had the previous morning. Maybe he figured he'd be undergunned with just Wade Palmer, Al Richie, and the Sun's two black hands, Samson Hoag and Little George Isley, but Odell speculated that it was more likely he didn't want to let anyone out of sight for fear they might also cut their pins.

Quinlin led them over trails Odell hadn't even known existed. They spent all morning climbing to a ridge probably seven or eight hundred feet above the Basin's floor, then immediately started back down in an easterly direction. Odell had no idea where they were or where they were going, and was as surprised as anyone when they came out at the top of a little flat not even ten miles from where they'd spent the night. Crowding forward for a better look, he saw a corral and an open-faced shed set back under the trees on the west side of the flat; a few seconds later he spotted a dugout burrowed into the side of the hill above the shed.

Art started cursing as soon as he realized the place was deserted, and had been for some time. The dugout's door was hanging open and a stove pipe that extended through the sod roof was scaled with rust. The corral gate had been left open, and the grass inside was tall and ungrazed.

Odell was surprised by the old man's anger. He would have thought Art would be happy to discover that at least one of the

North Rim squatters had taken his threats seriously. It was almost as if he'd been looking forward to finding someone on the place, and maybe venting a little of his frustration in the process.

They burned the shed and pulled down the corral, and Brownie and Al went inside to tie ropes around the dugout's support posts. They had a look around first, but claimed they didn't find anything of value.

"Pull it down," the old man ordered, and others took hitches around their saddle horns and eased the support posts out of the ground. The dugout collapsed in a cloud of dust and snapping roof poles.

"Whose place was this?" Miller asked Art as flames started to take a bigger bite out of the stock shed.

"Some goddamned Swede named Nilsson," Art grumbled. "Showed up last summer, but I guess he didn't have the guts to stick it out."

They continued south after that, moving steadily downslope, although with a continued eastward bent. Late that afternoon they came to another high ridge. Art motioned for them to be quiet, then he led them up a winding trail to the top. At the crest he ordered them to spread out so that they were all in a line, stirrup to stirrup. Odell's heart sank when he saw the place. Set in the middle of a wide, lush valley was a two-story log house with real glass in the windows and painted sills. A smaller cabin sat in its shadow, with a collection of additional log structures scattered beyond the main house.

Although he'd never been here before, Odell knew whose place this was by its tidiness—the perfectly straight corral poles and sturdy buildings, the just-starting-to-bud flowers that ran along a flagstone walk to the front door. Next to Max Ward's Flying W, Kurt and Sophie Schwartz owned the biggest homestead under the Rim. It wasn't a cattle outfit in the strictest sense of the word, but they ran more than a score of Holsteins in a steadily increasing herd, and had never made a secret about their plans for the future.

"Ve vill 'ave der largest dairy in der Basin in five years," Kurt had boasted more than once on his twice-weekly trips to Larkspur to sell his products. "Goot milk und butter for ever'one."

To Art Quinlin, they were just another rat's nest of shipyard refugees, barely understandable and offering nothing the valley needed.

"Like ticks on a dog's ass," was the old man's assessment. "At least the damned greasers know how to punch cows."

The family included two young sons under the age of ten, and Sophie's brother, Alois Neumann, who helped with the milking. From what Odell had heard, the whole family pitched in with the milking, twice each day—mother and sons, husband and brother.

"They got kids," Odell blurted, before anyone else could speak.

Art looked at him as if he'd just rattled off a batch of Latin. Odell quickly ducked his head, then raised it painfully. "Them milk cows of his ain't going to eat that much grass, Mr. Quinlin, and I kind of like butter on my bread in the mornings."

"Odell, ain't no one on the Lord's green earth gives a hoot in hell what you like for breakfast. Now shut your trap and let the men think."

Odell turned a panicky eye toward the Schwartz place. The cows were grazing across the far side of the valley, but already beginning their slow evening migration toward the milking shed. Smoke purled from the stone chimney, and a collie lay in a patch of sunlight close to the front porch, its long nose tucked into the shelter of its flanks, asleep.

"Palmer, take Richie and Hoag with you and get around

below the cabin. Watch that road close. I don't want 'em slipping away. Miller, you and Roth and Hillman and Isley can come at 'em from the front." He fixed Clint with an unwavering stare. "You're in charge, Miller, and you know what I'm wanting."

"Don't worry, Mr. Quinlin, I'll take care it."

"You'd damn well better." Then the old man put his cold eyes on Odell. "You're with me, Love." He grinned wickedly. "Just the two of us." Odell nodded dully, and Art turned back to Miller. "Give us twenty minutes to get into place, then move out."

Miller nodded and the group broke apart. Odell fell in behind the old man's buckskin, his mood riding down around his boot heels. They followed the ridge top for about a hundred yards, winding through scattered pines, then turned to come at the Schwartz place from above. Art shucked his rifle when they were close, but Odell kept both of his weapons sheathed. The pines were thicker up here, shutting visibility down to about thirty yards. Their horses' hooves weren't making much noise in the layers of dead needles under the trees, and the birds were silent. Odell flinched when the first shot rang out, but the old man kicked his horse into a trot. More shots drifted up from the house, along with shouts in both English and German.

Quinlin twisted in his saddle. "Get a move on, Love, before it's over." Then he pulled up, puzzled by Odell's startled expression. When he turned back around, Sophie Schwartz and her two young sons had already come to a stop in the pines not fifty feet away.

The woman's mouth was open and her eyes were wide with fear. She was plump and blond, dressed in gingham, her cheeks rosy from exertion. She had the hand of one of her children in each of her own, and they were staring as well.

"Son of a bitch," Art breathed. Then he threw the rifle to his shoulder and fired.

The woman cried out and took a staggering step backward, before dropping to her knees. *"Laufen,"* she gasped, shoving the boys away from her. *"Laufen!"*

The boys ran as instructed, darting like rabbits into the deeper forest to the west. The old man said "Son of a bitch" again, as if surprised by his accomplishment, while Odell stared in horror as the heavy-set woman slowly toppled forward.

Levering a fresh round into his rifle's chamber, Art growled, "Get your gun out, Love. I ain't doin' this alone."

"The hell you ain't," Odell breathed, but the old man was already spurring toward the cabin.

Odell rode to where the woman lay with her face buried in a carpet of brown needles. Her arms flopped limply when he rolled her over, and there was dirt in her still-open eyes. His breathing was quick and ragged as he brushed what needles he could from the woman's face, then gently closed her lids. He said her name aloud, then apologized for the fate that had befallen her, before pushing weakly to his feet. He felt wrung out, but knew he couldn't tarry. The old man wouldn't stand for it, and in his current mood, he'd as likely open fire on Odell as curse him for his tardiness.

He fumbled getting his foot in the stirrup, then had to haul himself up with both hands wrapped around the saddle horn. Quinlin had already disappeared into the trees, but Odell didn't have the nerve to ride in the opposite direction. Grimly, he reined his horse after the old man, winding down through the pines toward the log house. The shooting intensified and he moved his hand back to cover the scarred grips of his revolver, but he didn't draw it.

He came in sight of the house's north side and the old man in the same instant. Quinlin was sitting his buckskin at the edge of the trees, his rifle sloped across the crook of his elbow. Gun

219

smoke wreathed the house, partially concealing the bodies of two men lying in the dirt of the front yard. At first Odell figured it must be Kurt and Alois. Then he recognized Little George's coal black hide and Brownie Hillman's red boots, and pulled his horse to a stop.

"Goddamnit, get up here, Love," Art snapped.

"That's Little George and Brownie," Odell said, not quite sure if he believed it himself.

"I know who they are. Damned Dutch cowards must've ambushed 'em."

"Where's Miller?"

Art jutted his bearded chin toward the milking shed. "They got him and Carl Roth holed up in there and pinned down tight. I ain't seen the others, but they'd better haul their asses up here quick."

Odell guided his dun alongside Art's buckskin. "The others still in the house?" he asked, meaning Kurt and his brother-in-law, Alois.

"Be my guess," the old man replied with surprising calm. "There's at least one of 'em shooting down from an upstairs window. I ain't spotted the other yet, but I'd bet my best foal he's in there." He glanced at Odell. "We're goin' in after 'em."

"After them! Hell's bells, Mr. Quinlin . . ."

"Don't say it, Love. Just goddamned don't say it, because, boy, I am clean outta patience with you." He swung down, hesitated a moment, then returned his rifle to its scabbard. "Leave your long gun," he said. "This is gonna be close-up work once we get inside."

Swallowing past a cottony throat, Odell stepped to the ground and wrapped his horse's reins around the trunk of a slim pine. Art drew his Colt, then motioned for Odell to take the lead.

"I want you up front where I can keep an eye on you."

Or more likely, Odell thought, where he could be shot first if one of the Germans saw them.

They left the trees on foot and ran in a crouch across nearly forty yards of open space to the north side of the cabin. Odell didn't know if Clint Miller or Carl Roth had spotted them, but figured it was a good bet that neither Schwartz nor Neumann had; they would have opened up immediately.

They put their backs to the wall and stood there for a couple of minutes, Odell waiting and Art thinking. Odell thought the old man looked nervous; he kept licking his lips as if they'd dried out on the run from the trees to the cabin, and his eyes were darting erratically. Out front, the shooting continued unabated. Finally, Art motioned toward the rear corner of the house.

"Get movin', Love. We ain't got all day."

Odell approached the corner and peeked around the back. He was expecting a bullet to come slamming into his head at any second, but the rear yard was empty. The old man gave him a shove and Odell stumbled forward. Art slid around the corner after him, still licking his lips regularly, although now he was also cursing softly, under his breath, mindless little expletives that held neither rhyme nor reason.

There was a small porch with railing and a back door with glass panes. Odell kept his head down as he crawled onto the porch and sidled up next to the door. The old man was right behind him, looking kind of glassy-eyed now, like he was going to puke or pass out. Scuttling over Odell's legs, he put his back against the wall on the opposite side of the door and rocked the Colt's hammer to full cock. Nodding toward the rear entrance, he said, "You go in first, Love."

Odell looked at the door for a moment, then shook his head. "No, sir, Mr. Quinlin, I ain't gonna do it."

Art leveled his revolver at Odell's face. "You'll go in, or I'll by-God blow a hole through that empty skull of yours."

"No, sir," Odell replied stubbornly, but he kept his own revolver drawn, and when Art glanced at it, they both realized it was pointed straight at the old man's stomach. It was cocked, too, although for the life of him, Odell couldn't remember thumbing the hammer back. Then the shooting out front abruptly intensified, and Art shoved to his feet. He kicked the rear door open and darted inside.

Odell pressed back with his shoulders as if trying to embed himself into the logs. The sounds of the battle grew desperate. A man screamed defiantly, another screamed in pain. More shots, then a silence as thick as fog dropped over the broad meadow, and Odell uncocked his gun and returned it to its holster.

Gil returned to the jail alone. Hannah met him at the door, stepping to the side as he entered. Although she looked like she was trying to maintain a stoic demeanor, she wasn't doing a very good job of it.

"Did you find her?"

"No, but there was a hell of a mess in her bedroom."

"What kind of a mess?"

"Clothes scattered across the floor, a couple of drawers left open. There was that broken bottle downstairs that Peabody mentioned, too."

Hannah bit her lower lip and turned away.

"There were tracks of at least two horses behind the store, and tracks leading north. Any idea who they might've belonged to?"

Sighing, Hannah went to the window, staring through the dusty glass to the deserted street.

Remembering an earlier conversation with Doc, Gil said, "Is this about Earl Quinlin?"

"Maybe, I don't know. Peggy and Earl were friendly. Some of the people around town thought it was serious, but others . . .

well . . . others thought she might have been using him."

"Using him? Why?"

"Why does any young lady use someone?"

"Another man?"

Hannah smiled bleakly. "Your knowledge of a woman's wiles is limited, Gil Ryan, although not entirely flawed. It's not always men and it's not always money, but . . . in this case I think it probably was. A man, I mean."

"Quinlin?"

"Most people would agree that Earl Quinlin was the least of-fensive of Art's boys, but he was hardly the type to attract a girl like Peggy Somers."

"Not even with the Sun thrown in?"

"Because the Sun is the biggest ranch in the Basin? No." She leaned forward, squinting past the bars in the window. "Where's Doc going?"

"To ask Paul Offerman about horses." Gil closed the door. "Tell me about Earl."

"He was a Quinlin. Maybe not as mean as Les or as dumb as Joel, but he was like his father in that he thought he owned the Basin and everything in it. He was riding into Larkspur on a regular basis last summer, and Fred didn't like it. Then in late October they found him lying in the road a few miles south of town. He had a bullet in his chest and another in his head. Someone wanted to make sure he was dead."

"Any guesses as to who it might've been?"

"No, but Art is convinced it was someone from the Rim."

"What do you think?"

"It's possible, but not necessarily for the reason Art believes. Reece Ward had been coming into Larkspur pretty regularly, too. The town holds a Harvest Dance in the fall, and Peggy went alone last year. Earl was there, and he tried to keep her to himself, but later that evening she disappeared. They say she asked Earl to bring her some punch, but she was gone when he came back. It was kind of sad, really, watching him wander around the fringes of the dance with a cup of punch in each hand. He looked like a lost puppy. Finally, some of the younger men started jobbing him, the way young men do, and Earl threw the cups down and left. That was the last time I ever saw him. Art buried him at the ranch the next day, alongside Earl's mother."

"What about Peggy?"

"No one ever knew for sure, but it was rumored that she'd met someone else in the dark, and that her father caught them. I know she had a black eye the next time I saw her."

Gil scowled. "Who gave her a black eye?"

"Who do you think?"

"Her father?"

"Surprised?"

Gil hesitated, then shrugged. "Fred seemed like a pretty decent fellow, the little I knew him."

"Most of the men in Larkspur would probably agree, but the women have their own opinions."

"So who do you think she ran off to see that night? The Ward boy?"

"She never said, never talked about that night at all that I know of, but I know Reece was at the dance earlier, and then he wasn't."

Gil's frown deepened. "Where's Reece now?"

"Why, I don't know. He was here this morning. I just assumed . . ."

Her words trailed off. Peering through the window, Gil saw Doc heading their way, and he and Hannah went out to meet him.

"I don't know what to make of this," Doc said, climbing the steps into the shade. "Paul said the only man who's rented a horse all week is that stranger who came in on the stage this morning. Claimed his name was Servey, but that's all the information he gave."

Gil glanced across the street to the saloon, but the derbied man who had been watching them earlier was gone.

"Paul said he showed up shortly after he got into town and rented a horse and saddle, but that he didn't pick them up until about thirty minutes ago."

"About the time we went looking for Miss Somers?"

Doc nodded. "Here's something else to chew on. Both of Ward's horses are gone. Reece put them in our pasture last night, but they're not there now."

"The wagon, too?"

"No, just the horses. I went to check with Alma as soon as I noticed they were missing, and she wasn't aware that they'd been taken. She says Reece hasn't been back, and that Sally hasn't left the house all day."

"Max?"

Doc shook his head. "Max Ward won't be riding anything for several weeks." He glanced across the street to the saloon. "What now?"

"You have to go after Peggy," Hannah said. "Even if it means turning Joel lose."

"No," Gil replied. "I've already lost one prisoner today."

"Then shoot him. Do whatever you have to, but you have to find Peggy."

"Hannah, we don't even know for sure that she's been taken," Doc reminded her.

"Oh, the heaven's sake, Doc, we both know that girl's in trouble. Now you go bring her back, the both of you. I'll watch Joel."

Gil shook his head. "I can't ask you to do that, not after what happened this morning. We'll take Joel with us. That way, if we have to make a run for it, we'll have him with us."

"I'll fix something for you to take along," Hannah said.

"Make it something we can eat in the saddle," Gil said, but Hannah was already headed for the door.

Doc went outside to ready their horses while Gil went into the back room to fetch Joel. The younger man had quit his complaining and was reclining on the bunk. He barely looked up when Gil entered.

"Bet it's Pa that grabbed her. Gonna trade her for me, and there ain't a damned thing you can do about it."

"We'll see," Gil replied. He held up a pair of handcuffs he'd snagged from the desk on his way through. "You want to put these on, or should I do it for you?"

Joel swung his legs off the bunk and sat up. "Like hell."

"It'll be easier if you do it, but mark my words, one way or another, you're going to be wearing these cuffs when we walk out of here."

Joel eyed him closely, then swore and shoved to his feet. "I'm gonna have fun working you over, Ryan. Right up until Pa puts the noose around your neck."

Gil opened the door and stepped inside, and Joel obediently held out his hands. Gil put the handcuffs on him, then turned the locks and dropped the key into a vest pocket. "Let's go."

They walked outside with Gil holding firmly to the younger man's bicep. There was no one in sight. Doc led the palomino close and Gil told Joel to climb up. With the younger man in the saddle, Gil stripped the bridle from the stallion's head, then took a lead rope from his own horse and fastened it to the palomino's halter. Joel watched stony-eyed but silent as Gil and Doc climbed into their saddles. They were reining away from the jail when Hannah came out of the café carrying a sturdy cloth sack that bulged heavily.

"It isn't fancy," she confided, meeting them in the middle of the street, "but it'll stick to your ribs better than most." She handed the sack to Doc and told him to be careful. Then she came over beside Rusty. "I barely know you, but I want you to be careful, too."

"I will," Gil promised.

A faint blush crept over her cheeks. "You said yesterday you were looking forward to breakfast. I want you to know, that'll be on the house, too." Then her voice turned ferocious. "I mean it. Don't go getting yourself killed over the likes of Joel Quinlin, or any of their kind. Find Peggy, take care of your business with them, then come on back and have some bacon and eggs."

It was Doc who got them moving. "We'll be back as soon as we can," he told Hannah, securing the food sack to his saddle. "And we'll bring Peggy with us."

"Do that, Doc." She stepped back and gave Gil an impatient glance. "Well, don't just sit there looking lost, get on out there and find that girl."

Gil heeled Rusty forward, riding wide around Doc to take the lead. They rode to Doc's fenced pasture first, where Gil picked up the prints of Ward's two horses. As soon as the tracks were out of the gate, the trail split. On a hunch, Gil followed the set going north, and within a hundred yards they came to the spot where the trails rejoined. Only this time there were three sets of prints, all heading in the same direction. He glanced at Doc and wondered if he saw it the same way.

"Someone's got Peggy," Doc said quietly, "and someone else is following."

CHAPTER FIFTEEN

They camped that night a few miles shy of the foothills under the North Rim. The trail had been easy enough to follow throughout what remained of the afternoon, the tracks shallow but plain in the moist soil. They'd disappeared with the setting sun, though.

Although Doc would have preferred to push on at least as far as the edge of the pine forest, where there would be shelter from the wind and wood for a fire, he hadn't protested when Gil called a halt. He was along only to assist, and although he intended to do that to the best of his ability, as the miles fell away he began to wonder just how much help he was going to be if the chase lasted more than a day or two. He'd told Gil earlier that he could keep up no matter the pace, but he hadn't counted on the slow erosion of age, the stiffening of joints, and the softening of muscle and tissue that had gone largely unnoticed until he needed to call upon them. Twenty years ago he could have ridden for days without complaint. Tonight, after barely three hours astride a jogging mount, his back muscles were cramping and his tailbone felt as if someone had used it as a railroad spike.

Gil led them to an arroyo where a cutbank offered marginal protection from the stiff breeze coming down off the higher peaks to the northeast, where the snow was still deep, the cold unforgiving.

Joel complained about the lack of a fire, but by then Doc had learned to turn a deaf ear to the younger man's grumblings. Gil had apparently already developed the knack on the ride in from the Sun.

Doc took charge of the stock, picketing the horses above the cutbank where there was plenty of graze. He paused on his way back to stare at the Rim, but the fires that had burned so bright the night before were no longer evident, nor, apparently, had any new ones been set. The dark bulk of the range reminded him of a ragged smear of ink, the stars like frost.

When he returned to the arroyo, Gil was cuffing Joel to the wrist-thick trunk of a sagebrush. The Ensillado's new lawman wobbled slightly when he straightened, reminding Doc of how sick Gil had been not that long ago, and how exhausted he must be after his long ride to the Sun and back. Joel began to complain as soon as Gil started to walk away.

"You just gonna leave me here to freeze, Ryan?"

"It's tempting," Gil admitted. "Your bellyaching is getting tiresome."

"So is being hauled around the Basin like a fifty-weight of shelled corn." He chortled as a fresh idea occurred to him. "Turn me loose and I'll give you my word I'll go back to Larkspur and wait for you there. Put myself in a cell, too, if that'd please you."

"How about if I leave you right here, cuffed to that sage brush? I could pick you up on the way back."

"You'd probably do it, too."

Gil grabbed the palomino's saddle blanket and tossed it to the kid. "Use that if you get cold."

"You're real tough with me chained up like a dog, ain't you?"

"Hush now, Joel," Doc chided. "We're all tired."

"I notice you both got bedrolls."

"That's because we thought ahead."

That stumped Joel for a moment. Then he mumbled something that sounded vaguely sinister and lay back, curling into a ball before pulling the saddle blanket over his shoulders.

Doc eased down beside his saddle and began rummaging through the sack Hannah Brickman had sent along. Inside, he found a chunk of cold roast beef, a score or more of flaky biscuits, and a little crock of huckleberry jam to make it all slide down easier. Gil ate two of the sandwiches in as many minutes, then finished the feast with a long pull from his canteen. After that, he unrolled his bedroll and crawled inside without even taking off his boots or gun belt. Doc ate more sparingly, a single biscuit with a little jam and a few sips of water from his own canteen. When he was done, he made another sandwich and took it over to Joel.

"Here," he said, nudging the youth's heel with his toe. "Eat this. It'll help keep you warm."

"Another blanket would keep me warmer. Or a little whiskey," he added hopefully.

"We don't have any whiskey, and I wouldn't give you any if we did. I can loan you a blanket from my bedroll, though."

"Loan me two."

"I only have two."

"Yeah, but you ain't chained to a bush with your hand sticking out, either. You can walk around if you get cold."

Gil shifted in his blankets. "Shut up, Joel, and thank the man for what he's offering. If it was me, I wouldn't do it."

"Hell, I know you wouldn't, but Doc Shaw is a decent man. He's paid to look out for others when they're hurtin', and I'm hurtin' bad."

Doc's voice trembled as he held up his bandaged hand. "Do you know how hard it was for me to saddle my own horse this afternoon, Joel? Or to tie it off tonight?" He took a menacing step closer. "Or to even fix this goddamned sandwich for you?" He dropped the biscuit on the ground at Quinlin's side. "Eat it or don't, it doesn't matter to me."

"Hey," Joel said in surprise, but Doc was already walking away.

Loosening the bedroll from his saddle, he took it over beneath the cutbank and sat down with his back to the dirt wall. His pulse drummed and his face still felt warm. After pulling his blankets up to his chin, he leaned back and tried to get a rope on his anger. After a while he began to relax. As he did, a memory he hadn't thought of in a long time crept into his mind, so far in the past it brought along its own uncertain frown, as if he wasn't sure it was real.

It had been at the Harvest Dance last fall, with the young whirling and laughing across the flat ground north of the empty depot, the town's older citizens sitting on the sidelines digesting their dinners. Lanterns swayed from wagon tongues raised toward the sky like lances, casting an amber glow over the celebration. Doc and Alma had been sharing a bench with Roger Greene and his pretty wife, Tina, when Alma gently nudged his ribs and nodded toward Earl Quinlin, dancing a waltz with all the grace of a bear stumbling out of hibernation. Chuckling at the lad's clumsiness, Doc recalled his own awkward youth, his first tentative stabs at courtship. Then he noticed something odd, something he hadn't fully picked up on at the time, and that he hadn't mentioned to anyone then or since. Not even Alma.

Hal Keegan was lurking in the shadows behind the depot, the light glinting waxedly off his cheeks, his eyes deep and dark and kind of hungry looking. He'd been watching Earl and Peggy, but Doc sensed it wasn't Quinlin who had his attention. Doc looked at Peggy, her fine blond hair and laughing blue eyes, the upward twirl of her dress that, at times, nearly exposed her calves. Doc had watched her for a minute, then looked back at the depot, but Keegan was gone, so thoroughly vanished it would have been easy to imagine he'd never been there.

It had been Keegan, Doc recalled, who had found Earl's body south of town the next day.

Darkness was coming on swiftly, but the old man wouldn't be rushed. They'd hung the Germans—Kurt and Alois, at least— from the front porch. It didn't get them very high off the deck, but that didn't matter. They'd both been dead before Quinlin ordered them strung up. Odell had learned earlier that afternoon from Wade Palmer that Art's bunch had hung several men similarly the day before.

"The old man wanted to hang 'em all," Wade explained, "but the damned clod-jumpers wouldn't cooperate. They'd shoot at us and we'd have to shoot back, and the next thing you knew, they were all dead. The old man had us hang 'em, though. He was real serious about that."

Odell then asked a question he never thought he'd have to in his early years with the Sun.

"Did you kill any women or kids?"

"No, and thank God for that. I believe the son of a bitch would've, though. I'll tell you what, that ol' boy is mean clear to the middle."

Palmer's words still echoed through Odell's mind as he stared at the dead Germans, swinging gruesomely in the cool breeze coming down off the Rim. That was probably why Doug Hayes and the others had deserted last night, and why the three men Art had sent south that afternoon to cut off the Dutchmen's escape—Palmer and Al Richie and Samson Hoag—had taken flight, as well.

After Schwartz and Neumann had been killed rushing the milk shed, the old man sent Clint Miller south to find out what had happened. The gunman was back within twenty minutes to announce the betrayals.

"Don't look like they even stopped to talk about it," Miller observed. "Once they found the road to the Basin, they took off at a high lope."

The old man had cussed a blue streak for a while. Then he swung around to face the few who were left. "The next one of you sons'a bitches decides to run out on me, I swear I'll hunt you down like dogs." He had his Colt out, and let the muzzle sweep the four men still with him—Odell and Miller and Carl Roth and Little George Isley, who wasn't dead, after all, but who'd had his arm busted from a rifle slug.

The dairymen were still spinning slowly when Quinlin ordered his men into their saddles. "Let's get outta here," he growled, and reined his buckskin toward the Basin.

Odell lifted his head and his lips parted as if to speak, then he clamped them shut and looked away. Schwartz's kids were still out there somewhere, probably lost and surely terrified, but he was afraid to say anything out of concern the old man would order them found and strung up alongside their father and uncle. Odell decided the kids would be better off left to their own devices, adrift in a dark forest but with better odds than surviving Art Quinlin's burgeoning insanity.

It was coming onto full dark by the time they closed in on the hunter's shack halfway up the North Rim. Hal Keegan hauled up before leaving the rocky trail, eyeing the shallow concave of the Saddleback still several miles away. Although he'd never been that far before, he knew from others that the route would eventually take him over the top, then down into the Big Sandy River drainage—probably a week's ride with all the obstacles that would stand in his path. Even from here he could feel the icy caress of the deep snows lingering in the pass. For a moment he contemplated just pushing on into the night, leaving the Basin altogether and never looking back. Then he smiled and glanced behind him at the girl, and knew they wouldn't be going any farther tonight.

Flopping his heels against the springy ribs of his blue roan, Hal gave a tug on the lead rope to the black mare—one of the pair from Max Ward's wagon team—that he'd liberated that afternoon from Shaw's pasture. He'd had to slip back into town on the sly to do it, but figured the prize had been worth the risk.

Hal let the roan pick its own path over the rocky terrain. Although this was his first foray onto the North Rim, he'd once glassed the little hunter's shack from a distance, and had recognized Ira Bannerman's description of the place as soon as the saloonkeeper mentioned it in an offhand remark that morning while Hal tightened the roan's cinch.

If he could find Art Quinlin, he was confident the gnarled old rancher would set things right. He knew Art was going to be smoldering mad when he found out that Gil Ryan was not only back, but that he was wearing a badge and on his way to the Sun to arrest that fine, precious boy of his, even as Hal was being driven out of Larkspur like a common criminal. Art would likely want to blame Hal for everything that had gone wrong, but Hal figured he had a solution for that eventuality, too, and couldn't help another backward glance at Fred Somers's little bitch of a daughter, her hands bound tightly in front of her, Hal's dirty bandana crammed into her mouth.

The shadows of the pines at the foot of the ridge blanketed the shelter completely, turning dim into sable. The swift flowing of creek waters somewhere close to the trees reminded him that he hadn't thought to bring along coffee or a pot. He'd taken some food from the mercantile—sardines and crackers and a couple of airtights of tomatoes, along with a quart bottle of Old Tan sipping whiskey—but not enough to last for long.

Hal reined up at the base of the ridge and stepped to the

ground. After hobbling his roan, he walked back along the black horse to pat the girl's leg. "You stay right here, darlin'," he told her. "I'll go in first and start a fire, make it all nice and cozy."

She made a sound through the bandana that he couldn't decipher, and he chuckled and tied the black's lead rope to a springy sapling. Then he went back to the roan to fetch his saddlebags and bedroll. Feeling as graceless as an old woman, he climbed the rocky slope to the hut and dumped his gear on the ground out front. Leaning forward, he sniffed warily at the low entrance. He wouldn't have wanted to poke his head into a bear's den, but all he detected were the odors of old smoke and cold ashes. Drawing a match from his coat pocket, he struck it alight on the checkered grips of his revolver, burning the already-scorched wood a little darker, then edged inside with the sputtering lucifer thrust before him. He grinned happily when he spied the already-laid fire in the middle of the low-ceilinged hut. Scrunching forward on bent knees, he thrust the match into a wad of dried grass under the kindling, then sat back on his heels to watch the flames take hold. The wood was dry, and it didn't take long before he had a good blaze.

Satisfied that the fire wouldn't go out, he brought his blankets and saddlebags inside and tossed them against the rear wall. Then he started back down to fetch the girl. He cursed the darkness as he picked his way downslope, practically stumbled into the horses, then had to feel his way to the black.

"You ready, darlin'?"

The black snorted and pulled back.

"You try to run, you son of a bitch, and I'll shoot you," he told the horse.

The black snorted again and tossed its head. Then Hal grabbed the halter and gave it a hard yank.

"Hold still, damn you."

He moved alongside the animal, frowning as his hand slid

235

over the horse's back. He went all the way to the croup before he figured out what was wrong.

"Aw, no," he breathed. He ran his hand over the horse a second time, but there was no mistake. She was gone.

He whirled away from the horse, but even with his vision starting to readjust after the brightness inside the hut, it was still too dark for him to see more than a rod or two in any direction. He could just make out the black and his blue roan, but the girl had vanished. Turning to face the pines, he shouted, "You ain't gonna get far, darlin', I promise you that. You'll be lost before midnight and froze solid by dawn. Come on back, and I won't hold it against you."

Only the rushing waters of the creek answered him.

"You bitch!" he practically shrieked. "You little whore. I'll find you. Goddamnit, I'll find you."

They rolled out of their blankets well before dawn, Doc so stiff-jointed and sore-backed it took a couple of minutes before he could stand fully upright. After a couple of raspy "Good mornings," Gil went to bring in the horses while Doc fumbled through Hannah Brickman's cloth sack for breakfast. After their initial greetings, neither man spoke, not even as they saddled their horses. Both seemed lost in thought, tackling their chores more from habit than design. Joel Quinlin sat off to the side, shivering from the cold and now and then hurling insults like small stones. When Gil started to saddle the palomino, Quinlin cursed louder.

"You stay away from that horse, Ryan! That stallion'll kill you if you ain't careful. He ain't some gentle nag like that bucket of bones you're riding."

Doc and Gil exchanged glances, and Doc chuckled under his breath.

"He gets tiresome after a while, doesn't he?"

"He's been scraping my hide raw, for a fact. If he keeps it up, I might have to gag him."

"You can use my handkerchief," Doc volunteered. With his saddle cinched firmly in place, he brought the near-side stirrup down and walked over to where he'd laid out half a dozen biscuits, spread with jam and layered with meat. "I'm going to miss my morning coffee," he added wistfully. "A man gets used to the small comforts of a home."

"I've never had a wife," Gil confided. "Never had a home of my own, either. At least not since I was a youngster."

"Do you have family anywhere?" Doc asked carefully. He knew he was treading over dangerous ground, but Gil took the question without insult.

"I had an older brother who raised me after my parents passed away. When his wife died of typhus, we pulled up stakes and came West. I was maybe fifteen then. I guess I've been drifting ever since."

They ate in silence, then mounted up and rode out. Gil led, keeping Joel's palomino close on a short lead. Doc brought up the rear with a look that would have challenged an oak plank for expression. He was hurting all over in a way that only the elderly could fully appreciate, but it was his hips and his left hand—the one Quinlin's men had crushed with a hammer—that pained him the worst.

They rode back to where they'd abandoned the trail the night before and turned north. When the light grew strong enough, Gil eased his sorrel into a lope, dragging Joel's mount along with him. Doc stayed close, but the pace was taking its toll. If he hadn't been so frightened for Peggy, he might have insisted on a gentler gait; as it was, he gritted his teeth and tried to ignore the fire-like burn that coursed down both his legs.

They'd covered maybe two miles when a rider appeared suddenly out of an arroyo to the west. Gil called a warning and started to slow his horse. That was when Joel slammed his heels into his mount's ribs. The stallion lunged forward, and for a couple of minutes Gil had all he could do to hang onto the palomino without losing his own seat. Reining alongside, Doc grabbed the lunging stallion's halter to help bring the horse under control, hanging onto his own reins with his left hand. Pain lanced his clenched fist like a dozen angry wasp stings.

Grinning triumphantly as the palomino was brought to a lunging stop, Joel shouted, "I damned near made it, didn't I?"

"You little fool." Doc gave the kid a sharp rap alongside his head, and Joel howled and clutched his ear.

"Son of a bitch, that hurt."

"Try a stunt like that again and I'll throw you belly-down across your saddle and let you ride that way for a few miles."

Joel's expression changed in a flash. Staring into the youth's eyes for that brief instant was like meeting the gaze of an enraged monster bent on destroying everything within reach. Then the fire faded from the kid's eyes and he settled back in his seat.

"You're gonna regret that, Doc," Joel said, rubbing his ear.

"So will you, if you don't start behaving yourself."

"You're an ornery old codger. Pa said you was town-fat and wife-soft, but you still got a little fire left in your belly, ain't you?"

Gil had regained his seat by then and was sitting his mount calmly, both hands folded in plain sight over his saddle horn.

"Recognize him?" Doc asked.

"Looks like the guy who came in on yesterday's stage."

"That's what I'm thinking."

"What guy?" Joel asked. "It ain't one of Pa's men, is it?"

"He might be," Doc admitted.

The man riding toward them was slim and wiry, and sat his horse with a familiar ease. He'd exchanged his good suit for sturdy range clothes—canvas britches and vest, a heavy wool shirt, low-heeled boots—but kept his gray derby with its dark blue band, rare in that part of the country, although Doc had seen pictures of them in the Bloomingdale Brothers catalogs his wife loved to thumb through.

"Well, I guess the easiest way to find out is to ask him," Gil said, reining away from the trail they'd followed out of Larkspur.

Doc fell in at Gil's side, hanging onto the palomino's lead rope. The stranger was approaching cautiously. Like Gil, he was keeping both hands out front where they could be clearly seen. The word *professionals* entered Doc's mind, and he glanced at Gil and wondered, as he had so many times before: *Who are you, Ryan? What brought you here?*

They pulled up when the stranger was about twenty yards away, but the horseman kept coming. He stopped when only a few feet separated them, his greeting a curt, "Howdy."

Gil nodded in return.

"You'd be Gil Ryan?" the stranger asked.

"I am."

The stranger's gaze shifted. "And you're William Shaw, Larkspur's physician?"

"Yes."

"My name is Aaron Servey. I'm an assistant district attorney out of Santa Fe. I've come here to investigate the various claims and counterclaims our office has received over the past year, and to hopefully begin to install some semblance of order to the Ensillado Basin."

Slowly, as if aware of the distrust still aimed at him, Servey pulled an envelope from an inside breast pocket and handed it to Gil. Gil slid the contents of the envelope into the sun, scanned them briefly, then passed them to Doc. There were several pages, but the two that generated the most attention were near the front. One was a letter of introduction from the

District Attorney's office. The other was a form authorizing Servey to appoint an interim sheriff for the Basin, as well as to begin structuring a framework for a county government.

"Sweet Lord," Doc breathed. "Finally."

"We weren't unaware of the incidences taking place up here, Dr. Shaw, but everything takes time where the government is concerned."

"What are you doing out here?" Gil asked bluntly.

"The same as you. A potential witness was apparently abducted. I intend to retrieve her for testimony."

"Alive?"

The question pricked a flicker of annoyance from the attorney's deadpan expression, but his voice remained calmly detached. "She would hardly be any good to us dead."

"No, I guess not. Are you the law up here now?"

"I represent the law, as do you."

"I wasn't elected," Gil told him.

"Not officially, but according to the information I received from Misters Bannerman, Greene, and Fisher, you were appointed by a citizens' committee representing the town. In an unincorporated community like Larkspur, that would constitute a position of acceptance, and positions of acceptance are generally binding in court. Especially in territorial courts, where formal elections aren't always possible."

"You mean, he's legal?" Doc asked.

"Legal enough for our current situation. Before I leave the Basin I'll begin the process of making it official. Right now, I'm more concerned for Miss Somers's safety."

"As are we," Doc replied. "Have you seen her?"

"No. I've seen a trail, but I'm not sure it's the right one."

"It is as far as we can tell," Gil said.

"Then, if you'll permit me to accompany you, I'd suggest we get started."

Gil looked at Doc. "I'll take the kid's lead rope. You can bring up the rear."

Doc glanced uncertainly at Servey as the assistant district attorney refolded his papers and returned them to his coat.

"That's all right, Doctor," Servey said without looking up. "I can appreciate Mr. Ryan's distrust, and I'm not averse to accommodating it."

"Let's move out," Gil said.

Doc shrugged and handed the palomino's lead rope to Gil. Joel, he noticed, hadn't said anything. The boy was sporting a worried expression, as if finally starting to realize how much trouble he and his pa might really be in.

CHAPTER SIXTEEN

Hal Keegan began his pursuit of the girl at first light. The ground, still moist from the recently melted snow, made tracking easy. Her trail led downhill in a jagged pattern, now and then lurching clear of small boulders or prickly flora, occasionally leaving behind a few torn threads or a tiny patch of fabric from her dress.

Flight must have been difficult with her wrists bound and the night as thick as congealing ink. He saw where she'd fallen after crossing the creek, her knees planting dainty imprints in the wet soil, blood from a scraped palm leaving a smear across a small boulder. Her trail led up the opposite bank and into the trees. Hal followed grimly on foot, confident that she couldn't get far with so much against her, angered that she'd try. He was upset with himself, too, for not having checked her restraints before climbing up to the hut to kindle a fire. Back in Larkspur he'd tied her ankles loosely by running a length of cotton rope under the black's barrel, but he hadn't checked her bonds since, and one of the knots must have worked itself loose.

He had to slow down as he ventured deeper into the trees. Pine needles several inches deep covered the earth, making tracking difficult. From time to time he had to stop, then carefully backtrack to pick up her trail again. It was tedious, and his irritation grew as the sun began its arc toward noon.

Although the sky was clear, the light under the trees remained murky. After a while, that began to work on him, too. He kept thinking he heard something behind him, yet every time he spun around there was nothing there. At first he thought it might be the girl stalking him. Then he got it into his mind that it was a bear or a mountain lion, and the thought chilled him to his marrow. He didn't have a rifle, just his Colt, and he knew the revolver's .44 caliber slugs weren't going to offer much protection against a winter-hungry bruin fresh out of hibernation, or a big cat forced down from the high country by a lack of food.

Hal tramped on doggedly, his nerves becoming more frazzled. The slim trunks of the pines began to feel like prison bars closing in, and sweat dripped from the tip of his nose. The girl's trail seemed to wander aimlessly. He tried to picture what it must have been like for her last night, alone and lost in near total darkness, but the image failed to generate any empathy. He began to worry about the time, too, knowing the people of Larkspur must have realized by now that she was missing. It would be only a matter of time before they began to put it all together. He needed to find the girl quickly, then locate Quinlin before the town could organize a search party, so he pushed on doggedly, one hand clutching the scarred grips of his holstered revolver, the other batting inefficiently at the lower branches of the pines that kept grabbing at him.

Yet as much as Hal tried to focus on the hunt, he couldn't shake the feeling that he was being stalked. He kept looking back, scanning the timber. He wasn't sure how far he'd gone before he realized he was no longer following the girl's trail. Jerking to a stop, he stared dumbly at the needled forest floor. Then, shoulders slumped, he started back the way he'd come. He had only his own tracks to guide him now. Except for the rough bark of the pines and their still boughs, there was nothing to see, no landmark to point the way. The ground here sloped gently, but he no longer knew in which direction, and the sky remained a lacy motif of brilliant blue peeking through a canopy of green.

His pace slowed as he made his way downhill, and all of a sudden his scalp began to crawl. He halted to peer into the deeper timber before him. When the bear finally showed itself, he almost felt more validated than frightened; when the big bruin stood up on its hind legs and woofed loudly, his knees nearly buckled.

Hal began backing away slowly. He knew even less about bears than he did about tracking, but he could tell this animal was gaunted down to hide and bone, likely ravenous after a long winter denned up under the snow. It was a black bear, but a large one, and it looked angry. Either that or hungry, neither of which boded well in his current situation.

As Hal instinctively picked up his pace, the bear dropped to all fours. Panicked, he turned and ran. Fleeing was like a starter's pistol for the bear. It woofed again, louder this time, and dug in after him. Hal scrambled for traction in the slick needles. In a panic he drew his revolver and started throwing shots behind him. He wasted four cartridges without coming close. Then the fifth struck the dirt just in front of the bear and it skidded to a halt, snorting and pawing at the dust and dead pine needles flung into its face.

Hal kept running. After a while the ground leveled out, and he spotted sunlight ahead and to his right, a clearing of scattered aspens and green grass. He altered his course toward sunshine, legs still pumping, arms flailing. The bear had long since ceased pursuit, but he didn't care. He burst into the clearing and skidded to a stop, his eyes widening in surprise when he saw the girl huddled close to a buckboard-sized boulder, crouched in the sun as if using the stone's reflective warmth to leach last night's chill from her body.

Panting, his mouth hanging open as he dragged cool air into

his tortured lungs, Hal leaned forward to rest his hands on his knees. Finally, still puffing heavily, he said, "All this trouble, and it didn't do you a damned bit of good, did it?"

The girl didn't answer, but her eyes shuttled to one side. Hearing the sharp crack of a broken twig, Hal turned slowly, reluctantly. "Aw, hell," he whispered.

Gil led at a fast trot, and it wasn't long before Doc realized where they were headed. His gaze rose to the distant Saddleback, glistening with snow. A month ago he would have considered that high, shallow passage insurmountable for months to come, but Gil had proved him wrong on that count. Had proved them all wrong. It made him wonder who else in the valley would be so desperate as to challenge it in these conditions. Doc assumed Peggy's abductor—if she had indeed been kidnapped—was Reece Ward, but he doubted if Reece would feel any need to flee the Basin. With a sinking sensation in his breast, Doc began to wonder if he was wrong about that, too?

They were beginning their climb toward the pass when the echo of gunfire rolled overhead. Gil slid his heavy Winchester from its scabbard even as he brought his horse to a stop. Aaron Servey rode up on one side of him, Doc on the other. Joel sat quietly at the rear, staring toward the Rim. It wasn't long before they heard several more shots.

"It sounds like it's coming from those trees," Servey said, nodding toward a dense stand of timber less than half a mile away.

"A revolver," Gil said quietly, then looked at Doc. "Sounds like it might be pretty close to that shack I was telling you about."

A solitary revolver blast echoed over the trees.

"Do you think you can find it again?"

Gil nodded. "I'm sure of it," he said, levering a round into the Winchester's chamber.

Turning slowly, Hal Keegan whispered, "Aw, hell." The girl remained huddled close to the tall boulder, her expression nearly frantic with terror. "You goddamned bitch." Then he put his back on her, facing the lower end of the clearing where the Ward boy had appeared as if by some form of wizardry. Reece was carrying a rifle, and Hal slid his thumb over the Colt's hammer and rolled it all the way back.

Hal wasn't necessarily afraid of Reece Ward—he considered the boy young and untried—but he did wish he'd taken time to reload after his encounter with the bear. He tried to remember how many shots he'd fired. Four or five was his guess, but he couldn't be sure. With a young buck racing toward him with fire in his gut, it was something Hal would have preferred knowing. The kid was closing in fast, his face flushed from either anger or the exertion of running uphill at an elevation of nearly 7,000 feet. Hal raised his Colt to take careful aim.

"Reece, watch out!" Peggy cried, and the boy slid to a halt.

Hal grinned coldly. The dumb little turd should have taken his shot from the trees, instead of running into the Colt's range. Like he'd figured, the kid was inexperienced, and the mistake was going to cost him his life.

Reece worked his rifle's lever, but he was too slow against an already-cocked revolver. Hal fired and the Colt bucked. The kid spun from the bullet's impact and tumbled into the grass. The girl screamed and pushed to her feet. Hal thought at first she was going to flee, but instead she ran toward Reece and flung herself at his side. Hal started toward her. As he did, he methodically ejected the fired cases from the Colt's cylinder. When the gun was empty, he reached around behind him to extract a live round from his cartridge belt. It surprised him when the kid pushed up on his elbows. He'd thought from the way the boy had fallen that he was dead. It didn't matter, though. He soon would be.

The boy's voice was hoarse and filled with pain, but Hal could clearly hear him urging the girl to run.

"Get out of here," Reece gasped, but she shook her head and refused to budge. Her foolish loyalty to Ward irked Hal, and he grabbed the girl by the hair and roughly yanked her away from the boy's body.

"You little bitch," he growled. "I ought to smack you silly."

Keeping a handful of her hair wrapped in his fist, he glared down at Ward. "I should've killed you last year, too, 'cept I figured sure old man Quinlin would want to blame you for his boy's death."

Reece grimaced and pushed over on his side. Blood covered his ribs, pasting the fabric of his shirt to torn flesh. Hal muttered a curse. His aim hadn't been as true as he'd hoped, although it still didn't matter. Reece's Whitney-Kennedy lay several yards away, out of reach. Hal pointed his Colt at the boy's head.

"Here's something for you to ponder, Ward. I've only got one round in this pistol. How many times do you figure I gotta pull the trigger before a bullet busts your skull open like a melon?"

Reece didn't answer, but the girl did.

"No," she said softly.

Hal glanced over his shoulder. "Oh, yeah, darlin'. I'm gonna . . ."

He stopped and scowled and looked down. Then he looked at Ward, noticing for the first time that the boy's holster was empty.

"Son of a bitch," Hal whispered. Then something like a giant's fist slammed into his side, followed by a roar that all but drowned out all his other senses. He saw the earth speeding toward him and wanted to put out his hands to stop it. He didn't remember hitting the ground, but he must have. Pain surged briefly through his body. Then it faded, along with the light.

As the trail grew steeper, they had to fall back into single file. Gil ran the free end of the palomino's lead rope through the halter to fashion a crude hackamore that he handed to Joel.

"You try something stupid and I'll put a bullet through your spine," he told his prisoner, and the kid's face paled. It looked like young Quinlin was finally starting to comprehend the seriousness of his circumstances.

The thick pine forest south of the hunter's shack was hard on their right now, its shadowy interior looking nearly impenetrable. Gil kept tapping impatiently at Rusty's sides, and when they reached the trail leading to the hut, the sorrel turned off without guidance. Gil stopped when the small shack came into view. There were two horses standing below the hut. One was hobbled, the other tied to a sapling.

"Is this the place?" Servey asked.

"This is it."

"That's Max Ward's wagon horse tied to the tree," Doc said with a stricken look. "The roan belongs to Keegan."

Gil twisted around to motion Joel forward. "Keep an eye on this one, will you, Doc? And keep his mouth shut, even if you have to knock his teeth out with the butt of your pistol to do it."

"It'd be my pleasure," Doc replied, staring hard at the kid. "I'll consider it restitution for my broken hand."

"You do what Doc says," Gil told Joel, then heeled Rusty forward. Servey rode with him. Doc stayed back with Joel, his revolver drawn and resting lightly across his thigh, its muzzle pointed at the younger man.

Gil hauled up about two hundred feet away and dismounted. Servey got down, too. He didn't have a rifle, but he'd slipped a stubby Webley Bull Dog from a shoulder holster and was holding it like he knew what he was doing. Gil met the attorney's eyes.

"You're in charge, Mr. Ryan. I'll follow whatever command you give, short of murder."

They started cautiously forward. Ward's black raised its head when they drew close and nickered plaintively, no doubt hungry and wanting to be turned loose to graze. Gil and Servey dropped to a crouch behind a jumble of boulders close to the creek's edge and waited to see what would happen, but no one appeared at the hut's entrance, and no one called for them to stay back.

"It's empty," Gil said suddenly.

"Are you sure?"

"No, but one of us is going to have to go up there and find out."

"Cover me. I'll . . ."

"No," Gil said. "I've been here before. I know what the ground is like, and I'll have a better idea of what to look for if Keegan is inside."

After a pause, Servey shrugged. "All right. What do you want me to do?"

"Wait here," Gil said tersely, then slipped away from the boulders and began climbing toward the hut. He glanced back once and saw the assistant district attorney leaning forward over the rocks, the Webley held firmly in both hands, its muzzle leveled on the hut's shadowy entrance.

When he was about ten yards away, Gil leaned his rifle against a low bush and drew the Hopkins and Allen. If a fight broke out now it would be at close quarters, where the revolver would do him more good than the heavy Winchester. Yet the closer he got to the hut's entrance, the more convinced he became that the shelter was empty. Reaching its entrance, he paused with his back to the wall and ordered whoever was inside to come out with their hands in plain sight.

"I'm the law," he added, although the description sounded hollow spoken aloud. Aaron Servey was the law; his own brother had been the law, back in Idaho. Right now, Gil wasn't sure what he was, other than nervous and a little shaky.

Taking a deep breath, he swung inside with the Hopkins and Allen shoved before him. Then he exhaled loudly and dropped to one knee. The shack was deserted, but it wasn't empty. Gil stared silently at the blankets heaped against the far wall, the still smoking fire pit in the middle of the room. Several empty tins of sardines had been casually discarded in a corner of the shack, and dried urine stained the pile of firewood Gil had so carefully stacked inside, leaving a path through the dust and an acidic odor in the air.

Gil's lips curled in disgust as he backed out of the hut and holstered his revolver. He looked upstream along the winding path of the creek but there was nothing to see, and he finally waved the others forward.

Servey got there first. He peered inside, then leaned back with the same look of repulsion Gil had experienced. Doc rode to where the blue roan and the black were secured and dismounted. Joel said something and Doc glanced up the rocky slope to the hut.

"He wants to get down," Doc called. "What do you say?"

Gil didn't reply. His attention had been drawn upstream again, where a man had appeared suddenly from the trees, a rifle balanced across his mount's withers.

"Who's that?" Servey asked.

Gil didn't respond to that, either. He started downslope, snatching up his Winchester on the way but not stopping until he reached Doc's side. Servey was right behind him, the Webley still drawn. Gil couldn't see the rider from where they were standing close to the trees, and neither could Doc, but that didn't matter. Whoever it was would be there soon, and Gil wanted to be prepared.

"Keep the kid where he is," he told Doc. "We've got company on the way."

CHAPTER SEVENTEEN

There was a woman with him. Gil hadn't seen her at first, coming along on foot on the far side of the horse. She stumbled slightly crossing the creek, then hurried to catch up, keeping one hand protectively on the rider's thigh.

"Recognize her?" Aaron Servey asked.

Gil nodded and lowered his Winchester.

"What about the guy?"

"I don't know him, but Doc might." Gil made a motion and Doc came out of the trees, leading his bay and Joel's palomino, the younger man leaning forward in his saddle to see who was approaching.

"It's Reece Ward," Doc said as soon as he spotted the couple, still nearly a quarter of a mile away.

"So Ward is the culprit?" Servey seemed surprised by the discovery, as if he'd suspected someone else.

Neither Doc nor Gil replied, but Gil was thinking that if the woman had been abducted, she sure wasn't acting like it.

"He's hurt," Doc said, loosening the medical bag from the back of his saddle. He glanced at Gil. "Is there room in that hut?"

"There's room, but it's dusty."

"As long as it's dry." He nodded toward the still-damp ground. "I'd prefer dust to dampness."

"Go ahead and put him inside," Gil said. "I'll cut some pine limbs for a bed."

He returned the Winchester to its scabbard, then crossed the rushing creek and entered the pines. It took only a few minutes to cut off a couple of armfuls of evergreen boughs. Servey helped carry them up to the hut, spreading them out against the rear wall before covering them with blankets. By the time they finished, Peggy was leading the black horse up the slope. Doc walked alongside with one hand on Reece's waist, helping the younger man keep his balance. Joel was still sitting his palomino beside the creek. He looked like he wanted to get down but was afraid to attempt it; his demeanor had changed dramatically since Servey joined them that morning, although Gil wasn't counting on the transformation to last.

They slid Reece off the horse and carried him inside, laying him atop the sweet-smelling pine boughs before cutting his shirt away. Leaving Servey inside to help Doc, Gil backed out of the shack and stared at Peggy. She was standing next to the horse, her face pale and dirty, her clothing torn as she stared almost vacantly at the hut's low entrance. She only looked away when Gil spoke her name.

"Are you all right?"

She seemed unsure for a moment, then quietly nodded. Gil lifted the black's reins from her hands and led it down to where the other horses waited. After a moment, Peggy followed clumsily.

"How bad is he hurt?" she asked.

"I don't know. Seems like he lost a lot of blood, but I'm not a doctor. Let's give Shaw a couple of minutes to look him over."

She nodded absently and brushed a strand of hair from her face.

"Are you hungry?"

"Huh?"

"I asked if you were hungry."

"Oh, yes, I think so."

"We've got some biscuits and cold roast beef."

She nodded again, still in that distracted manner, and Gil lifted Hannah Brickman's cloth sack from the horn of Doc's saddle and set it on a low boulder awash in sunshine.

"You can sit down here if you'd like."

She didn't reply. She was staring at Joel with a look Gil couldn't fathom. Then, out of the blue, she said, "It was Keegan who killed Earl Quinlin last fall."

Gil's head snapped up. "Hal Keegan? Are you sure?"

"That's what he told me. Told us both."

"When?"

"This morning."

A chill slammed through Gil's chest as he stood and put his hand on the Hopkins and Allen. "Is Keegan up here, too?"

Looking him in the eye for the first time, she said matter-of-factly, "It was Keegan who kidnapped me."

"Keegan? We thought, when we saw you and Reece . . ."

"It was Reece who found me. He saved my life." She hesitated for a moment, then slowly related her ordeal. She told him how Keegan had slipped in the back door of the mercantile yesterday to surprise her while she was working on a prescription, then bound and gagged her before ransacking the store.

"He stole Ward's horse because he didn't think anyone would notice if it went missing for a day or two, but I guess Reece saw him and came after us. Came after me."

"Without telling anyone?"

"After what happened at the jail yesterday, I don't think he knew who he could trust." She paused to brush that stubborn strand of hair out of her face again. "He said that when he saw us leaving, he was afraid he'd lose us if he went for help. I . . . I really don't know why he didn't let anyone else know, but he didn't. He didn't catch up yesterday, either. Then last night, while Keegan was up there." She glanced at the hut. "I worked myself loose and ran into the trees. I was lost all night, but Reece found me this morning. He left me in a clearing, in the sun, while he went to get his horse. That's when Keegan showed up." She stopped again, the faraway look returning to her eyes. "That's when he told us he was the one who killed Earl. Not in so many words, but close enough that we knew."

"Where's Keegan now?"

"I killed him." She looked at him, tears collecting at the corners of her eyes. "I killed him, Mr. Ryan."

"Are you sure?"

"Yes, I'm sure. We left him in the clearing. There . . . there wasn't anything I could do. Reece was hurt and I wanted to take him home, but I thought we should come here first, so we could have another horse."

Gil nodded and began to relax. It was good to know there was one less gun he'd have to face.

"Would you swear in court to what Keegan told you, Miss Somers?"

She nodded. "Yes, gladly." Then her eyes widened and Gil turned and swore. He counted five men making their way up the creek-side trail. He recognized two of them even from a distance. One was Odell Love, the man he'd called Weasel on the night Les Quinlin and Tim Jackson accosted him in Larkspur. The other was Clint Miller, and Gil's blood surged when he recognized his old nemesis, the man he'd traveled over five hundred miles to find, while the puckered bullet wound in his shoulder began to throb.

"Get up to the hut," Gil ordered.

"That's Art Quinlin," Peggy whispered.

Gil nodded. He'd already spotted the wiry man with the long white hair and snowy beard riding at the head of the column, and knew it couldn't be anyone else.

"Go on," he said.

As Peggy scrambled up the slope to the hut, Gil walked over to his sorrel and yanked the Winchester from its scabbard. At the creek, Joel had reined his horse around to face the approaching horsemen.

"You stay where you are, Quinlin."

"Turn me loose, Ryan." Joel shook his wrists, the chain between the cuffs rattling faintly. "Come on, damnit."

"You stay put."

Joel laughed, his old cockiness returning in a rush. "The hell with you. Pa's gonna string you up, and I wanna get my hands free so I can help."

It was big talk, Gil thought, but he noticed Joel wasn't making any effort to join his father and the others.

"Ryan!"

Aaron Servey was coming rapidly downhill, skidding now and then in the loose soil but not slowing until he reached Gil's side. Doc stood at the hut's entrance, stripped of his coat and vest, his sleeves rolled up past his elbows.

"Who are they?" Servey asked.

"Art Quinlin and his boys."

"Yes, Dr. Shaw pointed out Quinlin, but I didn't stay long enough to catch anyone else's name."

Gil identified Clint Miller and Odell Love. "I couldn't say who the others are."

"The African is Little George Isley. I recognize him from a wanted poster in my office. I think the other one might be Carl Roth. If it is, he's come through our courts a time or two, as well."

Gil gave the assistant district attorney a thoughtful look. "Who's in charge here, Servey? I need to know before they get any closer."

"You're still sheriff by acceptance, Ryan. Until that changes, you're in charge. But I'll give you some advice if you want it."

"Say it quick."

"It's simple enough. Keep whatever happens here legal and aboveboard, so that I don't have to arrest you as well as the others."

Art Quinlin pulled up about twenty yards away. He glanced briefly at his son, then brought his wild gray eyes back to Gil. "Take them cuffs off my boy, Ryan."

"So you know who I am?"

"Yeah, I know you. You're the son of a bitch who shot my son last month, the same son of a bitch I'm gonna hang before this day is over."

Clint Miller had been hanging back. Now he guided his gray alongside Quinlin's buckskin. "Hello, Ryan."

"Miller."

"You're a little far from home, ain't you?"

"I'm here for a reason."

"Meaning me?"

"That's right."

"What the hell," Art said. "Miller, do you know this man?"

Miller didn't reply. He was looking at the star pinned to Gil's chest. "Is that Keegan's?"

"It was. I'm wearing it for the Basin now."

"Well, ain't you a noble son of a bitch."

Art's voice rose in frustration. "Damnit, Miller, I asked you a question."

"I heard it," the gunman responded, then raised a hand for Quinlin to back off and shut up. With the gesture, the fingers of Gil's right hand twitched involuntarily. It was a small move, but Miller picked up on it immediately. "Just so you know, Ryan, if you lift that rifle or reach for your pistol, I'll kill you. And this time I won't miss."

"You didn't miss the last time," Gil reminded him.

"You're still alive. I'd call that a miss."

Gil's eyes narrowed. "You're under arrest, Miller. All of you are. I want you to drop your guns one at a time. Quinlin, we'll start with you."

"The hell you will," Art replied incredulously. His gaze swung toward Doc, standing at the hut's entrance with his Sharps held across his chest, the forestock resting across his left arm. "Doc, get down here!"

"Stay where you are," Gil called, and Doc raised a hand off his rifle in acknowledgment.

Quinlin's eyes were like pale stones set in leather. He was a man used to taking charge, not being ignored while others conversed around him. Leaning forward in his saddle, he said, "What in the goddamned name of hell do you think is going on here, Ryan? You think that badge means shit to me? You think anything you say means horse piss? This is *my* valley, all of it. I'm the one who settled it, who chased out the grizzly bears and Apaches and made it safe for others. *Me*, Ryan, not a bunch of gutless homesteaders and townsmen. Now it's them same damned trespassers tryin' to take it away from me, and they got the gall to hire the son of a bitch who killed my boy to do the takin'."

"It was your son who drew first," Gil replied mildly.

"I don't give a whore's heart who drew first. My boy is dead, and someone's gonna pay." His voice rose. "You're gonna pay, and they're gonna pay, for Earl." He flung an arm behind him, toward the towering bulk of the North Rim. "Every goddamned one of 'em."

"It wasn't a homesteader who killed Earl," Gil said. "It was Hal Keegan."

Quinlin's lips parted as if to respond, then closed. He looked at Joel, his brows ruffling with uncertainty. "What's he talking about?"

"That's what that Somers' girl says, Pa, but you know she's a liar. Ain't a soul in Larkspur wouldn't lie to protect their own."

After a tense moment, Quinlin eased back in his saddle. "Why?"

"He wanted you to blame Max Ward's boy."

"Why?"

"I couldn't say. He kidnapped Fred Somers's daughter and brought her up here, but he's dead now. Likely we'll never know why he did it."

"Dead? Hal's dead?" Quinlin took a deep breath as if to clear his mind, then slowly shook his head. "No, Hal Keegan wouldn't turn on me like that. We was friends, damnit." His gaze hardened. "You're blaming it on a dead man, Ryan, tryin' to hide the real killer, but it ain't gonna work."

Servey eased forward. "My name is Aaron Servey, Mr. Quinlin, and I want to assure you that there will be an investigation into your boy's death. Both of their deaths, and others, as well. I'd urge you to wait until those investigations have been completed before jumping to conclusions."

"Who the hell are you?"

"Like I said, my name is Aaron Servey. I'm with the District Attorney's office in Santa Fe."

"Go back to Santa Fe, Mr. Servey," Quinlin said. "This don't concern you."

"I'm afraid it does, and I'm afraid Sheriff Ryan is correct. You'll have to come into town. You're under arrest."

Art laughed harshly. "For what?"

"For the murder of Fred Somers," Gil said, "and for whatever happened up there." He jutted his chin toward the Rim.

Smiling crookedly, Quinlin said, "Ain't nothing happened on the Rim I know anything about, Ryan, and I didn't kill Somers. I got witnesses to back me up on that." He looked at Miller. "Ain't that right?"

"That's right, Ryan. Mr. Quinlin ain't killed no one, not in

259

Larkspur nor on the Rim. I'll swear to that. We all will."

"No," said a meek voice.

At first Gil didn't know who had spoken. Then the weasel kicked his horse forward, riding wide around Quinlin and Miller.

"That ain't true," said Odell Love, his words quavering. "You killed Mrs. Schwartz, then left them kids of hers to wander up there alone. You ordered the killings of . . ."

Art's face grew dark. "Shut up, Love!"

"No," Odell croaked. He looked at Gil, his face pale and twisted with fear. "I'll stand witness to that, Sheriff. To what he's ordered and what he's done. To what happened that night in Larkspur when Les and Tim threw down on you." His gaze shifted to Servey. "Ryan's tellin' it square. It was Les who threw down first, but he missed and Ryan didn't. Same with Jackson. It was self-defense on Ryan's part, ain't no doubt."

"You little turncoat son of a bitch," Art snarled. "I'm gonna kill you myself, Love, and make it just as slow and painful as I can."

With Quinlin and the others staring so hard at Love, Gil slid his thumb over the Winchester's hammer. Art didn't notice the move, but Miller did, and went for his revolver.

"Don't!" Gil yelled, but Miller continued his draw. Gil swung the Winchester's muzzle toward the gunman and his finger tightened on the trigger. He was aiming from the hip, but close enough to be confident of his target. Miller didn't stand a chance, and in that brief instant between recognizing that and pulling the trigger, a barrage of images flashed though Gil's mind—*his brother Gavin falling through the Idaho snow, the blossoming of smoke from Miller's revolver; Gil's ragged cry of protest as he went for his own weapon, and finally the sense of failure as Miller's second bullet struck Gil like a sledge hammer; he saw himself spinning away and heard Miller's laughter*—and then he was back at the hut with the Winchester leveled on his brother's killer, and all he had to do was squeeze the trigger.

Gil couldn't miss, not at this range, but at the last second he swore and dropped the rifle's muzzle to fire into the dirt at the gray's feet. Miller's horse jumped backward and the gunman nearly lost his seat. He cursed and fired twice, both shots slamming harmlessly into the slope at Gil's side. The gray started to buck and Miller grabbed for the saddle horn with his right hand, losing his grip on the revolver as he did. The gun fell into the rocks as Miller jerked hard on the reins to bring his mount under control. He whirled the horse around to face Gil and his eyes swept the ground around him looking for the fallen revolver. Then he looked at Gil's rifle, pointed at his chest, and his shoulders sagged.

For a long moment no one moved or spoke, and Gil thought it was over, but he was wrong.

"No," Quinlin grated, his right hand reaching for the Colt holstered high on his right side.

"Don't do it!" Gil barked.

"No, you son of a bitch, *no!*" He yanked at his revolver, his eyes bright with rage. *"Kill 'em!"* he screamed. *"Kill 'em!"*

Gil started to bring his rifle to bear on the older man, then noticed Roth reaching for his revolver, and pivoted back to shoot the heavy-set ruffian through the torso. Art Quinlin's gun roared, the bullet passing close enough to Gil's jaw that he could feel the disturbance in the air. He threw the Winchester's lever to chamber another round, but Art was already leveling his Colt, and Gil unconsciously braced for the bullet's impact. Then another shot rang out, and Quinlin grunted as the heavy slug from Doc's rifle lifted him from his saddle. He flipped backward off his horse and struck the ground like a sack of wheat. Gil brought the Winchester back to Miller and the wiry black man behind him, but neither were going for their weapons.

Miller because his was lost on the ground, and Isley because he was staring down the bore of Aaron Servey's Webley.

Stepping close, the attorney lifted the revolver from Isley's belt and tossed it toward the creek. Gil turned his rifle toward Love, and Odell carefully drew his revolver and let it fall.

"I ain't gonna fight you, Ryan," Odell said. "I've seen enough killin' to last me a lifetime."

"Get off your horses, all of you," Gil commanded. He glanced briefly at Art Quinlin, sprawled across the trail behind his horse, then at Joel, who was staring at the body of his dead father with tears streaming down his cheeks.

"Get down," Gil repeated wearily. "It's done."

CHAPTER EIGHTEEN

It was early evening before they got back. It seemed as if all of Larkspur came out to watch as the tiny procession made its way down the street, then peeled off in different directions. Doc and Peggy went to Doc's house with Reece. Although Doc seemed confident Reece would recover, the young man was going to need time to heal. Doc offered to let him stay at his place, but Peggy suggested he would be more comfortable in one of the empty rooms above the mercantile. Doc hadn't argued.

Gil reined in at the jail and escorted his prisoners inside. He put Joel and Little George Isley in the back cell, and Miller in the one closest to the door separating the cages from the office.

"Where I can keep an eye on you," he told the prisoner.

He returned to the office where Odell Love stood with his head lowered. He looked up as Gil pulled the door to the cells closed.

"What am I going to do with you, Love?"

Odell shrugged. He hadn't had much to offer all day, but Gil knew if it hadn't been for him, the Schwartz children would probably still be up there, facing their second night alone in the forest. Instead, they had been placed with neighbors, an elderly man and woman named Johnson, who promised to look after the kids until Gil could make other arrangements, and to take care of the Schwartz's dairy cattle, too.

"Whatever you decide is all right by me," Odell replied after a long pause.

Gil shook his head and nodded toward the front door. "I'm not going to lock you up, but I want you to stay in town. I'll talk to Servey, but I'm thinking I might put you and Porfirio in charge of the Sun until we decide what to do with that."

Odell's face flooded with relief. "Whatever you decide, Sheriff."

"It's not going to be me who decides, Love. It will be a judge and jury, although I figure they'll go easy on you. Easier than they will on the others, anyway."

Odell bobbed his head and left the jail. Gil followed him as far as the veranda. Several townspeople had crossed the street and were standing curiously in front of the jail, their attention shuttling back and forth between the building and a couple of horses carrying grisly cargos wrapped in canvas. One of the townsmen went over to peer at the bundles. When he looked up, his face was ashen. "It's Art Quinlin."

A murmur of concern passed through the crowd.

"Art Quinlin and Carl Roth were killed while resisting arrest," Aaron Servey announced loudly enough for everyone to hear, including those citizens who had remained on the east side of the street. He was still astride his rented horse, watching over the corpses. "Joel Quinlin, Clint Miller, and George Isley will remain jailed until formal charges can be levied against them."

"Who are you?" the man asked.

Servey told him his name and his purpose, then asked for the speaker's name.

"I'm Arnie Hale."

"One of the men Dr. Shaw deputized to watch Keegan?"

Hale's face flushed with embarrassment. "I wasn't there when they busted him out. I would've tried to stop it if I was."

"So I heard," Servey replied mildly. He stepped down and pulled the two horses around. "I'm going to deputize you again,

Mr. Hale. I want you to look after these bodies until arrangements can be made for their burials. Will you do that?"

"Yes, sir," Hale replied, gathering the lead ropes to the two mounts. "Reckon I'll put 'em in the back room at the feed store. That's where they kept Les and Tim Jackson until they were buried."

"That sounds like as good a place as any," Servey agreed. He waited until Hale had led the horses away, then turned to Gil and sighed. "We have a lot of work ahead of us yet, Sheriff."

Gil cocked a brow in question. "Us, or you?"

"Both of us, I hope. You realize you can keep that badge, don't you? At least until a formal election can be held."

"We haven't talked about this, Servey, but I want Miller to stand trial in Idaho for the murder of my brother."

"Who was your brother?"

"He was the marshal of a little town up in the Sawtooths. Some of the big men around there didn't like the way he kept the peace. I guess it bit into their profits, so they hired Miller to get rid of him."

"Were you there when it happened?"

Gil nodded and his shoulder twitched. "I was there," he said.

"Stay here," Gavin said sternly.

"No, I'm coming with you."

"It's not your job, Gil. It's mine. Let me do it."

"Clint Miller is a killer, and he's got two others with him."

"I'm not worried about those other two. They'll cut and run when the time comes."

"Miller won't."

Gavin nodded soberly. "No, he probably won't. That's why I want you to stay out of it."

"You're the only family I've got left, Gav. I'm not going to let you face a trio of gunmen alone, even if two of them are cowards."

265

After a long pause, Gavin relented. "All right, but when we get to the Nugget, I want you to stand to the side and let me do the talking."

Although Gil said he would, he was lying. He had no intention of letting his brother face those three alone.

They left the small log jail together. It was early dusk and the snow was falling heavily, creating a silently gray, nearly featureless world. Although Gil wasn't looking forward to spending another frigid winter in the high country, he knew he'd stay if his brother did, and Gavin had been hired to bring order to the rough-hewn mining community, no matter how long it took. What neither of them had counted on was some of the town's toughest businessmen—owners of saloons and whorehouses and gambling dens—resisting his efforts so doggedly. Nor had they counted on these same businessmen hiring a professional gunman. But they had, and they made sure Gavin Ryan knew it, too.

"Leave town," was their advice. Either that or face the reaper.

They were on their way to face the reaper that night, but Miller had somehow gotten wind of their intentions and met them halfway between the jail and the Nugget, stepping unexpectedly out of an alley with his cohorts at his side. As far as Gil knew, Gavin never saw their attackers. Gil only caught a glimpse of them, before Miller's second bullet sent him spinning through the snow . . .

He exhaled loudly and looked at Servey. The assistant district attorney nodded his accord. "If he's wanted for murder in Idaho, I think I can help with the extradition. I'll want to be sure there's enough evidence to convict him, though. I'd rather he spend less time behind bars here than be set free up there."

"If I can get him back, he'll hang," Gil said.

"Then we'll do it, but with one provision."

"What's that?" Gil asked warily.

"What I said about that badge, I mean it. Larkspur needs a

good man to maintain order while its citizens begin setting up a local government. What about it, Mr. Ryan? Are you interested?"

Gil didn't answer. He was staring across the street to where Hannah Brickman was coming toward him, her expression almost slack with relief. Smiling suddenly, Gil stepped down off the veranda. "Watch the jail for me, will you, Mr. Servey? I'm going to have a slice of pie." Then he paused and glanced over his shoulder. "I'll try to keep from spilling any on my badge."

ABOUT THE AUTHOR

Michael Zimmer is the author of fifteen previous novels. His work has been praised by *Library Journal, Publishers Weekly, Booklist, Historical Novel Society,* and others. *The Poacher's Daughter* (Five Star, 2014) was the recipient of the 2015 Wrangler Award for Outstanding Western Novel from the National Cowboy and Western Heritage Museum, received a Starred Review from *Publisher's Weekly,* was included in True West Magazine's *Best of the West* (January 2015), and was a Spur Finalist from the Western Writers of America. *City of Rocks* (Five Star, 2012) was chosen by *Booklist* as one of the top ten Western novels of 2012. *Rio Tinto* and *Leaving Yuma* have also won awards. Zimmer resides in Utah with his wife Vanessa and their two dogs. His website is www.michael-zimmer.com.